Penguin Books
The Matriarchs

Susan Mitchell was born in Adelaide and began her career as a high school teacher there in 1966. After teaching in London and travelling in Europe, she returned to work at the South Australian College of Advanced Education where she is now a senior lecturer in the Literary Studies Department, teaching scriptwriting for the media and creative writing.

She has also worked for Crawford Productions as a scriptwriter and editor, and for the ABC as its first television critic on *Today at One*, and as presenter and writer of its radio programme *The Coming Out Show*.

She has written two other books of interviews, *Winning Women* (with Ken Dyer) which examines the issues facing sportswomen today, and the very successful *Tall Poppies*, in which nine women talk about women and success in Australia today. Both are available in Penguin. *Tall Poppies* was made into a successful television series.

By the same author

Tall Poppies: Successful Australian women
talk to Susan Mitchell
Winning Women: Challenging the Norms in
Australian Sport (with Ken Dyer)

The Matriarchs

Twelve Australian women talk
about their lives to
Susan Mitchell

Penguin Books

Penguin Books Australia Ltd,
487 Maroondah Highway, P.O. Box 257
Ringwood, Victoria 3134, Australia
Penguin Books Ltd,
Harmondsworth, Middlesex, England
Penguin Books Ltd,
40 West 23rd Street, New York, N. Y. 10010, U.S.A.
Penguin Books Canada Limited
2801 John Street, Markham, Ontario, Canada L3R 1B4
Penguin Books (N.Z.) Ltd,
182–190 Wairau Road, Auckland 10, New Zealand

First published by Penguin Books Australia, 1987

Typeset in Bodoni by Dudley E. King Pty. Ltd.
Made and printed in Australia by Australian Print Group

The Matriarchs
ISBN 0 14 008659 5

1. Women – Australia – Interviews. 2. Women – Australia – Biography. I. Mitchell, Susan, 1945 – .
305.4'2'0994

Promotion of this title has been assisted by the South Australian Government through the Department of the Arts.

For my Aunt, Marjorie Durston Hete, O.A.M.

Contents

Introduction

Here is a song, a celebration,
Let us sing in praise of Matriarchs

matriarch /'meitriak, 'maet-/, *n.* 1. a woman holding a position of leadership in a family or tribe. 2. a woman who dominates any group or field of activity.

Penguin Macquarie Dictionary

Many of the women in this book had to be convinced of their right to be called a matriarch. Apart from their natural modesty they often had a different understanding of the term. I took as my guide the definition from the *Penguin Macquarie Dictionary*. My main aim was not to focus on the interpretation of the term, but rather on the richness of the lives of these Matriarchs of our Tribe.

The twelve interviews in this collection represent the lives of women aged between sixty and a hundred from all over Australia, from different classes, different races, different religions, different cultures and different educational levels. Some of these matriarchs are well known to the public, some are not, but each is a leader in her own field of activity. I know that for every woman I selected there are thousands I neglected. We all know many matriarchs and generally agree that they are the backbone of the nation. Rarely, however, do we read about them. Our culture remains firmly patriarchal and when in 1986 I read a cover story in the *Bulletin* titled 'The Fifty Greats who shaped our Nation' and found that out of fifty only three women had been included, I became even more passionate in my desire to attempt to redress the balance. For too long our history has been dominated by stories of 'great deeds by great men', thereby totally ignoring the enormous contribution the other fifty per cent of the population has made. For too long these women have been hidden from history because their lives have been unsung and unrecorded.

I have purposely selected women whom I believe have blazed trails for others to follow. I have asked them all questions about every aspect of their lives – including their hopes, their fears and their dreams. The mood and the rhythm of each interview is different depending on the length of time we spent together, the circumstances under which we met, the person's state of mind on that particular day. The interviews vary in length, some are intense and philosophical, some light-hearted and jovial. They do however share common traits. Having completed all the interviews I did attempt to analyse whether in fact there were any similarities, and ask the question, 'What do their lives have to teach us in today's world?'

The most glaring trait the matriarchs have in common is the need to be busy. Their lives were, and still are, full of activity and they always have several pots on the boil, always wear several hats. There is not time to sit around getting depressed. Even if they had to keep going for sheer economic necessity, they still crammed as much variety and activity into their lives as they could and still do.

Secondly, they are always prepared to give anything a go. If they took on the traditional roles of wife and mother, they didn't ever think it precluded them from doing anything else. They continued to tackle new things and take new risks. Their cheerful, positive approach to life means you don't dwell on what you haven't got or haven't achieved, you just get on with the tasks at hand.

Thirdly, they were not focussed on the pursuit of 'romantic' love, finding Mr. Right and building your world around him. They were certainly never slaves to sexual passion. Such things were only part of the rich fabric of their lives. Alongside their commitment to their husbands or families they always tried to maintain another interest of their own. An orbit that was theirs alone.

The most powerful impact these interviews have had on me has been through the passion for living which illuminates them. The irresistible energy that bursts out of this book is like a blaze of sunshine, based in the firm belief that you have to take full responsibility for who you are, pick up your life in both hands and get on with it. These women have no time to think about the process of ageing – they're too busy, their lives are too full.

No nation can afford to turn its back on the accumulated wisdom of its matriarchs. Now that the extended family has largely disappeared, many people, especially the young, no longer have access to the knowledge of women of older generations. Many people, like myself, have never known a grandmother. Ours is generally a culture that is afraid of growing older because we associate age with powerlessness, loneliness and of course death. These women will not only challenge these fears head on, but will dispel them by catapulting you into a new perspective. These are modern, forward-thinking women who have an inextricable link with our past, present and future. In a country where the percentage of people over sixty years of age will increase from an average of 14 per cent now to an average of 22 per cent by the first decade of the next century, and more than half of them will be women.

It is imperative that we value this potential. Now perhaps more than at any other stage in our history we need to tap this collective wisdom and utilize all our resources. We need to rediscover the powerful pioneering spirit that is so alive in these women. My life is richer for having met and talked with these marvellous matriarchs. I believe we have a great need in our country and in our culture for such role-models. I hope people of all ages read their stories and gain strength and wisdom from them.

Now is the time to sing their praises and celebrate their achievements. I make no apologies for the unabashed admiration and pride I feel for these women, nor will you after you have read the stories of their lives.

Shaping the Community

Margaret Whitlam

Social Worker and Journalist

For a while I began to think Margaret Whitlam was the most elusive woman in Australia. After several unsuccessful attempts to ascertain her home number I left innumerable messages over the next month at her husband's office. I followed these up as requested with an explanatory letter. I began to think the silence was ominous. Then one day I returned from work to a message on my answering machine which said 'Hello, it's Margaret Whitlam speaking. You're clearly not home. I'll ring again'. Was there ever a more infuriating message? I continued to ring her husband's office. Silence. Finally with a deadline looming I left a message to say I would be in Sydney for the last week of February and that hopefully some arrangement could be made during that time.

My very first task on arrival was to ring her husband's office, announce that I was actually in Sydney and waiting by the phone. That afternoon, evening and the next day produced no result. By this time I was desperately phoning all my contacts in Sydney to find out the Whitlam's home number by fair means or foul. All to no avail. On the third day I went to the Blue Mountains to discuss a friend's forthcoming book and after a relaxed lunch and another bottle of wine revealed the cause of my despair. Never one to be defeated my friend said 'why not send a telegram? Women of Margaret Whitlam's generation always respond to telegrams. It has something to do with the war.' We agonized over the wording of the telegram as if it were a poem. Finally it read DESPERATELY SEEKING MARGARET WHITLAM.

SINCERELY, SUSAN. (With the appropriate phone numbers of course.)

Upon returning to Sydney the next day and discovering there was still no message on the answering machine I rang the office and was assured that my telegram had arrived. With only two days left before my return to Adelaide I began to compose an intricate plot in my head with Margaret Whitlam as the villain. Or was it the secretary? Or her husband's driver? Or her husband? Perhaps the Whitlams had split up and that's why the messages weren't getting through. I was becoming an obsessive bore, unable to talk of anything else. Late that afternoon a phone call shattered the silence. And there once again was that cheery warm voice that I had been longing to hear. She explained that she had been impossibly busy with several time-consuming projects like reading all the novels for the National Book Council Awards and taping a television program for the ABC. She was of course totally unaware of the panic and drama that she had created in my life.

The next day as I sat in her harbourside apartment, chatting and drinking coffee, I found it hard to believe that I hadn't known her all my life.

I was probably an obedient child, or wasn't unlovely. I was always tall. Until I was four there was Mother, Dad and me. And then we were four when my brother was born. I had a simple childhood. I was born one day at home – as people were in those days – in fact I think my grandmother was midwife. She was a professional midwife. At that stage my father was still a law student. It was just after the war and he had done his Arts. Then he did Law after and was associate to the Chief Justice. So he had to travel around a bit. Mother would have been left to look after me – although they took me in a basket. I was a babe-in-arms on some of the journeys to Melbourne. I remember her saying she hired a girl one day to take me out – they were doing other things – and Mother discovered that the the girl would take me down to the beach front at St. Kilda, meet her boyfriend and just feed me chocolates all the time. For a one-year-old baby that wasn't too bad.

We lived in a semi-detached house. It had an upstairs and downstairs and a nice little garden and every time I think of that I remember a picture of myself dressed as a fairy aged four down on the front lawn, wand and everything. Was it a fancy dress ball, or a concert or something? I can't think why I was dressed as a fairy. Probably because I wanted to be one and Mother thought 'she'd better have a fairy dress before she's too large'.

I went to Bondi Public School until I was ten and a half and then I went off to SKEGS at Darlinghurst. I was there for seven and a half years. I enjoyed that too but not to the sooky extent that some kids did. All those girls weeping around the place, crying out 'I don't want to go, I'll miss you!' In those days girls did that at girls schools. I didn't fool about. I was quite happy. I always feel when something ends, something new is going to begin, and it's all going to be so exciting.

I am fatalistic I think rather than optimistic.

Adolescence was OK. I was always doing things. I think it's terribly important for kids to be doing things. I remember my father used to refer to my activities as my uniforms, and he'd say, 'Good God, what uniform will we see the girl in next?' At that stage I think it was Greek dancing. He just couldn't quite come at that one. At school I always played basketball and hockey and while I wasn't a great runner I used to do the hurdles for fun.

I was always interested in drama at school and then at university. Strangely in drama somehow my height didn't seem to matter too much. There was always something I could do on stage or off. I could be a voice off in many things – and others I could be a handmaiden, or a servant. I could be the lead in play-readings, because you tended to stand or sit at a mike for that. I didn't feel at all frustrated in my interest in theatre. I had learnt ballet as a child. That was one of my uniforms. But I didn't learn after I was about eleven. I had too may other things that I was doing, but it satisfied my curiosity about what makes ballet dancers tick. You don't have to be a good performer to know how much skill and hard work goes into it. Much much later on when we were living at Cronulla, I remember going off to the Sutherland Evening College with a few of the girls, mothers of two or three, to do art, which really meant we were learning how to draw. Even learning the correct way to hold the pencil, the right pencil to use and learning to paint in oils, gives you an appreciation of the real professional.

Mother was very much a committee woman before and during the war. She was, for many, many years, President of the Red Cross in one particular city branch. During the war she worked for the Navy, because that was the service my brother was in. And I worked, I was a VA. When I was at University I was Commandant of the Sydney University VA's, in fact, I was supposed to go off to the Middle East with that first lot of VA's that went over, but Father put his foot down. He said he didn't approve of unpaid slave labour going off to war. So I stayed home and got married.

There was a family story that was always told, that went 'What are you going to do when you grow up?' And I said, 'Oh I'm going to be a social butterfly and go on moonlight exertions'. I'd seen it written up on the ferries or something, moonlight excursion. And anybody that doesn't hear the word spoken and who is young and impressionable, is inclined to think it's exertion.

I was a bit of a social butterfly. I did go out on moonlight exertions, with emphasis on the exertion.

University wasn't so deadly earnest in those days. But I know I wanted to be a journalist really. I started off in Economics simply because Journalism only offered social reporting. I didn't want to do that sort of reporting. I only wanted to do the socializing. I wanted to be the butterfly. So I did Economics and in the first year I also did English 1 and German 1. It was a bit too much. I passed half the things and repeated the other half the next year while I went to Business College and learned Shorthand and Typing at the same time. Then the third year I did Second Year Economics and I'd already decided I thought Social Studies was the thing for me, but you had to be 20 to do it. So at the end of that year I transferred to Social Studies.

I was always in team things. When I went to university I played tennis and I swam, inter-varsity, and that was terrific fun.

I was too busy to be keen on boys. Fortunately because I was so tall I don't think boys were really interested in me until I got to university. In fact, I used to go to lots of parties in my last two years at school – and really agonize. I loved the places and loved the people but there were always dances where we'd have programmes

Right: 'Margaret wishes you a Merry Christmas' from a family card, 1920
Below left: A fairy in the garden, 1922?
Below right: Girl Guide, 1932

and the boys would never want to dance with a great long streak. You know how immature boys are compared with girls of the same age. I really hated it.

The first year or two at university I was swimming competitively. I'd seldom be home for dinner. It was incredible. When I look back my parents were very forebearing. They would leave me a tray of something on the dressing table. Or a thermos of hot watered milk and a sandwich, in case I hadn't had any dinner, which was good.

My father was at the bar and he was a very busy K.C., which was King most of the time. Then of course he was a judge. He went on the Bench before I was married.

Both were influences. My father was marvellous to me as a confidante. As a mentor, he'd try and urge me into something a little more ambitious. For instance, I thought I'd do nursing because his mother and his sister had done nursing. And he said, 'If you're so interested, do Medicine, with a capital M'. So he took me out to the university and showed me around the Med. School and everything, the old darling.

He took me into the museum in the old Med. School with all these babies in bottles and I thought, 'Oh no'. It put me off for life. And then he took me around to the Economics Department and we saw the Prof. and we decided that a go at economics wouldn't be too bad. He said, 'Look, you'll have a good time at university. You're mad not to give it a go. Just for the year'. And of course after the year I was hooked. He was very helpful. Mother was very helpful too, very supportive, particularly later on, after I was married and had all the children.

We were living at Cabramatta at this time and Gough got a grant to go to America for three months. We didn't have much money and I wasn't included in the grant and I was really cross about this. So anyway I dug in every pocket. I had a little insurance policy and I went off three weeks after he did and took a week to get to where he was in the States. I spent all my savings doing it. I was bemoaning this fate and Mother said, 'You look in the paper all the time. The kids are nearly grown up', the youngest was 10 I think, and she said 'they're crying out for social workers. Why don't you go back to work part-time and then you'll never be short of the wherewithal if he's got to go on these things again'.

The accommodation always provides for two people but the fares and things do not. So when I came back from that particular journey, when I'd spent all my money, I looked in the paper and there were a couple of advertisements asking for social workers. So I rang up and said 'How old do you have to be? Do you want a fresh, new graduate?' They said, 'No, no we don't care. Age is of no importance really. It's qualifications. As long as you've got a Diploma of Social Work that's what we are interested in. Would you like to come over and talk about it?' So I said, 'All right'. So over I went. It was the Parramatta District Hospital, which wasn't too far away from where we were living. And they fell upon me and my Diploma.

I said, 'I can't work full-time, it would have to be part-time'. And they said, 'Terrific, you name the hours, and the days'. They kept to their word. They were wonderful. I got school holidays off. They gave me two weeks to just walk around the hospital and meet all the people in charge of all the departments and make myself known to them. It was a terrific job. And that was mother saying have a go. She was a frustrated, would-be academic, I think. She was very bright at Sydney Girls High, and got a bursary to the university, which included accommodation at the Women's College but she had no parents at all. Her father had been drowned several years before and her mother had died some years before that. She was the eldest of three who were being looked after by aunts and an uncle actually in the house when they were left. She was more or less responsible for the younger kids, so it was just impossible for her. Uncle wouldn't let her live in college and he wouldn't give her enough money to pay her fare to the university – so she left and got a job teaching at a little private school. She'd already met Dad. So she went on from strength to strength doing nothing, if you know what I mean.

Boys were never any problem. I met Gough at a science party. He and I had heard of each other from mutual friends and I think we knew that each would be at this particular party. And that was that. He was the most gorgeous thing I'd ever seen in my life. Sometimes he still is.

When he first proposed, I remember his words were, 'I wouldn't mind if we got hitched.' I hadn't really been waiting for it. Even though I felt at the time when I met him that he was really very much the one for me. I then went a little bit cold on the idea.

We were married in April '42 and I was 22 the previous November. He was a law student and at the time we were married he was on the Reserve of the Air Force, waiting for his call-up. In those days you had to go off to aircraft recognition classes and morse code things. He was doing that for about six months or a year and finally got his call-up for the intake of an air-crew. I think it was when he got word of his call-up, he said 'We might as well get hitched don't you think?'

When we were married I was in the second year of the diploma and doing the practical work in the vacations. Then I had to do six weeks practical work at the end of that year. It was rather protracted because I got scarlet fever. Gough was in camp at Sale and he had lots of relatives in Melbourne, because he was born there. So I got down to Melbourne for Christmas to meet him because he was out for a few days. I came back by train and sat next to a very sick soldier. I didn't know what was wrong with him. He was very feverish and 24 hours later I had scarlet fever, which wasn't very nice. You had to take what you could get in travel. I flew down but no way could I get a flight back. I was lucky to get on a train really. I eventually finished the practical work and then I got a job with the Family Welfare Bureau as a social worker.

I used to go out as a sort of field officer on all these home visits, advising all and sundry on how to budget and how to do without their husbands and how to care for their children in the absence of their husbands.

No wonder you had to be 20 to start that course. I can remember one woman when I went off to reassure her about the care her children were given in some particular home whilst she was hospitalized, saying, looking at me earnestly, 'Miss would you send your children there?' That was my gauge in future. I thought every place I look at for placements, it was mostly children, I'd grade it as to whether I'd send my relatives there. It made it easier.

I liked the work. It was a very good course then, because it made you know your community, know what was lacking in the community and know where to find aid. It was very useful in after life for instance, when Gough went into parliament I was doing welfare

University days. Margaret with her mother in the city

work all the time, showing people here, there and everywhere. Helping them with all kinds of problems.

I'd only been working about six months and I became pregnant on one of Gough's leaves, on purpose. I thought terrific, but I was as sick as a dog. I couldn't get up because I'd been so sick, and was coming late into the office. The chief social worker would say to me, 'Now Mrs Whitlam, you are coming in a bit late you know. I think you should come in a little earlier than this'. And I said 'Well Miss Moffat', I can remember her name, 'I won't be coming in at all soon because I feel so sick'. 'Oh, really.' 'Well don't worry, everything's all right. Whatever time you think you can spare us. I don't want you to do too much, or go too far. You come in when you feel allright'. So I left when I was about four months pregnant. These days girls keep on until they're eight months, which is good. Actually I was pretty silly, because by the time I left I should have been feeling allright and I might have been feeling all right if I'd stayed on and worked. As it was I continued to be sick morning, noon and night, until he was two weeks late. That happened with at least two, and I think the third one too.

There was quite a lot of reference to bringing up children in the newspapers as well as the weekly magazines and everybody read the *Womens Weekly* in those days and I mean everybody. The *Womens Weekly* was a family magazine. If somebody hadn't bought it, there would be all hell to pay. I remember, I used to buy it on the way to school or somebody would, and we'd all pore over it and if it had enough things that were good enough, we'd all buy our own copies.

The weekend papers had lots of articles on bringing up children and of course there was the inevitable Dr. Spock. Baby health centres were very big. Once you had the baby, it was absolutely obligatory to make your weekly visit.

I don't know whether they're fun in quite the same way now but there used to be one in every district and I went to one over at Rose Bay. You'd bundle the baby up, get it on the bus, and away you'd go. And you had your little book. We weighed every week, and there'd be hell to pay if it hadn't put on the right amount of weight. There would also be hell to pay if it'd put on too much weight. Then you'd have to do a test feed to see if it was a gobbler.

Gough was off at the war being a hero with the first one. And the second one was born just after the war had ended, December 1945. And he was busy working then. We were trying to build a house with the money that was going to take him to Oxford (as a post-graduate student) that his grandfather had left him. It almost covered the cost of our house. I remember how it cost more than it was supposed to. It cost eighteen hundred and fifty pounds. It was supposed to cost sixteen hundred I think. The land cost one hundred and ninety pounds and the house was double-brick with two bedrooms, separate dining room, entrance, little sort-of balcony thing, bathroom and kitchen. Incredible when you think about it.

I was a little bit put-out should I say, being left alone with the children a lot. At first. It takes a while to get used to it. There hadn't been any babies around in our family for a long, long while and I wasn't very *au fait* with the care of children. I don't find babies' company stimulating. But as they got older they became good mates. I got used to the routine. He used to go – even before he was in parliament – into the office six days a week and he'd come home on Saturdays in the afternoon. I was ready to play. I didn't want to produce hot dinners and things. I was pretty cross. Which was stupid of me. After all, if he didn't go in on Saturdays, he didn't get the briefs that were around.

Anyway when he got into parliament he was away from Monday night to Friday morning. I got used to that too, particularly after I'd been to Canberra and I'd seen how they worked. I was quite happy to listen to the debates on the radio and I really became quite fascinated by politics at that stage.

He joined the Party when we were living at Elizabeth Bay after the war. (The Kings Cross branch.) I knew he was interested in the administration of the Party but he wasn't particularly interested in being a candidate at first. Then he was asked to stand for the local council. I don't think he did. If he did, he certainly didn't get in. But he did stand as a state candidate and gave the local Liberal a great run for his money. He began to be interested in this and had an opportunity to join a great list of those for pre-selection for the seat of Werriwah, out of eleven candidates. When he won that, we knew he was in business. I didn't think he was destined to be prime minister. That was really never in our minds.

Frankly, I didn't think too seriously about it. Several wives of people within the business had tried to put me off and some had told me it was OK. Several people on Bob Menzies' side had tried to talk Gough out of standing as a Labor candidate. They thought he was the sort of material that they wanted.

No way could he join the Liberals. They were stunned to think that he would not join them. A lot of people spread around the world a rumour that he was once a member of the Liberal Party. He was never a member and never would be. He actually influenced me in my total acceptance of the Labor Party because he said, 'If you want to have anything to do with politics, you choose the party that has the most things with which you agree, with which you're in accord. There's no way you're ever going to be in accordance with everything that the political parties put up'. It was up to me if I wanted to join.

I must confess that meetings are a bit dreary and sometimes I wonder if they're necessary except at times of elections when you've got to raise funds. Although I suppose it's the natural way of putting some sort of philosophy in the platform.

I joined the Party but I didn't always go along when the children were little.

I spent my time reading, listening to music, knitting, friends mostly on the weekends, and local movies at night with friends. We had a good group down there in Cronulla and we'd mind each other's kids. Town was quite a distance away and there weren't all these decentralized shopping centres. The kids would go around to the other house after school or even before school, and we'd share things like boxes of oranges and apples and sides of lamb. We had a really good community spirit.

Even before Gough was in parliament, I was working with school things. He was also working with school things, the Progress Association and the Children's Library Association, and was very much concerned with that in Cronulla. We were always busy with some sort of community activity.

When we went to Cabramatta which was rather withdrawn from the life that we'd been leading, we determined to carry on as before. It was no problem. Actually at Cronulla I'd been doing WEA courses, discussion groups and things. I started them up at Cabramatta. There are always like-minded people wherever you live.

Somebody has to make a start. We had fantastic evenings in both those places where we lived the longest time. It was never lonely, no sense of isolation. Even the kids used to enjoy what they called 'Mum's culture evenings'. They'd slink in, from their rooms where they were supposed to be doing homework, and they'd sit in and listen on a discussion group on music or art or literature or politics. And when I'd suggest that they might disappear, I remember one in particular saying 'I'm enjoying the 'convo's Mum'. They would say, 'One of the culture ladies rang up today. Are you going to culture tonight Mum?'

These discussion groups tended to be just the women, so once father got home, if he got home late, he got his dinner plonked in front of him. 'All right you're on tonight, I'm off.' We'd take turns around the various houses. Apart from that I think he enjoyed being on his own to play his music, and read his books.

We were in Cronulla from 1947 to 1957 and then we were in Cabramatta from '57 to '72. I went back to social work in Cabramatta in '64 and I was there until '67. During that time I was doing – don't know how I got into it – some television panel shows. They liked the way I did them, so I got a chance to do a couple of presenting jobs in television too. Which was fun. That was in '73. We were pretty brave doing that, we didn't do a pilot or anything. It was an hour-long programme.

Looking back I was a bit of a pioneer in that regard. It was unfortunate that it was at the time that Gough was Prime Minister because there were those elements in the business world that didn't want the programme to succeed.

They did the best they could by putting it on later in the evening so of course the ratings failed. The sponsors couldn't afford to do another series although it was going really well and had really good reviews. Most of it was really OK. I had a couple of duds who had to be told it was due to a technical error that their part had not come out well.

I usually taped two at least in a day, mostly in Melbourne. I enjoyed it enormously. Sometimes I did three. I had really nice people working with me, and I got to understand, there again you see, what makes a television programme tick. Before that I was writing for two magazines. In the *Women's World*, it was headed

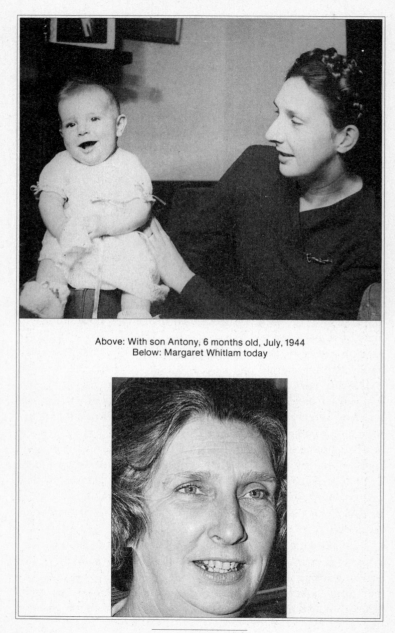

Above: With son Antony, 6 months old, July, 1944
Below: Margaret Whitlam today

'Margaret Whitlam says'. It was sort of Dorothy Dixer – letters would come in – giving social work advice. It was an extension of that. I've done lots of commissioned articles. I've done a great many book reviews and that's what I'm doing at the moment. You can do them in your own time. The deadlines are not difficult to meet. I enjoy doing them. It orders your reading, otherwise you flit from bough to bough like a stupid woodpecker. I don't know whether a woodpecker flits from bough to bough.

I do find I'm busy enough to keep up with my social engagements and Gough's and do the little bit of reviewing that I'm doing.

But I loved television. If you're not really interested in something, when in doubt, don't. Television is just being interested in people, wanting to know about them and wanting the world to know more about them. It was called 'With Margaret Whitlam'.

I had Antarctic explorers, racing drivers, pop music composers and publishers and on the very first programme, Leonard Bernstein. That meeting has been a continuing delight. Just before I left Paris, he was performing and I got tickets for the show. Then on the night I had to go to something diplomatic with Gough, and I was so cross. I gave the tickets to friends, and then I thought 'Blow this', so I wrote him a little note and sent it around to the stage door, saying that I had hoped to see him and hear him, etc. He rang the next day and made arrangements for me to come into a rehearsal because he was only there a couple of days.

I went into the rehearsal, and it was the Israeli Philharmonic Orchestra who had security, security, security. You could understand it in Paris at that time, but do you think I could get past the second lot of security blokes. They did not want to know me. He had left strict instructions that I was to be admitted. By the time I arrived the bloke wouldn't let me in for two reasons. He said nobody had given him my name, he knew nothing about me. I got into the hall and got up onto the floor where they were recording and he said, 'Apart from that Mr Bernstein's started recording'. I said 'Oh, well can I send a note into him?' and he said 'OK'. So I wrote a card saying I came, did not see and was conquered. So then – I had to go away. I was so depressed. But then the next morning at the crack of dawn, the most wonderful flowers arrived and he rang and said he was just off to Brussels or somewhere, and he was so disappointed.

He is such an emotional man. He said 'We will meet Margaret, you and I will meet and we will embrace'. Such a funny European expression.

When I met him in '73 he insisted on me going off with him to a party that was being given for him and the orchestra. I said 'I can't do that'. And he said 'you can, I can take whoever I like.' So off I swanned to this party, which was given by the State Premier, Rupert Hamer, at the time, who was a little surprised to see the Prime Minister's wife sweep in on the arms of Leonard Bernstein. Lenny and I had an instant rapport.

People used to ask me, 'How do you see your role as wife of the Prime Minister?' And I'd say, 'I'm still finding it.' If you ask me to do something I'll do it if I can and if I can't, I'll say that's not my role, not my job. You just do what you can of that job. Particularly since nobody's paying you for a job that has pre-requisites and requirements. You are not handed that job, with a salary and conditions that you have to do so many dinners, and so many receptions and so many morning teas a week and that you must change your clothes five times a day. You just do what you can.

It works out in different ways. I enjoyed a lot of it enormously but the part of having to be there – in Canberra – and on tap, so to speak, used to annoy me a bit. But I demanded to know what was expected of me a week or so in advance so that I'd at least make a programme for myself. It's all very well sitting on your thumb doing nothing for a week or so, but you don't want to do it for three months.

I made my little programme and said 'OK I'm seldom going to be available on Tuesdays when we're in Canberra because I'm going to play golf. Let me know if you're going to have these men's dinners or working dinners so that I can go out and see some of our friends instead of having dinner on a tray up in the room watching TV'.

You've got to stand up for yourself and make those little rules otherwise you find yourself living a nursery life, doing what you're told and not complaining. Being seen but not heard. I suppose simply because I answered the questions that were put to me I was always thought to be heard too often. Although that's not necessarily the public perception.

I just saw that role of Prime Minister's wife as being human towards other humans and not treating them badly.

Those people who are worthwhile make you feel so good anyway. The Queen makes you feel totally comfortable. There's no reason in the world to feel apprehensive of an audience with her. I do remember feeling that some people were being a little patronizing when they said 'How many people on the staff will you have?' I said 'They'll be doing what I'll be doing except that I won't have time to do it. I'll just tell them what needs to be done'. I said 'I've always done the house-keeping and a butler may not be necessary'. It proved right. I off-loaded the butler. We made do with the female staff and the house was run by women. Three wonderful house-maids, and a female cook, and it was no problem. If I wasn't there they knew what I expected to be done. They could set up the working lunch or working dinner for 50 people in for drinks or whatever. Same thing in Paris when we were there recently. That was a house-hold run by women. A female cook, Malaysian, one housemaid, a sort of butler/valet. One Chinese, one Sri Lanken. Our common language was English rather than French. It is interesting that those households were run by an entirely female staff. I was the house-keeper, I did the accounts and so forth. The cook used to check them out when the orders would come in and it was fairly rewarding to see that large households could be run in that manner. I loved living there. I don't mean the grandeur and the fact of having staff. I could well be without that. In fact on the weekends we always did for ourselves and we always did our own breakfast. So there was nothing superimposed that was uncomfortable. Who wouldn't like living in the most beautiful, the most sophisticated city in the world? The most tempestuous city in the world? But not for ever. That's why I'm glad to be back and trying to settle into my small quarters with my stored and acquired goods – still not unpacked.

Public occasions can be really rather fun. Sometimes you get out of control. You can be at something pretty toffy and it's so ridiculous, people are so pretentious and you can have a bit of a giggle. It's a bit like giggling at school. Sometimes Gough and I can't look at each other or we set each other going. I think a sense of humour is absolutely essential. And a sense of not being the greatest thing since sliced bread. You musn't have too great a sense of your own importance because really nobody else will have.

1975 – not the best experience in the world. The worst thing about it was that we weren't together when it happened. I was in Sydney at a meeting, and he was in Canberra in parliament. Sometimes people say what would you have done if you had been there? I say, I would have torn up the document of dismissal. I really would have. Also a mini-revolution would have helped. I can't see how they could accept that proclamation. I really can't. I just don't know why they didn't walk inside and say 'That's what you say, but here we are, we are the elected people and we're going on with our business?'

I was staying at Kirribilli House and when Gough rang, I said 'I'm moving out of here?' He said 'Well perhaps you could go to the flat?' We had just bought this place as a weekender. The women staff at Kirribilli House said 'Don't go, don't go'. When they saw that I was determined they said 'We'll help you'. And they went off and lined the kitchen cupboards and filled them up. Our daughter and our doctor were with me. He had called in to see if I was allright. He was very worried about the shock – which I was probably in at the time. We all had a slap-up dinner with lots of wine. The next day my English daughter-in-law, who was absolutely stunned by it all, came with me to town to buy a television to see what they were saying about us. She lived in Woollahra and couldn't believe the behaviour of the pretentious conservatives in the eastern suburbs. My friends rang up and said 'Don't go hiding yourself – we'll have lunch here and dinner there'. Then Gough arrived and from then on it was all work for the elections – which we really did believe we were going to win. We thought people would be so angry, even though they were displeased with some of the things that were happening or not happening. I remember my mother saying to me at the time 'Isn't there something that Gough could do to make him popular'. I said 'No, he's too honest'. He said when he went in that it was going to be difficult to do popular things apart from the withdrawal from Vietnam. Mother could see that things weren't going too popularly. She suffered too. In three years she had stayed one whole night in Kirribilli House and that was after she had been in hospital. When she went home somebody rang her up and abused her for using the Prime Minister's facilities. People are awful.

It's not fair to take it out on other people. I don't think Gough was ever aware of the victimization that our kids had at school, until afterwards.

I was angry not only with the injustice of it but the ungainly, unmannerly way in which it was all done, by people who regard themselves as being leaders of society. If my children behaved in the manner in which they behaved, I would have beaten them. They were just so unmannerly, so ungentlemanly, so rude. In a country like this, how dare they? That really did rile me terribly.

I became very snaky afterwards. I've had a couple of opportunities to throw back in some people's faces activities and sayings that were done on purpose to hurt not just me, but my family. Quite unexpectedly on several occasions I've met people who I know have been more than unkind to my kids because of their father's position. I think to visit the sins of anybody on anybody else is ridiculous but in that particular regard it is just awful. I met one eastern suburbs matron who was smarming up to me and said she thought we'd met many years ago and did I ever go to such and such. I said 'Oh yes, I go there quite often. That's the place and that's the occasion when you and some of your friends caused me so much unhappiness. Do you recall such and such and so and so?' And she said 'Oh'. Somebody else came up to talk to me at that time so I just turned away from her. I thought thank goodness I've got that off my chest to that one anyway. Now she knows, she won't smarm anymore. They think you forget when you don't forget and don't forgive. If something comes on that reminds me of it I think 'Oh yes, it's that person and that one. Right I've got ammunition for you today mate'. I can be a good hater if I have to. I feel they deserve it – some have been getting away with it for a long time.

I thought the Women's Movement was terrific in that people became more aware of women's needs, women's lack of facilities, lack of opportunity and lack of means. But I have never been keen on aggressive feminism. It doesn't get you anywhere, even though some of the best of the so-called aggressive feminists made some marvellous moves. I think Germaine Greer made some wonderful pronouncements, but she's made some disastrous ones too. She was initially our Joan of Arc. If you look around you do find many more women in meaningful positions and that's good. It's not so hard for women to be considered for jobs any more. Equal pay for equal work didn't make it easy for women to get jobs because they just closed those doors, knowing they would have to pay the same amount. Now with the Equal Opportunities Act, it's probably less of a problem. I think that the people who did the best work in the early days for women were the Women's Electoral Lobby.

I am a feminist in so far as I don't want to be trodden on and I don't want to be used as somebody's handbag. I am not an accessory. I'm not an active feminist – probably too lazy to stride out and sing songs and make demands. I don't know whether I'm too lazy or too shy.

I used to be a shy person. I really was. My mother would get so cross with me when I'd go with her to big do's that maybe Dad wouldn't. She always had great confidence going into a room and bounding up to people and chatting away to them. I used to think I don't know any of these people. It was awful. Now it doesn't worry me at all. She jollied me out of it, and said, 'Just stand there by the door, look around, and if you know anybody go up to them, and if you don't know anybody, find out who they are. You know full well Margaret, that you look just as good as anybody in that room so off you go'. She was right really. So now it doesn't bother me I find the reverse – too many people talking to me. I'm not averse to going to the theatre, the opera, ballets, concerts alone, if at the last moment whoever I was going with can't go. I cannot be bothered ringing up people and saying 'Oh look, so and so can't go tonight, do you want to come?' I just don't want to hear their excuses. I'll just go. Some of my family are not too keen on my doing that. They say 'why are you wandering around by yourself?' I say 'I usually meet somebody I know'. It's terrific. I remember being jealous only once or twice in my life and that was when I thought I wasn't having enough attention paid to me and somebody else was and I thought that was a bit unfair. I'm not a jealous person really. I really find it difficult to dislike people, but I don't burst into flames on first acquaintance either. Even people whose reputation has gone before them and not been the greatest, I'm prepared to form my own opinions of those people and hold to it.

When I get a bit sorry for myself and think 'Oh I'm creaking and I'm not as agile or as active in many ways as I would like to be.

Maybe I haven't got that much longer'. I'm comforted when I suddenly see old so-and-so and she's ten years older than I am and she's going like a train. Or somebody else who is twenty years older. I wouldn't mind being like my aunt who is nearly ninety-two. She's got all her marbles, but she can't get around that much. She's dependent on the television and talk. She can tell you who won the golf yesterday, and whose going to spring everything tomorrow night on television, all that sort of thing. She's right up with politics.

I had looked forward to being 40 and enjoyed it enormously. It's a terrific age. My father knew I was looking forward to it, so he called me up on the eve of my birthday and said, 'What are you doing for lunch', and I said 'I don't know, I'm going out at night'. He said 'I know you're going out at night, but what are you doing for lunch? I'll take you to Usher's. I said, 'Oh terrific'. So we had a terrific lunch and I said to him, 'This has been very nice, darling, what have I done especially? I know it's my birthday but I've had other birthdays?' He said 'It's your fortieth birthday and you told me you're always looking forward to it so I thought I'd make it a really good one'. And I said 'I've got news for you, old boy, I'm 39 today'. So we did it again next year. Mother came too. He needed a witness.

I wasn't too keen on the thought of fifty but as it turned out it was OK. The forties were the great years but the fifties were OK and the sixties are surprisingly good. You don't worry about things. The way you don't worry when you get married because you no longer worry about whether you're going to have a partner for this or that. You've got an in-built partner. It's fantastic. And then I guess afterwards you worry about all sorts of other things to do with living together. At this stage you're just happy you've got somebody you're living with. My sixties are definitely the best so far.

Dame Roma Mitchell

Queen's Counsel and Supreme Court Judge (retired)

It is not that the first woman Queen's Counsel and the first woman Supreme Court Judge in Australia is a daunting person. On the contrary Roma Mitchell is a warm, charming, extremely easy person to talk to. Why then was this the hardest interview of all? Why did I make two attempts to try and find the private person behind the public mask? Perhaps she is a product of a generation unused to discussing its private life in public. Perhaps it's because for so long she sat in wig and gown and refrained from making personal statements of any kind. Perhaps she is simply an intensely private person. Whatever the reasons, the questions remain.

After the second interview, which took place in her living room overlooking the Adelaide parklands, I reminded her that in a recent newspaper article the journalist had inferred that her failure to marry was the result of someone who had died in the war.

'He's quite wrong. Quite wrong. Certain things in my life are private and that's that. Now, is it time for us to have a drink?'

Each time I see Roma Mitchell I get to know her a little better. I now believe that with some people, and she is one of these, the private and the public have almost merged. My pursuit of the 'private face behind the public mask' was based on a wrong premise. With Roma Mitchell, what you see is in fact what you get. Her passion is the law. One would not obsessively question an opera singer, who had devoted her life to her talent, about some secret private person behind the public performer. For

Roma Mitchell there was always the law.

I'm someone who has always steered a pretty even course. I didn't really get into awful hassles at school but if there was ever any question of having to speak up for somebody, I always found myself doing it. I was the one saying 'That wasn't fair'. I usually got away with it because I was brought up to be a courteous child and I always tried to put the argument courteously and, I hope, well. I was a good student who got A's and enjoyed it. But I was hopeless at sport. I was skinny and small until I was about 13 or 14 when I sprang up. I think I was a fairly late maturer physically and emotionally too, which is probably an advantage.

My father was killed in World War I when I was four. He was a solicitor who didn't really like practising the law so we lived in Renmark and he liked to spend time on his bit of property outside the township. I do remember the news of his death. We were living in North Adelaide at the time and a telegram arrived, 'Missing, believed killed in action'. Everybody hoped it was wrong but in due course it was confirmed as right. My sister, Ruth, who was seven at the time, was at St. Dominic's Convent and I was allowed to walk up to the corner to meet her, not crossing the road. I told her. When we arrived home, mother told her and she burst into tears and said 'I know, Roma told me.' Afterwards mother said to me 'Why did you tell Ruth?' And I said 'I wanted to save you having to do so'. I had a very strange protective feeling. My mother and I were very close. My father's death had a very traumatic effect but not as much on me as on my sister. My mother had the most enormous economic struggle. She didn't remarry and had no profession. I think she probably would have been very keen on a career but she hadn't been brought up to work. She was a great believer in tertiary education and realized how difficult it was for women without it. She had to struggle along, keeping up appearances. Nobody cares as much about 'appearances' these days, which I think is a good thing.

My mother always felt that my father would not have stayed in the law had he survived because his heart wasn't in it, but mine always was. So my mother and sister and I grew up in this very small household. A cocoon really.

I didn't ever regret wanting to make a life of law. Some people do regret it. Adelaide University was pleasant. I was just 17. It was Depression years so although there were a few people there who came from wealthy families, nobody had any money. It was a nice, small university. We knew people from other faculties. There was only a sprinkling of women from anywhere in those days. In law we had quite a number, really. There were about thirty altogether out of about 160. It wasn't a bad proportion. Six of us started the year I started. It's a lot more now. For a long time it wasn't. Now it's at least 50 per cent, perhaps 60 per cent. The only eating place was the old refectory, which is downstairs. There was one top table for professors and then the rest of it was for all and sundry and they used to eat the pies and pasties. There were some quite distinguished people. You were cheek by jowl much more than these days.

I never dreamed I would be in the hierarchy of anything, certainly not the university. Sir George Murray was Chancellor of the university when I was a student and for some years afterwards. He was the one who purchased the beautiful Chancellor's robes that he then presented to the university. I often think when I wear them, poor old boy, it would be hard for him to know that a woman was wearing them.

We had romantic songs – they're wonderful and they still evoke memories of course. I think we pandered to the men a fair bit too. It didn't stop us from being competitive as far as work was concerned. We used to do things like debating, and French plays and things like that. I used to worry about how I looked – I think that was the time if you went to something and you thought it was going to be a long dress and it was a short dress, or vice versa, you suffered agonies. I think they are much more sensible in that respect now. I thought I was too thin. I used to try to put on weight until I was about 25. It maddens me now, while I do nothing but try to take it off. I don't think I ever had any illusions that I was any great beauty. When I look at old photographs I think I was better looking than I thought I was.

I was admitted to practise in mid-December and it was very tough

Above: 10 months old
Below: 23 years old, with sister Ruth

times for anybody to get anything at all, of any description. It really was very difficult. And more by good luck than anything I think, I discovered that Joe Nelligan and his firm were looking for somebody, and I applied to them and then he couldn't make up his mind – I thought he was never going to make up his mind, but I started there on the 19th February. That shows how important it was. I've never forgotten the date. I went there as what was called a managing clerk, for about three months and then they took me in as a paid partner and then eventually I became a partner and I stayed there – with the firm changing – right until about '61 and then for various reasons, it broke up and I had my own firm. Then I went on the Bench in '65. So I didn't move around very much.

When I began there weren't any areas of the law barred to women but I did virtually no criminal work, because we didn't have any women on juries until after I went on to the Bench. In my early days I felt that I would be a curiosity and that it would be a disservice to my clients. I suppose you could call it a self-sacrifice, I didn't regard it as such, but I still think it was a good judgement for that time because it would be a disservice to the client to have the barrister looked at more as a curiosity than otherwise. It was a deliberate choice. I was doing other work, but I was always interested in criminal law and I never had any problems with it when I went on the Bench. Some judges find it terribly difficult when they go on to the Bench.

Just before the Labor government took over from Sir Thomas Playford, I was asked if I would lead a deputation of women to argue for women on juries. They had had other deputations before and he had always said 'I wouldn't like my wife to serve on a jury'. So I prepared for it. I thought up all the arguments that would please Playford, like the National Council of Women was in favour of it and that represented however many thousands of women. Also they would get a lot of women serving on juries who weren't employed and anyway women weren't getting the same wages as men so those who served would be cheaper. I thought of all these beautiful arguments at the end of which he said, 'Yes, well I can't see any reason why women shouldn't serve on juries. I think it would be a good idea'. And much to everybody's surprise he went off cheerfully and talked to some of his ministers, who said 'I wouldn't like my wife to serve on a jury' and he dropped it. Of course when the Labor government came in they introduced it. I always felt a bit sorry for him because I knew he was all ready to do it. But in fact women didn't come onto juries until the beginning of 1966. It was ridiculous. And then of course any woman could simply say when she was served with the notice, 'I don't wish to serve', and that was it. I remember the then sheriff coming to me in despair and saying, 'I don't know how to work this because I've got to have the same proportion of women as of men as are on the electoral rolls in any panel, yet women can say 'I won't serve'. I said, 'Well, if people pass silly legislation you can expect silly results, and that's what they'll get.' But in fact they didn't because the women didn't take advantage of the loophole.

In the early days I did a lot of work in the field of domestic problems. I've acted for women who couldn't leave a violent, drunken husband because they had young children, he owned the house, nobody could order him to get out, nobody could order him to transfer the house to his wife. There were no women's shelters and no pensions. It was a pretty tough state of affairs in those days.

My main goal I suppose when I started was to be a good barrister. I was always a keen debater and liked a good fight. I certainly didn't see myself as a female Rumpole, even though I had a keen competitive spirit.

Barristers' work is exciting. You are either in the heights or in the troughs but it is never dull.

After the Depression there was the War of course. Those of us who were here worked very hard trying to keep other people's practices as well as our own going. We really worked quite hard during those years which was probably just as well. It gave us something to do. I didn't even go overseas for the first time until 1955. I was too busy. It was always tomorrow as far as I was concerned. I always worked hard. It was very much a consuming thing because I could never bear to be behind with anything. Once you get busy, you are almost always behind with things.

Circumstances dictated the fact that I never married. It wasn't a matter of a definite decision. Gradually one path closes and another one opens. I'm not prepared to go into the details because I think it's my business and nobody else's. I grew up at a time when you believed there were parts of your life that were your own. I don't think anybody does that now. Nowadays everybody tells everything, don't they? I would probably have different ideas if I were young now. There are areas of my life that I haven't discussed with anybody except the person concerned. Although my sister and I were very close, until she started the illness from which she finally died four years ago, there were people that I wouldn't have discussed with her. Nor she with me. She was very respectful of people's privacy. It was the way we were brought up. Ruth was even keener on her privacy than I am. I would just preclude certain areas. I heard a radio programme about Miles Franklin where it was suggested that Miles had consciously turned her back on getting married but I'd have doubts about that. I love reading books about other people's private lives but I wouldn't reveal such things myself. People confide in me, but I don't find myself confiding in them. Even people of my age now tell you things they would have not said twenty years ago. I'm always interested but I feel no urge to reciprocate. I think I have managed to keep my private life pretty private. Probably not as well as I think I have! I don't have any regrets. I don't think marriage in itself is an ideal. I have certainly never sat down and thought 'Oh dear, oh dear. I haven't reproduced'. I've never been lonely and I don't think I ever will be. I've always had lots of friends, the young as well as my generation. I don't think anybody really need be lonely. It's only people who are very self-centred who get lonely. There's always somebody to be interested in and if you're not a thorough bore, people are usually willing to put up with you, aren't they? I did however make a conscious decision when I went onto the Bench when I was asked whether I wanted anybody invited with me for formal occasions. I said 'No'. I've never been willing to have somebody come with me as an official companion. I wouldn't have inflicted it on anybody. They seemed to have a lot of State dinners at that stage. They are terrible because they seat you, husband-wife, husband-wife and I remember on one occasion when Joyce Steele was a minister and she took her daughter along. One night there were a lot of people absent. Somehow various people kept getting moved up and we were left at one table, just the three of us. I said 'Let's get up and shout "Votes for

Women"'" but she didn't think it was a good idea. I think it's less boring at these official functions if you can walk around and talk to people and that's easier to do if you are on your own. I usually find if I ask someone a question they'll rattle on. Of course if I get tickets to something good at the Opera, for example, then I would ask a friend along. I really am rather gregarious by nature.

As far as my career was concerned I certainly didn't ever think of becoming a judge because I wouldn't have thought anyone would have contemplated appointing a woman as a judge. I was conditioned to an acceptance of the situation. That's why the Women's Movement was so important.

I have followed the Women's Movement with considerable interest and I always thought it had to be supported. Whenever people moaned about it to me I'd say 'Look at the suffragettes. If they hadn't carried on the way they did, women wouldn't have had the vote.' I know they had to draw attention to themselves in the same way. Mind you I wasn't always convinced about the need for affirmative action. I always thought that if you quietly infiltrated the system then gradually women would just be there and discrimination would go away. It became clear to me that this quiet method of infiltration was not going to be very effective. You can't just let things drift along. You've got to do it by affirmative action. The publicity that my appointment to the Bench received really shocked me. There still hasn't been one other appointment of a woman to a Supreme Court Bench anywhere in Australia. At the time when I was appointed, the English were about to appoint the first woman to the High Court. There was a great performance over what she would be called. They first of all said she would have to be called Mr Justice and eventually they decided on Mrs Justice. I didn't think that sounded too good and Miss Justice was just as bad, so I decided for myself that I would like to be known as Justice Mitchell. Of course I'm delighted by the appointment of Mary Gaudron to the High Court. I first heard of her when she was an outstanding student. She's had good experience as Solicitor-General. At least the publicity surrounding her appointment focussed on her so-called political associations rather than the fact that she was a woman. She is very young but she doesn't have to stay there if she gets bored. She won't be able to be there as long as Sir Mellis Napier on our Bench. He went up at 42 and stayed until

Dame Roma Mitchell today

he was 84. Mary will have to retire at 70. I'm sure she will make an excellent contribution to the High Court.

You know when I started at the Bar there were no women's lavatories at the Supreme Court. I always had to walk down to my office. It was absolutely ridiculous when you think about it. I think my main reason for not wanting to draw too much attention to myself was in case they put other obstacles in my way. It was a conscious tactic on my part. I still think it was probably right for the time, but I don't think it would be right for now. It wasn't until the mid 50's that they installed a women's loo. Ridiculous!

When I went to the Bench I chose chambers that had a loo, a dressing room and an airconditioner. I had to have a separate lavatory from the male judges.

In my last few months on the Bench the Chief Justice Len King went overseas and I was Acting Chief Justice. He was keen for me to use his chambers and it suited me because I retired two days after he returned. In fact he came back early for my retirement. So I cleaned out my chambers and moved into his and then left. It wasn't quite so traumatic. All I said to the men about the loo was, 'Put a latch on that loo downstairs so we'll know if anyone's in there.' It was as simple as that by that stage.

There was certainly no problem about my being a woman when I was put on the Bench, but I didn't find any problem when I was in practice, I must say. There had been a few women elsewhere who had done court work and tried to play on their sex by asking for concessions. I think that's fatal. You neither ask nor give quarter. You don't play that sex game as far as your work is concerned. That can be left for other times. I think the young women now have too much sense to fall into that trap. But in the past there were a few who played that game.

Being on the Bench is not exciting, but it's not boring. I think the unhappiest time of my career was the six weeks when I knew I was going onto the Bench because I had agreed to do so. They were the professionally unhappiest weeks of my life, because I thought I'm going to hate this and I'm really going to miss what I'm doing so much. But I thought if I didn't accept it then, I'd probably be sorry later. I think I would have been too. I really felt I was going away from something that I did enjoy and certainly life on the Bench is not exciting. It's nothing like the Bar. It has its compensations and I was never bored with it. I had the good fortune to spend a lot of my time on the Bench when John Bray was Chief Justice. Some people from other states call that the Golden Era of the South Australian Bench. Certainly I was a part of that Bench and that mood but I would attribute it mainly to John Bray. Being on the Bench didn't make a great deal of difference to my life, except you didn't hear the legal gossip so quickly. I remember getting a congratulatory letter from one of the Melbourne judges which said 'You'll find it's a lonely life'. I thought lonely! My chambers were like a railway station with the number of people shunting in and out and I really didn't notice any difference. I believe in compulsory retirement ages. And so when my time came I simply went on to the next thing which was the Human Rights Commission. I don't believe in looking back. I was told to get a high profile for the Commission so from a life spent trying to avoid publicity I had to create it. I adapted to it. I really liked the work. Its all part of the legal system and part of the essential search for justice. I'm a fairly middle-of-the-road person in politics. I am very interested, however, in political issues even though I've never belonged to a political party. I never had any urge in that direction.

I do however think that a Human Rights Commission ought to be fairly controversial. Otherwise people would talk about human rights as though it's a nice comfortable thing and certainly everyone should have them. But when you realize that other people's human rights are going to impinge upon you, they're not nearly as comfortable as you thought they were going to be. It's good for people to know that. We had about 10,000 complaints altogether, I think a lot of people who wouldn't have had any redress got something they wouldn't have and they're so-called 'unimportant' people by and large.

My life is still extremely busy. I thought when I retired that I'd have some spare time and be able to do some work for Meals on Wheels. I think that kind of work is very important for the human contact it gives people who need it. But I haven't had a spare moment. One door closes and another one opens. I hardly ever watch television. I'm out to dinner most nights with friends. I go to music and theatre and opera whenever I can. I do cook when I'm at Carrickalinga where I share a beach-house with two women friends. I love to spend time there on week-ends, swimming and walking along the beach. I have many friends in Sydney, Melbourne and Canberra. I love spending time with them. I have very warm feelings for people I'm fond of and have a great capacity for loving. Although I've got a quick temper, I'm pretty good-natured and don't easily lose my cool. I like to get on with people. I probably have more real friends than most people but that is probably because I don't have any family. I have some cousins around the place but we're not a close-knit family.

My mother used to say she'd seen enormous changes in her lifetime but I don't think she saw half as many as I have. The Women's Movement is very largely responsible. Just had the wireless on for something the other day and I don't even remember what it was about, but the speaker said 'Oh that was when I was living with so and so, naming a man'. I thought, 'Well, you know, when I was younger, they would have cut that out'. Now it just comes so naturally. I think it's a good thing. This may sound contradictory to you, but I think it's a good thing that people don't find it necessary to conceal things. I don't think that people should tell you 'all' whether you want to know it or not, because that could be very boring and oppressive. Women now as a matter of course go on with their careers after marriage, and particularly after children. It was the rare bird who could do that in my time. Virtually all gave up their careers. And even a more interesting thing is now the wife or woman takes a job somewhere and the husband or companion follows her. That would have been unheard of. We had a few people in the Human Rights Commission who were working part-time and who had a husband or friend who were also working part-time, so they took their turns in looking after young children. I noticed it more particularly then because of the people in our office I came into contact with. I wouldn't see that sort of thing much in the life I've led otherwise. The legal profession has been conservative. Although nowadays they're coming around to the notion of part-time work. I've never thought that there was any innate attribute that was particularly related to males or to females. Upbringing in many cases has led to the men feeling important, and you certainly see examples of it, plenty of them. But they're not necessarily the people you value. I do think on the whole women don't value themselves as highly. That's why if you were making a high academic appointment you get plenty of applications from men, some of whom are unsuitable, but virtually none from women. I think that a lot of that is due to the fact that they haven't had the experience to fit them for it. But the point is that some of the males haven't either, but they put themselves forward.

I am, however, concerned about women in the university field. In Adelaide, we've only just appointed our second female professor. Now there is something the matter there and it's going to take time to remedy it. Traditionally, how much you have published has been one of the main criteria. A lot of young women haven't published because they've been having children, but if you looked at them and said take her at 35 and the top contender of the men and ask who has the most potential. That's how we have to start persuading people to look at it. How we do that I'm not sure. I know I wouldn't have reached the level I did in my career if I had married. Many women are prepared to put up with their husband never being at home. It's still hard for them to ask a man to put up with it. And then there's the old-boy network. I would still rather break down the male network than start up an alternative female network, but that may be the only alternative. What worries me is the creation of yet another elite.

I don't think I've lived by my instincts. I have found at times – coming back to people again – somebody that I've been very attracted by at first sight, that I've been right. But then there have been people, that you meet, and you think – I'm not very interested in this person, and they turn out to be somebody you really value. So I don't always think that your instinct tells you. I mean some people are instant bores. Sometimes you get pleasant surprises, sometimes you get unpleasant surprises. So I don't trust intuition.

When you're young it's very hard to understand that old people feel exactly the same as they felt when they were young. Things get a little less, quite a lot less acute, both in misery and in joy, and certainly in expectation. But otherwise you're essentially the same person.

Above: Justice Mitchell (centre) with Mr Justice Hogarth
(Left) and Mr Justice Mayo (right)
(Photograph: Vern Thompson, *The Advertiser,* Adelaide)
Below: University of Queensland graduation ceremony, 1984

I don't think anybody looks forward to the idea of dying, because somehow you feel, you, the essential you, can never really go, don't you? You have the egotism. But I certainly don't sit and count the years and think – this is it, this must be it.

A lot of my friends have died. At some part of your life you know only two or three people who have died, and now you think, more people I've known and loved have died than are still living.

But you feel it's a very long time ahead even though the years start flitting by quickly. That's where I think the hope of something afterwards, and of meeting the essential quality of the people that you've loved is strong, but it can't be anything more than a hope. It would be nice if that is what will happen. Then you think, how could it happen with all the millions who've died. Then you think, I'm not God; it's not for me to determine how.

I think it's much better to let people go on doing their own things, while they can. No, I don't think people get any wiser. They get more experienced, but that's all.

As soon as feminist became a term to label certain women, people would say to me 'Look at what you've done. And you're not a feminist'. And I would say 'I am a feminist'. I think the feminists probably thought I was a bit old hat in the beginning, but I refused not to be associated with them. When people go on against affirmative action it usually takes the wind out of their sails when I say 'I might have thought that way fifteen years ago, but I've moved on.' And that's what you must do, keep moving on.

Betty Makin

Community Worker

You won't find Betty Makin's name in the *Who's Who of Australia* – yet. She is one of the matriarchs of South Sydney and in particular the suburb of Redfern. She had no formal education yet government architects now ask her advice before they design public housing.

I sat with her in the living room of her Housing Commission flat where she and her husband have raised their five children. Her connections with the area date back to her great grandfather. When she decided that the New South Wales Housing Commission was not going to destroy an area she and her family had grown up in and loved, the fight was on. She joined with concerned residents in other areas to stop the building of highrise developments. She taught herself and others the skills of lobbying politicians and government departments. The ensuing years involved visits to Parliament House, organizing petitions, barricading the streets against demolishers and above all attempting to keep up the fighting spirit in her fellow residents. It was a twelve-year battle and she won. She is living proof that ordinary working class people do not have to be powerless in the face of an uncaring bureaucracy. Although she shrugs off praise for her amazing efforts, her success in reviving Housing Commission policy is a truly great achievement.

Everyone in the area knows Betty and the phone never stopped ringing the whole time I was there. She remains the shining light in the community to whom others can come for help. In 1974 she helped organize a meeting in Redfern Town Hall out of which grew the South Sydney Committee of the Australian Assistance Plan, which was the mainspring for numerous self-help community activities. A rich community spirit has returned to the area and even if she had the choice Betty Makin says she wouldn't live anywhere else.

My teacher, Miss Lucy Woodcock, had a great influence in my life. In my first year at high school she was the Head of the Teachers' Federation in New South Wales. She taught us girls that we must always stand up for ourselves. The greatest thing I remember is her saying that men were no different. In fact, they weren't as clever as us. That we are the ones who have the babies and rear them with no training and we are the clever ones. She used to instill that. She was a gorgeous lady. I think she got the idea by seeing so many downtrodden women in our area. Every woman you saw had a baby on her hip.

Most people that were born in Waterloo and Redfern usually married women within a mile around because they never went any further. They worked there because there were heaps of factories and you knew everyone as you were growing up. Both my mother and father were born and grew up in this area.

I was born in 1926 and grew up in the Depression years. Mum was having babies and Dad wasn't getting any more money at work. You didn't get any child endowment in those days if your husband was working. We always had Nanna living with us and lots of aunts and uncles who couldn't afford to live anywhere else. The kids were just piled into beds, on floors, anywhere we could put them. I was the second one out of nine children. My elder sister was a very quiet, sensitive person, more arty. I was a real get-up-and-go-get-it. At primary school one time the teacher decided that everyone had to put on a concert from their class at Christmas. They asked if anyone could sing and a lot of girls put up their hands. I knew I'd have no chance at that but when they said did anyone learn dancing, I put my hand up. I went on in that concert and danced my feet off. They must have had a real laugh. I thought I was doing splendidly but I bet the teachers thought I was a real little horror. But I enjoyed myself. There wasn't a thing I thought I couldn't do.

My mother was a wonderful lady. She kept us all in control. We learnt to understand that you have to give to people and help each other. But she also told us that we had to stand up for ourselves in life, otherwise you would be trampled on. She particularly did that to the girls, because of her life. My father was the type of man who thought all he had to do was work, come home, have his meal and not worry about whether the kids had shoes. When I was about thirteen or fourteen, Mum had the third youngest so I had to leave school and look after all the others. My sister had a job and we needed the money. Mum had to be in hospital for a month. Without my Nanna I don't know how I would have survived getting the kids to school and washing and ironing. Nanna was blind but I'll never forget her sitting washing socks. She'd say 'Get me a dish of water' and she'd put them on her hand, wash both sides and throw them into another dish of water. I'd chop the wood and boil the copper. At that time, we had our gas cut off. My sister needed a new shawl. Nanna said 'Betty, will we pay the gas bill?' because we had a fuel stove, 'or buy Barbara a new shawl?' I said 'Let's buy the baby a new shawl'. When Dad came home and I told him, he went mad. But it didn't matter. When Nanna's little pension came in, we paid the gas bill. Everyone in the area helped each other and if your gas had been cut off, then someone would cook at their place, or they had that penny-in-the-slot gas and you'd run around there and say 'Could I just put a shilling in your slot?'

I loved where I lived. We had so many friends and relatives that you could never be lonely. I thought it was the most beautiful childhood you could have. We were good together. We all were allocated our own babies. My eldest sister had the first boy and I had the next, and so on. We adored them. Even now, our babies are still our favourites. When we played, we always had a baby on the hip but it didn't matter because so did everyone else. That's how our mothers managed. They would never have been able to light their fuel stove or cook their tea with all those screaming kids around. The boys never wore shoes and the girls had sandshoes. Mum had to buy them in turns and if it wasn't your turn you had to put cardboard in the bottom. On hot, sunny days, when they had black tar footpaths, if it was bubbling you'd have to walk along the kerb because your feet would be burning. But this happened to every family, not just ours.

Above: Betty Makin, 15 years old (with dark hair)
surrounded by brothers and sisters,
and Mum sitting at the back
Below: Demonstrating against high-rise
developments at Haymarket in 1975

I remember being a happy child. I was sorry about never having any pretty clothes. And I always felt very sad about my poor Mum who would have to wear old shoes of Dad's around. That still makes me teary. I used to argue with my Dad and he'd say 'She's so cheeky, this girl'. I mean, don't get me wrong, my father wasn't a drunkard or anything, but he never helped her. He was so full of his own importance because he managed to work all through the Depression. He always had his suits and collars and ties and my mother had nothing. She had all the worry and always tried to make everything nice for us kids. It still upsets me. It was so unfair. I'm sorry about these tears. But it's still in my system. I swore it'd never happen to me. I've had five children and my husband will get down and scrub the floor and wash up and do messages for me. I've been going to meetings now for fourteen years and even my youngest son, Steven, knew there was no way I was going to always be there as a mother. He had to learn to do things for himself.

When I was growing up here, the average family was nine or ten. I don't know whether there was any contraception or not. People didn't talk about it. Even if they had known a doctor who would abort them, they didn't have the money. I'm not saying it wasn't going on but if they had it done, it would have been from a loan and by the time they'd paid it off they'd be pregnant again. Until about 1937 Mum had all us kids at home with the mid-wife coming in. It used to be a lovely time because she would paint all the kitchen chairs and make the bedroom so beautiful for the nurse.

My Dad was a real conservative. The boss could have stood on his neck and he would have said 'That was very nice of you to do that'. He called me a communist when I was thirteen because my ideas were different to his.

When I first went to work we weren't allowed to talk. And you weren't allowed to go to the toilet unless you asked the forelady who sat up in a box that was like a stage in the middle of the floor, looking over all of us all day. You had to ask her if it was all right to turn the machine off if you needed to go to the toilet. And on Friday we had to scrub around the wooden floor where our machine was in our lunchtime which was half an hour. If the Union people came around they were told to get out. If anyone spoke to them they'd be sacked. There would be three or four waiting to step into your job. I used to say to the other girls 'We shouldn't have to do this'. I wanted to join the Union but if I'd been sacked, then Mum would have suffered. Miss Woodcock told me that Russia was a beautiful country and not to believe what I read in the papers. She said things weren't as bad in Russia as they wanted you to believe. I knew things weren't too good where we were. Once I had to go with my aunt, who had nine kids too, and lived at the back of us, to the Town Hall to get handouts. They threw this bundle of blankets and things at her. I'll never forget one woman who was given these awful orthopaedic built-up shoes for her girl. There was nothing wrong with her feet but that's all they had in her size. My other aunt who didn't have any children gave most of her money to Mum. We always sat around reading at night. Mum started us off with *Coles Funny Picture Books* which I loved and then for Christmas and birthdays she would get us *Anne of Green Gables* or *What Katie Did*. She loved reading. I was mad on history and very good at British history at school. I loved learning about the mills having their strikes.

But we knew that none of us could ever go to university – there was no subsidy then. Miss Lucy Woodcock said at a Mothers' Meeting one day that we were the brightest children and it was a tragedy that we wouldn't be able to advance ourselves through education. But all my family have done well within the opportunities they had. The brains were there but not the opportunities. I knew that you didn't have to just accept everything. You had to learn to ask the reason why.

I was never ashamed about where I came from. I was angry that my mother and all the other mothers in the area had to suffer. My eldest sister was very resentful. She hated the poorness of the area. She went to Sydney Girls High School and there were only two of them – her and Daphne Stiller who came from this area. All of the other girls came from the eastern suburbs and when one of the girls in the class had a birthday party, my sister and Daphne were the only two who weren't invited. It really got to her. She was so upset that Mum had to take her away from that school and send her to live with my aunt at Rockdale. She was so ashamed that she would never tell anyone we lived in Waterloo. She said we lived in Redfern which was only a stone's throw away. I used to think it was so funny.

When I was working at the box factory during the war, one of the young blokes was called up and he asked every girl to write to him. So I did and one day he rang and asked me and one of my sisters to go to the army camp at Parramatta. I thought it was like going to Russia. We hadn't been outside a three-mile radius. Anyhow, that's where I met Fred, my husband. He and another bloke called Reggie took me and my sister to the pictures. I really liked Reggie better and my sister thought Fred was nicer, but the men must have made their minds up because Fred walked with me. I thought 'I'll sort this out later', but I never did. I'm only joking. I made the right choice. He went away and our courtship was conducted mostly through letters. Most people who got married in wartime didn't really know the person they were marrying. He came from the same kind of background but only had four children in his family. His mother told me that she got money for five abortions from her mother-in-law. She told me she nearly died a couple of times.

We got married in 1945 and lived with Mum. Then my sister got married and she came back to live and Mum had a three-bedroomed house with lounge, dining room and kitchen and out the back was the bath and things like that. It was a big, double-fronted place. June's husband was a carpenter, and he built in the two sides of the front verandah. Well, Dad stuck a couple of the boys out there, then he built in the back verandah and stuck another couple out there. My sister and her husband had one room, Dad and Mum had the other room with the youngest of theirs in the bed, and Fred and I had the other room and two sisters in the loungeroom – they put a three-quarter bed on one side and a single bed. In the daytime we put covers so that they looked like loungy looking things, and when the Housing Commission came out, I will never forget this, he said 'Mrs. Lewis, who sleeps in the bath?' That's how many were piled in.

My mother must have been a very strong lady. She said 'I will have no arguments in my house. You all either get on together, or else you will have to leave' and all the time we were there there wasn't one argument from any one of us. She did all the cooking. She used to light the fuel stove during the winter as well as having the gas stove so she could cope with the whole lot, because in the summer time we could have salads and things. She would have two huge pots of potatoes on if she was boiling or she would have two great big huge baking dishes in each oven doing potatoes if she was baking. She was marvellous as far as cooking and her cake tins were never empty, because that day was her cooking day and she did nothing but cakes or tarts and if someone liked one cake better than the other or didn't like a cake, she would have all these different sorts. She cut everybody's lunches.

I used to do the washing. June's husband was wonderful – he kept the backyard clean for which we were very lucky, the backyard at one time had been stables and everything else. It was a huge yard. Fred planted the vegetables – everybody got in and did, except Dad.

My younger brothers would go in and scrub floors and Mum always told them when they got married their wives would come first – whatever happens they have to do for their wife because she never had it and she would have loved it. And every one of my brothers are wonderful husbands. They never go out without their wives, they wouldn't go and stand drinking in a pub, if they want a drink they will bring it home and none of them are drinkers actually, they are like Dad there. And they paint, they build things, whatever their wife needs, they do.

I continued to work until I got pregnant in 1946. Fred decided it was too much for Mum. My youngest brother was only eight months older than my first child. Grandma Makin had offered a place out at Paddington – to go out there and stay with her. But you could never do anything right. If I made a bed she would strip it off and say you make it this way and that way. One day I said to Fred, 'Would you go around to the shop Fred and get some things?' And she said 'All work and no play makes Jack a dull boy'. I said 'Very sorry Grandma, he was dull before I married him'. She said 'How dare you say such a thing'. I said 'Don't you ever talk to me like that. Don't try and stand over me like you stood over my mother-in-law. I will not cop it from you or anyone else'. I got a couple of things and I left. I told her she wasn't standing over me. She was nasty and went and told my mother-in-law that I was going to hit her. I had waved my hands 'Don't you ever speak to me like that', and my mother-in-law said to me, 'Betty, I've been frightened of her all my life, I've never been game to say what you've said'. So whatever's been in me, I will not be stood on by anybody. I don't care who they are. I don't care if they're the richest person in the world, or the poorest person in the world – Aborigines, New Australians or Australians – they will not stand over me. I'm a person. I'm me. Why should I be hounded? That's what Miss Lucy Woodcock taught me. That lady, I loved her. Isn't it nice when you can feel that towards someone?

So I went back to Mum's. She said 'Move over everyone, here's Betty'. She never asked the 'whys' or 'wherefores'. She knew that if Fred and I had come back, there must have been a good reason. We put our name down for a Housing Commission place and it took seven years. Fred was working as a plumber and I was dreaming about getting a place in the country. When the telegram came – it was Redfern. Now I'm so glad. There's no way I would move from here. I can walk into the city in fifteen minutes.

I was working in a printing place just around the corner here. Then I worked down at Eveready batteries because it was night shift and I found it was good for the kids. Fred would mind the kids. He would come home as I was leaving and I'd have all the things pre-pared. He would only have to bath and shove them in pyjamas and feed them. I would chuff off to work and it was giving us more money. We needed it. I read in the papers, 'Cleaners Wanted on the afternoon shift at the Main Roads Department from 5.00 to 9.00. Apply at quarter to five tonight.' So I said to Fred, 'They're not going to bypass me. I'll go down at 9 o'clock.' So down I went to the Personnel Officer of the Main Roads. I said 'There's an ad in the paper this morning that you want cleaners for the night-time down here'. 'Oh' he said, 'I'm very sorry but that's run by a contractor'. I said 'I need the money so badly. I've got four little kids.' He got so upset he said 'You come down at quarter to five and I'll personally take you down and introduce you to the fellow'. Which he did. And this young fellow who had the contract didn't like it. Anyhow he said 'All right, I'll start her', but I knew he didn't like it. And he said, 'Righto, there's the ladder, you get the water from here and you wash walls,' and the Main Roads ceilings are miles high and there's a massive amount of walls. He said 'I want all those walls cleaned.' I thought, 'You don't like me, but you think you're going to beat me'. I got up and for three hours no break, scrubbing those bloody walls down. So when I got down from the wall I went in and said 'Excuse me' and he said 'Yes'. And I said, 'Do you know it's against union rules to be up a ladder? Do you know it's against union rules to have your arm above your head?' And he looked at me. I said 'I'm just letting you know because if anyone falls you are up for compensation and that would be your fault and you would have a lot of money to pay out'. 'Oh' he said, 'All right, thanks for letting me know'. Next day I go in and he said 'Oh Mrs. Makin, I've decided I'll put you in the legal section. You've got your own floor and the library'. It was a breeze. All I had to do was sweep and dust and then a fellow came in with a polisher. I really wanted the money – I needed it for gas bills, light bills and everything. My husband and I go to a Club – Souths – a League Club. One of our friends always says 'One thing with Bet and Fred, they always start the dancing off at the Club', which we do. I can't stand people who sit and listen to the music and won't move. I say 'Come on Fred, let's start it', and up we get. We do rock 'n' roll and everything at our age. And then they all have a ball. My son, Steve, writes his own music for his band. I love it.

Because I've always lived in this area, everyone knows me and always comes to me for advice and information. The phone never stops ringing but I don't mind. If people are in distress and need your help, then you give it.

I have heaps of problems from people. Yesterday I was on the phone to the social workers about one fellow and his wife who were in the high rise and moved out. He got diabetes very bad and a very bad liver complaint and he's on a pension. They can't afford the outside rent which is over one hundred dollars a week. They came on Sunday and she was in tears, the collectors were knocking at their door because when he left work he had borrowed through a credit union and the credit union were after him to pay and each time you don't pay they raise the bloody interest. He should have gone to Legal Aid. The Legal Aid people will just say to the credit union they can only pay you so much. But most poor people don't know these things.

In 1972 when Whitlam was in, they started giving out grants to communities for self-help. It was called Australian Assistance Plan (AAP). I went along to the first meeting. I think if anything is going on in the area, you've got to be there so you know where you stand. At first they only gave us enough money to cover the cost of papers and pens and leaflets. I've hand-delivered millions of leaflets around this area. We have a ratio of about one thousand leaflets to one person turning up at a meeting. It's a bad area to organize. A lot of bad drinking problems.

In 1973 the battle with the Housing Commission began over the high-rise developments. They had already built one at eight storeys which I fought. I said 'Where's the kids' playgrounds? All you've got is carparks'. Everyone said 'You can't beat the government'. Then we all got this glossy brochure, showing how our homes would be carparks and the 26 acres in Waterloo would be razed to the ground so they could build six thirty-storey tower-blocks with little rows of units around for pensioners. They were paying people who owned their houses a pittance to get out. They came to us and said 'Now, Mrs. Makin, you've seen the brochure. You can pick where you would like to live'. I said 'I'll have Double Bay'. He said, 'No, you can't have that. We haven't any places there'. I told them that if I had wanted to go I would have put in for a transfer and that if they wanted to get rid of me they would have to throw me out. Marg Barry, who is really a lady I admire, came over from Waterloo and said, 'We are going to fight for ours, what are you going to do?' I said 'We're going to fight too'. I went around the area, door-knocking and getting petitions signed. I said, 'If we are going to fight, we mustn't move'. One of the Commission officers told the lady upstairs I was moving. I was out the back sweeping and she said to me, 'They're going to put the same tiles we have now in the new place'. I said 'Are you leaving missus?' She said, 'Yes, aren't you?' I said, 'No'. So on the Monday she went down to the Housing Commission and told them 'Don't ever come telling me lies again. I'm not moving. If Mrs. Makin's staying, I'm staying'. She's eighty-four now and still goes into town every morning. We are all like a family. We've only got five of the old stagers left in my road but at least those that have left are in houses. Twelve years is a long time to keep fighting. They conned a lot of them into moving into flats. I've met some of them and they say they really miss doing their lawns and sitting out in the yard on a Sunday morning, having a beer.

One of my sons was an organizer of the Builders' Labourers' Federation (BLF) and he said, 'Mum, are you going to fight?' I said 'Too right, I am'. He said, 'I'll go and see Jack Mundey tomorrow.

You're not losing your house, why should you? Just because you're poor why should they be able to toss you out?' So they slapped the green bans on but that meant that no repairs were done to any of the houses. They also said that even people who owned the terrace houses were not allowed to do them up or they would be fined. We were lucky because others were fighting in other areas at the same time – like the Rocks and Victoria Street in Kings Cross. We had a phone-tree and got organized. So that wherever the bulldozers were, we'd all be there. We had to keep it going from area to area. I could see people over the years getting more and more tired and saying 'We can't go on'. It was very upsetting and emotional for some people. I could understand their feelings. They were getting harassed every time they went to pay their rent. We kept saying 'Look it's going to be better. We are going to win. We've got to win'. And finally the bureaucrats in the Housing Commission changed and Woolloomooloo went ahead. That was our first victory. Margaret Barry was really wonderful. Every time our hopes would flag, she'd bolster us up and say 'We can do it'. It was really run by the ladies, that fight, because the men had to go to work. So we were the front line.

I think the Housing Commission decided they couldn't keep fighting. They were getting nowhere. We weren't going to give in. We were getting down to our last little groups, some of the meetings had only ten residents. All of a sudden the Housing Commission decided to come to the party with us. They knew they were getting no building done, the houses were left wide open and being vandalized. We told them to board them up or someone might get hurt and the Commission would be to blame. They were hoping that only shells would be left and they could bulldoze them. Once they decided to talk with us, we started to consult with them. Now they're doing them up, they're really beautiful and because of what we've told them, they've got things like their own laundry and clothes line. Most of the arguments in this area between the women were over laundry. Mums with babies couldn't dry their clothes. In the high rises, for every six flats they have a tub, a drier and a copper. There's always fights over the same bloody thing. The Housing Commission has finally understood that if they listen to what the tenants are saying instead of imposing what they think we should like, they're going to save their managers a lot of problems. Some of their rules are terrible. I said, 'Bugger them. I'll have fowls'. The little kids came from the flats to see the chickens coming out of the eggs. The kindergarten saw the kids looking at my chicks and so they got two. Do you know what they found out? The kids were very cruel and rough with them. One got its wing broken. They had no idea how to handle them. Children must have something they can pet and love. If you've got something you have to look after, it gives you a sense of responsibility.

Redfern was named after the ship's doctor who came with the First Fleet. It was also the first railway station. I'm very proud that my family has always lived here. I have been asked many times to stand for local council but I would have to conform to the Labor Party machine. Even as an Independent you get beaten by the Party machine. I'm better off using my clout on the outside. If the Labor Party doesn't do the right thing by the area then I'll back the Independent who will. It's true there are a lot of trendies moving in because it's so close to the city. The poor are being forced into the outer suburbs. I'm not against people with money, don't get me wrong, but I am against things that are unfair. Anyhow I door-knocked for the Independent woman who's in now, even though she is a trendy. At least she understands what we are on about and will back us. She swept the Labor bloke out.

In 1974 I helped organize a public meeting at Redfern Town Hall – out of this grew the South Sydney Committee of the Australian Assistance Plan. It's a strong community group which covers things like the factory in Raglan Street; home help run from the Women's Centre in Chippendale; Family Day Care and Occasional Care; Magic Yellow Bus; South Sydney Community Aid; a radio station; Redfern Legal Centre. I'm so proud to be associated with all the people who have worked so unselfishly, giving of their time. We also started a dance for young people from thirteen to seventeen. It was a great success. At one dance at Erskinville Town Hall we couldn't fit them in, but we had to stop the dances because of lack of help from the parents themselves. I was also a committee member of both the Cyclone Tracy Fund and Child Care Committees of the South Sydney Council. In 1977 I became involved in the Community Youth Support Scheme (CYSS) which was commenced when the

Federal Government was approached for funding. CYSS began at the Congregational Church Hall in Belmont Street, Alexandria, it is now housed in George Street, Redfern, in an unused section of the Rachel Forster Hospital. One of the programmes we started was the young unemployed serving hot meals to senior citizens. It was a great success, a boost to the morale of both the old people and the young. Great understanding was developed between them. But we were stopped again. This time because there was no compensation laws covering such activities. I have been Chairperson of the Management Committee of CYSS since 1981. The programmes have been aimed towards giving the young unemployed skills to prepare them for the future and to give them support when they needed it the most. We hold classes in woodwork, music, typing, photography, sewing, screenprinting and cooking. This is a good example of the community helping the community. If one person in the community employs just one of these young people for just a day, they are helping everyone. Don't forget our young are our senior citizens of the next decades and help for all is an ongoing thing. But I don't want you to think that it's been a grind – I've loved it all.

Me and my friends have started a lot of good things – like home help for the aged or the sick. We fought hard for that. There were a lot of deserted wives around here who never got a chance to get out. So me and two of my friends, Denny Powell and Lil McNeil set up childcare at night for them. We took fifteen kids, that's five each. We ran raffles to buy them orange juice and biscuits. Every Friday night I'd take the portable TV and we'd all have a beaut time. Their mothers dropped them off at 7 pm and we'd say we'll let you stay out until one o'clock. They were always there on time. It was so good for them to get out. It worked really well for six weeks and then some bastard rang the Welfare and said there was no toilet inside the Church Hall where we held it and that the kids would get wet going to the toilet outside if it was raining. So we shut it down and I went on the Childcare Committee to try and get a grant. They finally decided to put in a daycare centre. I went to a big seminar and told all these childcare experts that it's wrong. We have a beautiful childcare centre in our area but no one here can afford to use it. Most of the people using it are from outside the area.

I was very honoured to be awarded the City of Sydney Australia

Day Community Award 1985. They sent me a letter to say I had been nominated as so many others had from this community. We were being invited down to the Sydney Town Hall so would I mind ringing and saying how many people could come. I said I've got five children, ten grandchildren and four in-laws to come. They said that's a bit much, just let your five children come. My eldest son at the time was living at Muswellbrook and he said 'That's it, I'm not working today. I'm going down to see Mum'. He went to Grace Brothers and hired himself a beautiful suit and he looked delightful in it. Fred was all dressed up and so were all the girls, but young Steve said 'Blow it', and he went in his jeans and his runners. He couldn't care less about the award as far as dressing was concerned. But he was just as proud as the others. I couldn't have done any of it without all my friends who have worked side by side with me. One of the things we did that I really loved was a mural of the area for the Redfern School. I drew the outline for my old street. Above this, there are the Aboriginal carvings and below it the high rise which now stands where my street was in the 1930s. I went to Redfern School for the opening and told the children to be proud of their area. They loved it.

The whole mural is a fascinating study of the area as seen by the diverse people who live here. I also had some input into the visual history of South Sydney. The incorporation of Aboriginal and industrial history has enlightened many people to the past of this area. Not only will the people of South Sydney benefit from it but all people, including those from overseas. It shows what makes this area one of the most unique in the world.

No, I haven't always had good health but I've battled on. Steven was four when I had my two heart attacks. I have diabetes which is kept under control. About three years ago I had a serious throat operation to remove a growth. I was very lucky. It would kill me not being able to talk. I'm on a real high when I'm at a meeting because I can voice what I want to say and help people understand. Meetings are as good as going to the theatre for me. A lot of people don't understand when I tell them I love meetings. I usually get up about 6 am because I've always had to go to work. I can't sleep in. I get stuck into the housework before the 'phone starts ringing. People have got to have someone they can depend on. People who are poor can't just throw a worry off and go to the theatre or a restaurant. They sit down and worry and worry. They know they can ring me and I'll help them. I can refer them on to Legal Aid or the social worker or the doctor. If nothing happens, I ring them up and say 'Get off your butt and get down here quick'. They all come. Just before Christmas a woman came here and said 'I think someone is gassing themselves in the back flats'. I ran over, got the fellow on the second floor – he's a painter and I've known him all his life. He ran up the ladders and the poor girl was saved. She would have been dead in another ten minutes.

Fred takes messages for me and cooks tea when I'm at meetings. He supports me in every way. I couldn't have done it without him or without Steve. He never put on acts and said I should be at home more. I'll always live here. I'll always be involved. Australian women have got to stand up for themselves. I reckon feminism is a good thing for family life. Men have to wake up to the fact that they have to take an equal share. The way women are moving into the Peace Movement is fantastic. I think the world would be a better place if women ran it.

The main thing I've learnt is that people count more than material things. Everyone is not the same and you've got to consider people's feelings. A lot of people have no feeling for the other person. I always say 'Reverse the situation. If it was happening to you, how would you feel?' And I've also learnt that if you link your hands together and form a chain, you can beat anyone. The minute you let a chain break, you've gone. And if you believe it in your heart, you'll stand together. And like Miss Lucy Woodcock said, 'You can do anything, if you really want to'.

Edna Ryan

Author and Political Activist

Edna had told me to come early in the morning because that's when she was at her best. At 9.30 sharp I knocked on the door of her unit in Glebe and it was immediately opened by a sprightly woman in slacks and a shirt. Although I had heard of her and her work I had never actually met her before.

Her first words were 'Would you like a cup of tea or coffee? Now what exactly do you want? I've been up since five making a few notes'.

'Edna I didn't want you to go to all that trouble. It's simply meant to be a casual chat about your life.'

'Well I've made a few headings and jotted down a few notes. Do you want me to start at the beginning or treat it thematically?'

What followed was the most logically structured, incisively analysed, anecdotally highlighted, smooth flowing narrative that I had ever encountered.

I hardly needed to ask a question. I settled back into the cushions, basking in the early morning sun while Edna wove for me the rich tapestry of her life. So fluent and confident was the speaker that I could allow my attention to wander around the room, and observe the paintings and the books and the posters. It felt like the room of a young student. Postcards from all over the world were stuck to the pin board. This was what Virginia Woolf had meant by a 'room of one's own'. Everything in this small unit is an expression of Edna, chosen either for its function or its pleasure. This is a room for working and for living – not a room full of faded photos and memories of the past. Edna lives totally in the present and the past is only important in terms of its historical relationship to what is happening now.

Meanwhile the narrative continued its steady flow and by lunch-time I had to drag myself away for another appointment. She came down into the street and hailed me a cab. I knew I had been given so much good material that the main problem would be agonising over what to cut out. Edna's interview is longer than all of the others for this reason. If I had stayed until dinner time I would probably have had to write a separate biography just of her. There's certainly something to be said for 'late' blooming.

Once Jack, my husband, died it never occurred to me to remarry. I'd had a satisfactory marriage and Jack would have preferred to die rather than live as an invalid. It might sound an awful thing to say, I don't mean it that way, but once I was alone I seemed to find myself. I found another dimension to my life. I became a late developer. It's no use regretting that I didn't get on with a lot of things earlier. I didn't realize my own potential. On the other hand, I had a lot of practical experience that other people, like academics, don't get. When I was writing this last book on my own, I thought how I would love to have a supervisor. I longed for that.

I don't have any special philosophical theory about life. It's simply what's happened and where you find yourself. You might have some control when you're my age but you don't get much before. Now it's different. A lot of women no longer follow the set path.

I was born on the waterfront at Pyrmont into a poor, working class family. My earliest recollections are of the family talking about the bubonic plague, which had been rampant in 1900. It must have been a terrible panic. The plague was brought by rats and until then they hadn't put those cones on the ropes to stop the rats coming ashore. The City Health Officer was given complete control and he whitewashed everything in sight. They quarantined an area around the wharves and employed men to clean it up. Once you got inside this area, you had to stay there. Unemployed men were jumping the fence to get work.

I spent a good part of my childhood wishing I was a boy. I had three brothers immediately senior to me and they had complete freedom. In fact the men in the house, who were my father, my bachelor uncle and the three boys, were never home except to be fed and looked after. The boys would play in the lane or go off and play football, whereas the girls were always at home. The only thing they played was hopscotch or jacks, which are the knuckles from the leg of lamb. We used to paint them sometimes. I don't know at what age I heard this one, but it's very sexist: that it wasn't a good idea for girls, because you developed big knuckles.

I regard myself as a political animal so what was it that did this to me, what made me political? I came from a Catholic background, but I could never say that my mother was a good Catholic. I never saw her go to church. She was very disillusioned actually and not at all religious but her mother came from Ireland at about the age of sixteen or seventeen. She could have been one of Caroline Chisholm's group of Irish girls brought over to Melbourne to fill the gap for the lack of servants. She did go to Ballarat to work in a hotel on the goldfields. I worked it out that my grandfather was better educated than my grandmother in an academic sense because he was a Danish German who came from Altona which had been Danish then became German, and was a craftsman. He had that dignity and pride that craftsmen had in those days, not horribly superior. He was a lovely person, but he was very particular and when my grandmother wanted to investigate her father who had been sent out here as a convict, he forbade her to do that because he was ashamed. Men could forbid their wives to do things in those days. My father was also better educated than my mother. She had been sent to a Catholic school, and as far as I could judge, all of the family were semi-literate, but they all knew their catechism and their prayers and their Hail Marys. Sometimes they wagged school and put their school money down the drain. It always used to amaze me when she told me that. I thought fancy throwing money down the drain. Their conscience wouldn't let them keep it. They had these fears and threats of punishment in hell hanging over them.

I had six sisters a lot older than me. I'm number ten out of twelve. They had all gone to public schools, and were better educated than my mother. In any case the education system had been improved enormously since my mother had been a child.

I mention that as a factor because it is the women's influence that prevailed upon the family. My mother and her brothers and sisters were all absolutely blatantly Irish and anti-British. Very firmly. And, of course, that was translated through my mother to me and the rest of the family. Whereas the men had little influence on the children I think my father had some influence because he was an atheist. There was never any argument or tussle about it. Everybody just said their own thing, or did their own thing. Even my grandmother married a German who would have been a Lutheran I presume but never was there any question of an argument in the family. She decided where the children went to school.

It was a very outspoken environment and we tended to adopt my father's politics and beliefs. Living in the city you are also exposed more to political life. This was the nesting ground of two of our most famous politicians. Billy Hughes who revived the Waterside Workers' Union after they had been beaten in the 1890s, he was a brilliant Labor leader. The other one was Holman, and they both lived in Balmain which is just near the waterfront. My family knew these people, they were part of the district, and the community, so we were rubbing shoulders with Labor politics. And then, of course, the IWW began to thrive prior to World War I. Industrial Workers of the World was an organization that as far as we are concerned, came from America where in that period they were jumping the rattlers, travelling on the trains. The same kind of thing was going on here. If you were on the breadline you might wander up to the country.

Then came World War I. Having been born in 1904 I was ten in 1914 and well aware of the war. I remember being very, very involved and worked up about the conscription campaign. I didn't find out until much later in life, that in New South Wales the voting was actually in favour of conscription. It was Victoria that turned it down. Staid old Victoria.

My father was a committed socialist. We used to go to the Domain

Edna Ryan

Above: Edna Ryan in 1984
Right: About 12 years old, 1916?

because we weren't living far away and the IWW would speak every Sunday and they were the most popular propagandists of the time.

During this wartime period, they were framed for burning down buildings. Actually, what was happening was that a lot of buildings were being burnt down by people who wanted to claim the insurance on them. IWW men were framed, and twelve of them were put in gaol.

My sisters were working as tailoresses and especially on Saturdays, one of them would be sewing, making a dress to go out that night. Being able to sew, they looked pretty stylish and snappy. They made our clothes as well. Everything was made or handed down. Suddenly one Saturday there was this man, this tailor, in the dining room, as we used to call it. It was one living room which was a lounge and dining room combined. It was a female-dominated household and the men were always out. They would be down the pub or somewhere, and here was a man sitting at the machine, sewing. He was a very sympathetic, happy sort of person and a member of the IWW, I discovered. When you are in a poor situation, you have no expectations – you might have dreams – but you don't have any practical steps about getting out of it or improving. I dreamt for years that I was going to be able to earn a lot of money for my mother, but I never put it into a positive plan for earning the money.

When we would talk about the material or what we were going to wear, he would say 'Only the best is good enough for the working class'. And that hit me like a rocket. I was so humble it never occurred to me to have that much pride. Of course I remember it to this day. I'm sure it gave me a lot more expectation. His influence was enormously valuable to me.

Although I was very good and happy at school, my mother always described me as sensitive in the sense that I was tongue-tied and quiet and timid. But school was a world of my own and it was a haven really from some of the discord at home. I got a bursary to go to high school and it was a fortune. Two pounds ten a quarter. It was a lot of money to be bringing into our house.

I went to high school for four years. In those days high school was a five-year term. There were only two pupils at Newtown School that got bursaries – another girl and I. But what I didn't have and what I needed was somebody who could give me the kind of encouragement and take the kind of interest that a student needs. I knew nobody.

At one stage when we had left my father, he went to the headmistress of Fort Street School unbeknown to me, and asked her how I was getting on and told her he was my father. One day I was told in class that the headmistress wanted me. Well, of course, if the headmistress wanted you your knees would quake. I went to her office absolutely in terror – knowing I couldn't have done anything wrong. She said my father had been to see me and that I didn't have to say a word. And, of course, she would have done better not to have mentioned this. I was struck dumb. I didn't know what to say, what could I tell her? I just said nothing. It was a non-event, except that it had a very bad effect on me.

This tailor, who subsequently married my sister, made me my tunic for Fort Street Girls High and I had the best tunic in the school, but it was an awful thing to happen. It was a square neck with the box pleats, and being tailors, they hated this pattern. So they made me a beautiful serge tunic that had a round neck and it was not pleated at all. It fitted beautifully. I suffered over that. Because I was different. I couldn't possibly say I didn't like it. I couldn't hurt them. I was sensitive. There were plenty of kids that would have been quite cheeky about it and kicked up a row. I couldn't do that.

Well, the next thing that I remember, being political, is the Russian Revolution. I must have read the *Herald* every day. I don't know how it happened. My father wasn't home, then, but the year before I went to high school, I remember writing an essay on the Korinsky Government in Russia and I would have got it all from the *Herald*. I'm only sorry I haven't got it now.

By my fourth year, all of the family were married and we lived in my brother's home rent free while he was paying it off until he got married. My mother was working as a cleaner at the Haymarket Theatre and then we moved into rooms in Stanmore. Nobody said anything to me about going to work. My mother never suggested it, nor did anyone else.

I needed someone to advise me what was the best thing to do. I now realize it would have been better for me to stick it out for another year and get my matriculation. I was also finding the work a bit tough, especially the maths. I lost heart a bit and got a job in an office. Like most people of my generation, whatever dreams you may have, they never had any air of reality about them. My sisters always said that their little sister was not going to work in a factory like them. It was obvious I would get a job in an office.

I was realistic enough about getting work but not about achieving anything special. So I found during the course of my working life that I was always in a rut and I changed my job about every two years, always to get a better job.

The theory has prevailed about the workforce that women were unreliable. They're not in fact, but they left jobs like I left them, not because they weren't good workers. Any time of my life I wanted a job, I was never out of work. There was always that kind of work for women. Even now a good secretary, shorthand writer and typist can get work. I don't say she'd be satisfied, but it was always possible.

I joined the Clerks Union. I was still very politically motivated. I was still saving the world. I had read all the socialists who believed in the great dream. There were a lot of women around including my sister, who had married this member of the IWW. And we read Havelock Ellis and Edward Carpenter and Olive Schreiner and Bernard Shaw and H. G. Wells and then it was Marie Stokes and Margaret Sanger. During the 1920s I was around the Trades Hall and I was noticed by a woman who was the organizer of the Printing Trade Union, Mel Cashman. Mel was a Catholic and a sincere one called after the saint of course (Imelda). She would have been by then in her forties, and she encouraged me enormously. I think she wished I was a member of the Printers Union quite frankly, because she used to organize functions and I was often invited to go along. I was, unofficially, a printer a few times. And we went for a weekend school once, which was an out-of-the-way, unusual happening in those days where they had working girls, factory women, always called girls of course, meeting women who were higher up the social scale, and getting to know one another. Going around town to meetings, I became not exactly vulnerable but waiting for someone to come along and take notice of me. The fellows were very attentive.

Never in the whole of my life had I ever been in the position where I feared I might be raped, it didn't occur to me. I knew it could happen – that terrible rape case had happened in my lifetime – in the pack rape – and God knows the community was corrupt and rough enough. It was a case of luck. I would be out at all hours of the night by myself, talking about the Russian Revolution of course.

I was invited to a Women's Meeting there by Hetty Whitesold, a schoolteacher in Sydney. There was a proposition put to me, why didn't I join the Communist Party? I seemed to have been made for it. The training I got there is what really brought me out of my shell. I developed very, very quickly. It was all rather heavy and I got very busy. In the end, I remember, they said, 'You've got to speak somewhere or other', and I said, 'I can't speak', and they said, 'Oh yes, you can'. It just came out. I knew what I wanted to say and it was there. I'd gone to classes and all the rest of it. Of course, the average term for anyone to be in the Communist Party we worked out subsequently, was about five years. Some of the old hands hang around all their lives, but five years was about an average and that proved to be so in my case. Things changed. We fell foul of each other. The war was coming up by then, and I'd been married and had a child in 1930. I married a Communist. He was one of the top boys, a bright young man.

I never intended to get married. My mother's life was such that we didn't envy her. Of course, none of our marriages was going to be like our mother's. In fact, none of them were. They were all reasonably happily married. But none of them had the obsession I had about wanting society to change. It was like a religion I suppose.

I don't remember getting married being a great passion, but it was a very good partnership. He was a bit more advanced for his time. He'd never played sport – he wasn't an ocker Australian at all. He was a good character and an intelligent bloke.

His father had a butcher shop in Melbourne and he would normally have stayed there and learnt the trade, but he had a stepmother and he was a very unhappy child and kept on running away from home from the age of about eight or nine. He'd run away and sell matches down in men's lavatories. His father would have to go around scouring Melbourne looking for him at the weekends, because he had to work all the week. During the war he used to run down to the waterfront on ships and they'd feed him. He did learn his father's trade, but he didn't stay. He came up from Melbourne to Sydney via the Victorian mallee and worked in the country on and off for some time. In Sydney he worked as a butcher and became a unionist like me. That's how we met. He was a delegate to the Labor Council, a good speaker. He went over to Moscow as a delegate and to the All India Congress and met Nehru.

Jack Ryan was a well-known name in Sydney. We were regarded as the two bright sparks, but soon after we were married (within a year), we were both out of the Party. He left before me. He was billed as a right-winger because the Party line had changed. Well, that's a long story and it was a blow to us. As soon as we met and went around together, we had to live together because neither of us had a free night in the week. You had the union meeting, and you always had a caucus meeting before that. You had one or two classes that you might have been attending. And then there might have been a women's group and meetings. It took up all your spare time.

When we were put on the outer, we were a bit isolated. The party members wouldn't like to be seen talking to you. We would have been glad to talk and argue with anybody. In the course of time there were quite a number of dissidents so we did have colleagues. They used to come out and plague us a bit. Jack was out of work when all this happened. I had to go to work. I was the breadwinner. We had the baby who went to Woolloomooloo Day Nursery while Jack was looking for work. A lot of the Labor Party people were delighted at him being kicked out of the Communists and it was immediately suggested he join the Labor Party. They all predicted a great future for him. I could not come at it for a while. I did eventually, but it took me much longer.

My sexual knowledge was quite backward. Before Jack, I had only had one man as a lover. He was about fourteen years older than me. I had read Marie Stokes but I knew nothing about birth control, so I didn't do anything about it. He looked after that side of things. I was very much sheltered and taken care of. He used to withdraw mostly. Once or twice I thought I was pregnant, but I never was. Jack was just the opposite. He said it's the woman's job to look after birth control. I couldn't believe it. So I got pregnant straight away. I just automatically thought that I would have to have an abortion. But to my astonishment, Jack said he would like to have a child. I was determined it would be a girl, but it was a boy. Jack said he knew it would be a boy. But I got my way, I subsequently had two daughters. I remember my sister saying to me, 'I often wondered what you'd be like with a baby'. I was hardly the type-cast mother. But I obeyed all the rules to the letter. Four-hourly feeding, not picking them up. The kids turned out all right.

I don't think there's a parent in the world who doesn't say to herself or himself someday, what have I done? I've been particularly fortunate in my family relationships. You have your share of wondering whether they're going to get a job, whether they're going to get a scholarship or whatever they want. You go through all that with your kids. But, we encouraged the kids, without pushing them. They didn't have to achieve. They were never interfered with. Very few rules. We didn't consider ourselves to be in the crazy series of people who gave kids carte blanche to do anything they like. I'd say, 'Go outside and make that noise, go outside and kick that ball and play'. We always reckoned parents had to have a fair go. And we put that to them. Apart from that, we didn't hold any rein on them, not even on the girls. They just went their way. I never made all those rules about having to be home by a certain time, because my theory was if they were going to do anything, they could do it just as well at seven o'clock as twelve o'clock.

Kids don't want to kick over the traces if they're not on the leash. I remember both my daughters at university, particularly the younger one, where all of her friends at uni were unhappy with their parents. She said she was the only one that wasn't having any friction.

When the first one was little, I was working. Then we had the butcher's shop which flourished, and I was at home and then I had my daughter. By the time she was about two, I was going around the bend; feeling so guilty, and wondering what the hell was wrong with me. Jack felt quite disturbed about the way I wasn't prepared to be happy looking after the house. He was good in the house, better than I was because when he came up to Sydney on the breadline without a penny, he had to find a live-in job in a boarding house so he could eat before he got a week's pay and he learnt how to clean a house. I never learnt how to clean a house as well as he did. He would notice that the windows were not cleaned and I'd say, 'Why do you notice the things I haven't done? I've done a lot of other things'. I used to think it was so unfair. So there would be periods of a good deal of discontent. You had day nurseries only for the mothers in need like I had been when he was out of work. But you had to be really a lone mother to even attempt to put your name down anywhere. I don't know how I stuck out the period until the second child started school at the age of four instead of five. I had been a very good mother in training them. They were really almost able to write.

I think a lot of young women say 'My children are going to have an opportunity. My children are going to get a go. Mine did get a go. I have to say that. There's a blank in my mind about the years before I did actually go back to work. It was a long time, because the war was on and we were very busy in the shop. There was rationing. And Jack had a bad hereditary record. No man in his family had lived much beyond the age of 40 and he had had this hanging over him. When the war broke out, I just couldn't get madly patriotic. I was in a political no-man's land. Nobody could possibly not be against Hitler, but on the other hand, the war wasn't working to pattern. My old training was that the enemy is at home, and that wartime is an opportunity for the workers really to bring down the ruling class as they had done in Russia. This was very difficult and not at all practical. And so I didn't know where I was, politically speaking. I couldn't be hypocritical about it. So what did I do? I had a war baby.

There were a number of people petrified with fear and there was a great exodus to the country. And Jack said 'Do you want to leave?' And I said, 'Good heavens, we've only just bought a washing machine' and that was such a great boon. I said I wouldn't leave the washing machine. I'd sooner face the Japanese.

I do remember one night, when the child was still a baby, I was awake and something was going on. I took her out. We had a little front balcony overlooking Cooper Park, and I could hear these things whistling. I thought 'If I didn't know any better, I would think those shots or whatever they were, were coming towards me. But it

can't be that. They're firing out to sea', says I. Little dreaming that
in fact we were being shelled and it was up the street from me. Half
of the neighbourhood was down in the air-raid shelter. I don't know
what Jack thought. I don't think he woke up. He had been stricken
with deafness which was a big handicap and probably he would not
have heard it anyway. He used to have a hearing aid that was like a
camera, a little box camera, a Brownie, and being a bit of a character, my sisters or someone would come and see us, and he would get
out his gear and put the box on the table and say, 'Now talk sense,
this is costing me money'. And that of course would have the immediate effect of stifling anybody.

The war was a great strain on him because of the rationing in the
shop, and he was a very, very popular person with the women. Most
butchers are pretty good at talking to the women – part of the game.
But they used to confide in Jack. My God, everything about their
private lives. Most of the women had reason to look for a counsellor,
to look for some shoulder to cry on.

He got on well with the Catholics in particular and they knew he
was no longer a practising Catholic, but he was still a Ryan. They
used to say, 'Don't send your children to the university, they'll lose
their faith'. We decided that we would rent the shop out, lease it to
somebody else. He never liked the trade, but it was a great standby
– it had given us a very good living by this time. I was better off than
I'd ever been in my life in a sense that I didn't have to just live from
week to week. We weren't rolling in money but we had as much as
we needed.

Jack thought he'd look for something else in the Labor Movement
or in the unions and he became an organizer for the Workers' Educational Association. This was another thing I had taken up again.
There were lots of them and they were always on current affairs. I
had gone back to the WEA in the dead period of being a mother at
home with a child, and organized a class up at Bondi Junction. I
organized two or three classes with great success and they were on
Drama and English and Current Affairs. Jack became a WEA
organizer but he had an occlusion, a sort of stroke. He came out of it
quite luckily but he was diminished by it. The Sister at the hospital
said to me, you must never cross him or argue with him. Just go
along and do whatever he wants. Treat him gently. Well, he was lying

in bed daydreaming about what he wanted to do. He wanted to get away, to be a poultry farmer, have a little farm. If anything was unsuitable for me, it was a little farm. However, we did in fact do that. We didn't go very far out. It was in Liverpool electorate.

So guess who fed the chickens? Edna. I took a course at the Agricultural College by correspondence. I was breeding my chickens by the book. Day by day. And I'd become very good at it. And I kept on breeding chickens until we had a whole farm full of chooks. I was living up there between the age of 44 and 50. I remember telling somebody I was 49, and she said I hope I'm as lively as you are when I'm 49. I felt very old.

While I was doing this poultry farming I had been asked by two of the Labor Party boys if I would be on their ticket for the local council. Well, there wasn't an election so I became an alderman and then I had nine years as an alderman. There were elections for the two subsequent three-year periods. We had also set up a branch of the Labor Party and Jack was the President and I was the Secretary. Then he did become ill and he died while I was still an alderman. I became the President of the Branch in due course and I was also the President of the State Councils.

After my stint as an alderman and being widowed during that time, the third and youngest child left home because she graduated and went to Canberra, so here I was with a fairly large timber cottage still on the site of the farm. I looked for some kind of place to get for myself. I was a bit hesitant about doing this because the home was a base for the kids. Two of them were married and I felt that if I had only a unit, then it wouldn't be a home any longer, but it was a burden to me. I never was what you would call a very houseproud housewife.

In the meantime my two daughters had become very active in Women's Liberation and, of course, when I moved into the city, one of them invited me to a meeting the women were having in George Street. I felt a bit timid about going and she said 'They're a little bit scared of you coming', which seemed amazing to me because I'd been nothing more than an alderman and an ALP activist. I wasn't really well known in that sense, but it surprised me a little.

The women got out a magazine and one Sunday they came all day long and interviewed me about equal pay. They didn't know how to deal with it. This was the first time that I knew I had something that I could tell them.

I did, however, ask my daughter why they went around without their hair being combed and looking like nothing on earth. I was never a fusspot, but I was intrigued by these girls. She said to me 'Look some of them put on makeup and do themselves up because they went to a convent and they were not allowed to use lipstick or they were deprived and they wanted to express themselves. Some of them are just the opposite because they were at home and their mothers wouldn't let them go outside the doors unless their hair was done and they were made up and they always had to look all right if there were men around. And so this little rejection is part of self-expression.' And they used to talk about sex and orgasms and I said 'Well, quite frankly, I don't let my consciousness get raised on this issue'. I was a bit prissy I think.

I then said to my daughter, 'You've had an education, you have been to the university. What are you complaining about? You've got the world at your feet'. I believed that if girls were educated they'd be home and dried. And she said, 'Don't be silly, there's sexism prevailing within the university the same as everywhere else'. I didn't think college men would be so afflicted. That was an eye-opener to me. And even though I had all this experience and regarded myself as a feminist, I had still some way to go in under-standing.

It was all very heady and I found these women a bit hardline to my taste. They were mostly very politically revolutionary, and I said, 'Look, we've got to get somewhere, long before the revolution comes. Don't think the revolution is going to emancipate us because it isn't'. I'd already been disillusioned with the revolutionaries. So that didn't go down with me.

But in 1972 we had the federal election. I was still working then and like many women of my time, if you had to go back to work, you put your age down. It was taken for granted. So I put my age down by ten years and by this time, in 1968, I was 64 wasn't I? Well, by 1973 I was in my late sixties. I was classified in 1966 as a male clerk before Whitlam's equal pay decision. Under the state regulations you could be classified as a male if you did the same work as a male, and we were able to prove that. I was very active in the union, by the way, on the executive and all that.

I had been reading about the Women's Electoral Lobby. In my time, I'd organized a lot of street meetings but that was before the onset of television, which just about killed outdoor meetings, and most campaign meetings in a hall. But the Women's Electoral Lobby had the bright idea of inviting all the candidates in an electorate to come and meet the electors and of course, they all had to come. The candidates daren't stay away, and this impressed me no end. I went to one meeting and thought this is for me. In January, the Women's Electoral Lobby had its first national conference of women in Canberra, so I went and I joined up the day before. I knew it was my thing. They were a political lobby group. Politics is what I'm on about. Well, I took off from there. I never noticed the difference between the ages. First of all, I was accepted. They must have noticed it, but I didn't feel as though I didn't belong because I was so much older and of course my experience turned out to be quite valuable.

I had never experienced anything like this. It was so alive. It was just so wonderful and I thought, oh, blow this, I'll give up work and I did that in '72. I had my ten-year long service leave and I was going to work for my fifteen. I rang the Personnel Office and said 'Will I get my proportionate long service leave if I don't wait the five years? They said 'Yes'. So I said, 'Take my notice, I'm going'. I spent a lot of time in Canberra because my daughter was there. It was so heady.

That was where I met my dear friend Beryl Henderson. She's older than I am and she had translated a book from the French on the great Bobigny trial. Bobigny was a village in Paris where they had a famous abortion trial. There were about four women in trouble over this young girl's abortion. They had an Arab woman, Giselle Halimo, as their lawyer and she got prominent women as witnesses to admit to having abortions. She got well-known doctors, Nobel prize winners, the lot. Simone de Beauvoir wrote the introduction to the book. The first thing I ever read of Beryl's was an article about how terrible St. Paul was to women. I was fascinated by it and got my daughter to introduce us.

Beryl was an Englishwoman who had been one of the millions of women left without men after World War I. She once told me that she had never had a lover who wasn't someone else's husband. There simply weren't enough single men to go around. She had worked in the Abortion Law Reform Movement in Britain and in Israel teaching English and was retired. Somebody suggested she should come to Australia. Thomas Nelson, the publisher, had taken her book and kept it for a year. By this time, Anne Conlon and I had published our book, *Gentle Invaders* – that was what the judge called women in the ragtrade. But it was really the other way around. It was men who invaded the sewing trade.

Anyhow, I gave Beryl's book to Pat Woolley who was half of a publishing firm, Wild and Woolley. She gave it to a reader who said 'No, don't publish it'. Pat was about to tell me when she started to read it. At midnight she rang me and said, 'I'm going to publish it'. I knew she didn't have any money so I got a fund together and we raised $2500 in about eight weeks. That's what you could do in those days. And so it was published. I was enchanted with Beryl because her experiences were so totally different from mine and yet we had so much in common. We called ourselves the Later Tubers, as we had both had a book published in our old age.

From then on I seemed to take off. I did a lot of things I didn't know I could do. Like writing another book. It's hard to write. You need a lot of time to yourself. And it's lonely. But I couldn't stop being active. And so I wrote my second book, *Two thirds of a man* – another judge's words. While I was researching the first book I had stumbled across a couple of people I wanted to follow up, particularly a woman who was an organizer for the laundry workers in Sydney. I followed up the Arbitration cases that concerned women between 1901 and 1908. I found only four cases that affected women and they were all significant.

The remarks of the judges, the actions of the union and the employer advocates – all adds up to a clear picture of how women were patronized and ill-treated at the time.

Since the book was published in '84, I've done assignments, like chapters in anthologies. I did a chapter for *Labor Essays* two years ago, and I was very proud of that. I was thinking it wouldn't be good enough, but I realized afterwards that it is quite good. I've also got a chapter in another anthology that came out this year, from Oxford University Press. This is *New Feminists' Perspectives*.

It is a new perspective in the sense that we had this set picture of the family and you'll still find leading Labor men today talking about the breadwinning male in the family but in fact he never was all that common. Women always worked. They had to do something about making money. I found evidence in my lovely Arbitration transcripts of what they were doing about the need for women to earn and how they were preventing it and how they were saying it didn't happen. I was pleased about this new evidence that nobody else would have thought of using except a woman.

The really greatest surprise I suppose is Sydney University giving me an honorary doctorate of literature. Beryl Henderson was visiting me when a letter came from the Vice-Chancellor. I was so glad I had someone to share it with.

I just think I have a lovely life. I'm lucky. I'm old but I keep good health. It's not enjoyable to be getting old, but for somebody that's my kind of person, the little bit of medication that they have these days is very effective. My legs don't swell because they have multi-national pills for these things now and I can contain blood pressure. You have to be careful not to overdo things and to know how much you can or can't do. And this annoys me a bit now. My eyes get tired, but I've got good eyesight. My hearing isn't good but I have a hearing aid for that. I can't imagine not working, not having an objective.

I buy season tickets for the theatre. One thing about being on the pension, if you are lucky enough to be able to own your dwelling, you can live all right. I don't buy new clothes. I wear the old ones out. But the theatres do have concessions. I think the theatre has an enormous impact and value in society. We could make a lot more use of it. Also, I'm a bit of a film buff because it's another medium.

When I first moved to town and retired I began to catch up with the art shows, but I couldn't keep that up. It's just so ridiculous to be so busy. It's a pity because I'd like to have more spare time. I don't have time to be lonely. I might write some short stories. I would dearly love to be a playwright. There's so much still to be done . . .

Dame Beryl Beaurepaire

Social Reformer

Beryl Beaurepaire is a member of what is known as the Melbourne Establishment. She married 'well'. She became the Lady Mayoress. She chaired the management board of the same private girls school she attended. She is a close friend of many well-known members of the Liberal Party and has just retired as Vice-President of the Victorian Branch.

Armed only with facts of this kind, I drove down to her charming new home on the Mornington Peninsula. She and her husband Ian have semi-retired and like any new home owner she showed me around. Ian was gardening and the dogs attempted to knock me down with enthusiastic leaps. Behind the 'facts' and the 'image' lay the reason why many of Beryl's peers often think she is a bit 'mad'. Why would a woman who had all this want to bother with anything except bridge, tennis lunches and charity work? Why would she want to mix in the sordid world of politics and the even more suspect world of feminism? Beryl answered these questions for me in the most forthright manner.

Ian joined us for lunch and we shared a joke over the wine. In the recent move from Melbourne some of the wine was misplaced and the only bottle of red that Ian could readily lay his hands on was labelled Andrew Peacock and had clearly been part of a fund-raising campaign some years ago. 'Is it off?' Ian asked. After careful sipping and consideration I replied, 'Just on the edge, I'd say. You could probably make do but it's been around a bit long'.

Beryl roared with laughter. Now that she's no longer an office bearer in the Liberal Party she feels freer to speak her mind, although I doubt that much would stop her doing that anyway. Beryl has used all the privileges which life has endowed her with to help those who are less privileged. She once sent me her 1940 Prefect's Pledge, a code of 'honour', 'duty' and 'service to others'. However old-fashioned these words may sound in the 1980s, Beryl's life has been an honest attempt to live by them. In fact she has taken these words out of their somewhat restrictive casing and placed them in the context of social change. Such words are often used by the powerful to support the status quo; she has used them to challenge the existing system and make it fairer. Beryl has used her position of power to help those who remain powerless in the society.

I am a Liberal and not a Conservative and I think a lot of people in the Liberal Party are forgetting the meaning of the word liberal. If you are liberal in your views then you are willing to be tolerant of other people's lifestyles and other people's views. The Liberal Party, which Bob Menzies formed, accepted that there must be change, not like the Conservative Party that insists that life will go on the same way.

I disagree strongly with people like Sir Joh and Andrew Hay and John Elliott who say 'If you don't agree with me you must be wrong.' All my life I have had many friends with vastly different political affiliations and I think tolerance and liberation are words that are very close to each other.

I get really wild when I hear certain people putting down others who are more disadvantaged than they are. Whether it be a man putting down a woman or a person putting down someone of another race. We don't choose where we are born. We are lucky if we get the genes that give us the opportunity to take advantage of what we've been given and if we've been born into a situation where we can take advantage of what we've got. I know I am privileged but when I hear conversations like I did the other day between two Dames of the Realm who said, 'We didn't need equal opportunity legislation and all that sort of thing, why do you need it now?', I get really angry. Those two Dames came from two of the most privileged families in Australia. How dare people who have had all the advantages put down people who have not. Sometimes the cream will rise to the top but there are some people who have had no chance from the day they were born. This is why I get very annoyed with people who talk about 'dole bludgers'.

We all know that there will always be people who use the system, but there is no doubt there is a certain percentage of Australians who have just never had a chance. People will say they went to school and didn't do anything. But if they come from parents who don't care whether they go to school or not, they won't do anything at school anyway. We must be tolerant of those who just haven't had a chance and it's a great pity in our country that there are still those who haven't had a chance. I don't have a solution. When people have attacked me saying I want to send all the married women to work, I say 'I don't want to send all the married women to work, but what I want is an economic situation where every woman who prefers to be a full-time homemaker and mother may do so, and every woman wants to be in an outside situation has sufficient satisfactory, childcare available to her so that she can do it without feeling guilty'. I've been fortunate in that I have never had to earn a living to survive, but I know many women who are doing extra jobs to send their children to school.

We've got to remember that in our mothers' day you bottled your own fruit, you made your own curtains, you made your own clothes, you did all these things. Now for the young people there is no point really in making their own clothes, they can pick up the things at Target or wherever it is cheap. Fashions change so quickly, the kids want new things all the time, it's better to buy cheap things. It's not the old idea of buy something good and it lasts for ever like in our day.

Why would you bother to do all those things our grandmother did? We grew tomato crops and bottled tomatoes in those Fowler things and I burnt myself every time and it was a terrible business. Why would you do that when you can buy a can of tomatoes cheaper than you can buy a kilo of tomatoes? I remember rubbing the eggs of the chooks we kept with Kepeg and putting them down in boxes. No point in any of that now.

Many women have finished their housework by 9.30 or 10.00 in the morning. Now what are they going to do? If they don't get out and do something they get into this – they're on the sherry or Valium and looking at the television.

Australia can't afford to lose those people. When we brought in supposedly equal education opportunities for girls, and I say supposedly because there are still many families where if they're a bit short of a few bob the girls leave school early and the boys continue. When we brought in the chance for girls to have education, those girls are going to be bored to sobs if they can't continue with their education. They've got to do something with it. They'll be frustrated, and I'm quite sure it's a frustrated Mum that will be bashing the kids or getting on the drink.

I've been very fortunate that so often I've been in the right place at the right time. I would never have had the opportunity of being convenor of the National Women's Advisory Council if it just hadn't happened that I was chairman of the Federal Women's Committee at the time that Malcolm Fraser won the prime ministership. Because I've worked closely with him and we've got on well and seem to speak the same sort of language, although a lot of the community didn't seem to think that we did, I was there at the right time. I was asked the other day why I was made a Dame and I said, 'Just because I happened to be there in the position at the time'. To me that was a great honour but it doesn't fuss me and very seldom am I called it because I don't ever introduce myself to anybody in that way.

I had a very happy and contented childhood, but always at the back of our minds was the shortage of money. Nobody outside would have realized this because my sister and I lived in a large house and went to independent schools. My father was part of Bedggoods', a shoe manufacturing business, and he went through a terrible time financially, partly because his father believed he was the wealthiest man in Melbourne and used to spend money very generously. His sons nearly went broke twice trying to save the business. Particularly during the Depression years it was very hard.

My mother hated sewing and she used to try and make our school clothes. I can remember one day when Dad came home and Mum was in tears trying to put collars on school blouses. He said 'You're just not going to do it any more. We will just go without something else'.

My mother was probably spoilt by her father. He was W. C. Craigie, the tailor in Little Collins Street. Mother did what was then called 'Senior Public' and then she was supposed to sit at home and wait to get married. I don't know whether she did anything but make the tea, but anyway she used to go in to my grandfather's shop to get out of the house. She was very supportive of anything that I've done.

My mother sent me to Fintona Girls School because even though she had been to M.L.C. (Methodist Ladies College) she thought we should go to a school near where you lived so you would have your friends nearby.

It was the most marvellous school and Miss Cunningham, my headmistress, was the first feminist I ever met. She claimed she wasn't a feminist but she was first woman to go with the Student Christian Movement to China in 1919. She started the superannuation scheme for women teachers when she discovered one of her staff members who was leaving didn't have enough money to live anywhere except in a rented room with shared facilities. Teachers in those days were paid a pittance and she managed to get the salaries raised. She only died two years ago but she left the school to the old girls of the school in her will. I've been Chairman of the Board of Management for the last thirteen years. We are truly an independent girls school run by women for women.

I still believe in single sex schools for girls. In most of the co-ed schools the boys still tend to dominate. For example, I went to Geelong Grammar to talk to the years eleven and twelve and when I asked for questions at the end, not one girl asked a question. At lunch I said to the Head, 'Mr West does this always happen when you have guest speakers?' And he said 'Yes, the girls never ask questions'. I still think that these schools have a bit to answer for in the attitude these young fellows have towards their women later on. They are still taught that the male is superior. If you say that to any of them they don't agree with you, but I think it's still there.

I started school when I was too young and when I was in sub-intermediate year Miss Cunningham decided to have an innovation. She selected fourteen of us who were struggling socially because we were a year younger than the others in the class, and she said, 'You're going to virtually have a year off from formal classes'. We had a year where we did current affairs, languages and art. Now that

Above: 6 years old, with sister Gwenda aged 8
Below: Fintona Prefect

was a most important year for me. I won every prize in the school practically for work, sport and character. It gave me an opportunity to consolidate and from then on I had no trouble at school. I was a prefect and I matriculated and I was in a couple of teams.

Miss Cunningham taught us to be confident. She kept saying to us there's nothing you can't do if you want to do it. That is the point. We debated against a lot of the boys schools, which was very good for us, so we didn't only have social contact with males as we were growing up. We even played sport against them occasionally. But she always said 'Don't let me hear you say that you can't go into this profession because you're only a girl'. And with that, I left school, and went to Melbourne University for one year before I joined the airforce. There were only two of us out of eighteen that matriculated that went. The rest went to do secretarial courses or what were called professional courses – that was what was expected of them. The war had just started too. Some of them went to work in munitions.

Dad had joined the airforce and I decided I would join the WAAF just as soon as I could. I wasn't old enough and so I went to the university and started to do science because that was what I matriculated in. I'm sorry now I didn't have the urge after the war to go back and do more. I should have done, but I got married and had children, which was in accordance with the pattern. If I'd said then to my parents and my in-laws that I was going to university, there would have been an uproar. There was enough problem when I went to cooking lessons and wine tasting lessons because you weren't supposed to do these things. All you were supposed to do was look after the children and do charity work. Even though I had a live-in nurse, you just weren't supposed to do these things. I now realize I wasted so much time – I guess I wasn't strong enough to buck the system.

I did an interview the other night to mark my retirement from various things, and we started talking about AIDS and condoms and contraception and family planning and so on, and I just said 'Well I believe there should be slot machines for condoms in secondary schools' and the interviewer said 'What year?' and I said 'Well look I just wouldn't know about that, but certainly for year twelve'. So the next day my headmistress rang me and said 'What am I going to do when the mothers ring up and say the chairman wants to put slot machines in the school' and I said 'Well you can put them on to me if you like. Do you object?' and she said 'No, but I think we need them at year ten.' I think it's terribly important that they should be told about all these things as early as possible. Nobody likes having abortions, but if these kids had enough knowledge then we wouldn't have so many.

I had knowledge about sex from science classes when I was in that special year in sub-intermediate so I knew exactly what happened and then of course the minute we joined the WAAF we were given a very good going through by a female doctor. But I certainly didn't know very much until then. I never discussed it with my parents. Mother didn't say anything even before I was getting married.

There were certain things you never discussed – sex, politics, religion and money!

I wanted to get into the airforce but there were so many restrictions because you were only eighteen and female. There were only two choices for me to join. Either as an office orderly or a drill instructor. I wanted to get into the meteorological service and the only way you could get in was to 're-muster', that was the word I was told. I did join as a drill instructor and was quite interested as it involved sport and it was quite fun. We really spent all the time during training partly in a very nice old house in Toorak and then in a terrible place which had been the working man's college in West Melbourne, where they used to ring the bell at three o'clock in the morning and we had to troop out and go into the slit trenches used as emergencies for bombs, across in the gardens. Then I transferred to the meteorological section and once again there were three of us in a course of about twenty men. We had lessons and an exam at the end and of course the three girls topped it. It wasn't very difficult because we'd had to have qualifications of final year school maths and science and the fellows had only to have two years before, which we called intermediate qualifications. I was stuck in the Weather Bureau writing charts and things and that was pretty boring, so I decided I would apply for the next re-muster. There were four girls that time and we all came top again. Again we had to have much higher

Passing out day of the Officers' Course—Meteorological Officer

qualifications than the fellows and then we got shoved back into the Weather Bureau. It really was not what we intended. We wanted to be out on the airfields taking the weather and helping with the forecasting.

One of my friends, Lois, and I were sitting there one Saturday afternoon and we decided we would ring up and complain. So we tossed and I rang up and said 'Please, we would like to be graded'. I explained that we were fed up to the back teeth, sat in there with civilians, we hardly got paid anything, we had to work such terribly long hours and do all their hard work and we'd had enough. So down we went to see the squadron officer and we both thought we could be sacked, or court martialled. But when we got there we were given cups of tea and biscuits so we decided it must be all right. We had a long talk with her and explained what the position was and she took up our cause and then we were both posted to stations.

Lois went to Mt. Gambier and I went to East Sale. Having led a very sheltered life until then, I think the whole experience was very good for me. I had to mix and cope with communal living – dreadful food and tinned plates and knives and the showers and toilets had no doors.

We couldn't even get tampons because they were being used for cleaning the engines! Every time the officers came around they said what's the matter? What are your complaints? We'd say 'No tampons or Modess'. Everybody was finally given one box of Modess a month. That was all. Occasionally you could pick up some tampons down at the chemist. It was dreadful.

After the airforce I was going to do law and then decided to get married instead. I had known Ian on and off for a long time. We got engaged before he went to Borneo as a pilot and then when he came back we decided we would get married almost straight away. We'd both have to take up new methods of living when we got out of the airforce, neither of us had any idea of living at home again and also for a girl to live away from home was just not done.

So we went househunting, and got married. Three months after we were married I was pregnant and that was the end of law, and that pregnancy produced twins. We moved house a couple of times, altered houses, I worked for charity, did the things I was supposed to do.

There was no time but that was my choice. I did things such as the odd cooking lesson and learnt to make hats, and tried to do some dressmaking at which I was hopeless. There were certain activities connected with school and I seemed to be driving the station wagon full of little boys all over the place. There just wasn't any time.

On and off I had help. The majority of the time I didn't. Once the boys went to school, we seemed to be forever looking for sitters and house-cleaners and what have you. We travelled overseas a lot and that always meant putting the kids into boarding school or getting someone in. I just saw it as my duty and had to do it. Ian often says that I had three careers. We had to entertain a lot and travel a lot. I enjoyed it.

Ian's father died and that created a great change in our lives, as Ian had virtually become head of the big company (Beaurepaires Olympic tyres) at thirty-three. There was no room for me to do my own thing of any description then. He just needed all the support. It was very grim.

Ian's father's colleagues persuaded him to join the Melbourne City Council and again that was a pretty torrid time for us really. That was in 1956 and his father died just before the Olympic Games. So we had all the Olympic Games business to cope with. His mother was very upset, because she thought she was being ignored because her husband had died. He was the one who had got the Olympic Games for Melbourne and then we had amusing scenes when people from all over the world started turning up, saying that Sir Frank had invited them and we had to accommodate them and find them tickets.

I started to become interested in politics and I think I possibly resented it a bit that I couldn't do more of my own thing. But I just couldn't and that was it. I certainly wasn't bored. The first time we went overseas was 1952. My father-in-law said to me 'I'm going to send Ian away next year' and I said 'No you aren't'. And he said 'What to you mean?' and I said 'If Ian goes away next year I go with him'. And he said 'Oh no, we don't do that in our company'. And I said 'Well, sorry you will be. Have you forgotten?' And he said 'Forgotten what?' I said there still is a rule in Australia that husbands and wives have to sign a document to allow each other out of the country on their passports and I won't sign it. What's more I don't think you should send any ex-serviceman away without his wife. A lot of them are just learning to live together again, they've been separated sometimes for three and four years, and then you want to send the fellow off to live in luxury hotels and travel around the world for three months without his wife. I think you're being very foolish and I'm not going to be a party to it.'

Not only did I go but Ian's sister offered to mind the children.

Most of the girls I went to school with who got married when I did and we all went to each other's weddings and so on, they all think I'm mad now. They can't understand why I don't just want to play golf and tennis and cards and do things like that. I would be bored.

Ian was Lord Mayor 1965–67 and when he was just finishing his term, and this is name dropping, we went to Government House to dinner one night and who were there but Sir Robert Menzies and Sir Henry Bolte. They were sitting on a couch together and they called me over and said, 'Now what are you going to do when you stop being Lady Mayoress?' And I said 'I really haven't got around to thinking about that yet, I'm just getting things tidied up'. And both of them said, 'Will you join the Executive of the Liberal Party?' And I said 'I'd never get on. I've been too busy to go to branch meetings, nobody would vote for me or anything.' 'Don't worry dear, we'll fix it'. And they fixed it.

And so I was put on the Executive of the Victorian Division of the Liberal Party. And then a couple of years later I was Chairman of the Women of the Liberal Party, and then I was Chairman of the Federal Women's Committee and that was occupying a large amount of my time. That was really when I was first able to do my own thing. I liked it because most of the meetings I chaired and that's a different matter. I got more and more involved. I tried to get the Liberal Party's attitude changing. It took an awful lot of doing. Bill Snedden was very supportive of women, but strangely enough he wasn't as supportive as Malcolm Fraser.

When I was Chairman of the Federal Women's Committee, we were at Ballarat at a State Council. This was the famous meeting where all the good Liberals stood up in the hall and clapped Billy Snedden when he came in and Malcolm was sitting down in the front row and all the press were taking much more notice of Malcolm. It was generally around that there would be a challenge next Friday and Malcolm had the numbers. That was a most uncomfortable meeting. Anyway they duly had their party vote on the Friday and Malcolm became the leader.

We were meeting in Melbourne on the next Monday because I was using Ian's boardroom, and we had invited Bill Snedden to come to morning tea. I thought 'Oh hell, what am I going to do now?' So we tried to get Bill Snedden's office and couldn't raise it, so then I rang Malcolm and said 'Look, you will have to come to the Federal Women's Committee Meeting on Monday. We think Bill Snedden is coming for morning tea, will you come for lunch?' And he said 'I can't possibly come'. I said 'Why can't you come' and he said 'I've got a meeting with Doug Anthony in Canberra'. I said 'Well if I were you I would change your meeting with Doug Anthony in Canberra'. He said 'you're not going to tell me what to do'. I said. 'Well I'm telling you it's for your own good. Those women are very fond of Bill Snedden and if you are aloof and don't show them the consideration you will lose them for good'. 'Oh' he said, 'I'll think about it'. About half an hour later he rang back and said 'Doug Anthony is coming to Melbourne to see me, I'll come to lunch'.

Finally on the Sunday night I got hold of Bill Snedden and he said he'd like to come to morning tea just the same.

Well fortunately there were two lifts and two doors in the office and we had to get Bill Snedden out one door and Malcolm Fraser in the other door so that the two wouldn't meet. It was touch and go by about five minutes but Malcolm was extremely supportive to the women of the Liberal Party and I think we probably didn't ask for enough change.

When we did the policy speech for that election Malcolm said he would set up some machinery of a consultative nature regarding the needs of women. It took until June next year before any progress was made and then the Working Party was set up and we worked for about four months and presented a report and then it took a lot longer again before we got anywhere. I was retired as Chairman of the Federal Women's Committee by then and I kept meeting him around the place. I'd say 'When are you going to set up this Advisory Council. You said you would'. And he said 'I don't know who to put on it. I could put all my friends', and I said 'That's not what you could do at all. Why don't you ask some of your senior ministers to make suggestions'. He said 'Do you think I should have women from the women's organizations?' And I said 'No'. This was a bone of contention with the National Council of Women because I felt that whatever number we had, ten, twelve or fourteen, ought to be women who could make a decision on the spot. Not have to go back to their organization and then come back, because that could take months and often you did have to make a decision quickly.

One day he said to me 'I'm nearly up to it' and I said 'All right I will hope to hear soon'. My mother and father were both alive, and they were both pretty sick and I used to go there for lunch every second day. I got there this day and they said 'You must have done something. You've got to ring Bob Ellicott urgently at this number'. So I rang Bob and he said 'I'm going to a luncheon in Adelaide tomorrow, and I'm going to announce the members of the National Women's Advisory Council, would you like to be the first convenor?' and I said 'Yes, thank you very much, I would.' He said 'I'll tell you who the others are' and he read them out. I only knew two. I put the phone down and Mum said 'What was that about'. So I told her and she said 'You must be very pleased' and I said 'Yes, I am'. Dad said 'Do you mean to say you said you'd do that without asking Ian's permission first?' And that was the difference between the two of them.

Ian gets a bit cranky when I'm away for too long now, but he accepted it all. When he was so busy in business quite often he could organize that he could have a visit at the same time. For example when I went to Mt. Isa he managed to go and see the copper mine. We did quite a lot of those sorts of things together. But he would never have said I couldn't go anywhere.

There are some women who think I'm left-wing and some left-wingers who think I'm right-wing. So I suppose if you have each group thinking like that you must be somewhere in the middle and be reasonably acceptable. The women that I've had most difficulty with always, as long as I can remember, have been the very right-wing. I don't think I've ever had any difficulty with union women and in fact one day I went to speak at a union meeting of the Shop Distributors and Allied Industries. That's a very right-wing union and I was asked to open a conference in which they were trying to encourage their shop assistants to seek further training and get into supervisors positions. I said 'There's just something I would like to ask you. Are you all losing a day's pay for being here? Put your hand up if you are?' All but two were losing a day's pay. So I said 'Could you tell me something else, if the male shop steward goes to a conference for a day does he lose a day's pay?'. 'Oh no.' So I said 'that's exactly what I thought and that's most unfair. You ought to go back to management when you go home and put your point of view'. Next Saturday Ian's playing golf with one of the managers of the Coles stores and he said 'I wish you would keep your wife out of my business'. They were so male-dominated and afraid if they complained they would lose their jobs. But now they get the same conditions as the men.

Remember that terrible so-called 'Lusher Motion' that hospital benefits were not to be paid for abortions. One of my friends in Canberra rang me and said 'Do you know that they're going to debate that Lusher Motion on International Women's Day'. I think it was '81. So I rang Malcolm. He respected a lot of my judgement but I think he may have been sorry he accepted it on this occasion.

I said to him 'You are stupid to debate this on International Women's Day, you will get terrible flack if you do that'. But he said 'there are lots of people who are in favour of the Bill.' I said 'Malcolm, you come from a very good Catholic electorate and that's why you're being pushed into doing this. You vote how you like, that's got nothing to do with it, but the point is that you should not have this on International Women's Day. It's very, very stupid'. He said 'Oh well I'll have to talk to Ian Sinclair.'

That was about eight o'clock and about eleven-thirty he rang me and said 'We're not going to debate that for three weeks'. I said 'Well thank you very much.' Of course three weeks later he didn't thank me very much, because I think he got about 3000 letters. It gave time for everybody to get ready and get going on it but Bob Ellicott was extremely helpful. He spoke very well and we attacked it not from the point of view of whether we believed in abortions or not, it was the fact that abortion was a State matter and if your State law said it was legal to have abortions you shouldn't have Commonwealth people telling you you couldn't have the hospital benefits.

I got a ring from one of the most conservative members on the National Women's Advisory Council, and she said I think we ought to make a statement against the Lusher Motion. Will you ring Bob Ellicott and tell him. So I rang him and said that I had had this put to me and he said 'Well, do a ring around and see if you can get a unanimous decision because I knew you've got some Catholics on the Council and if you can get agreement from them, it will carry a lot more weight'. So I did and I got absolute unanimous approval that we should make the statement, that we felt it was wrong for the funding to be stopped. Bob Ellicott spoke very eloquently in the House about it and so did Andrew Peacock with my pushing and shoving.

Just prior to that I was somewhere with Dick Hamer, who was Premier, and he agreed entirely with my view on the situation and he wrote to all the Victorian members of parliament urging them to vote against the Lusher Motion.

Now that created quite a bit of a problem for him because somebody asked him in the House who suggested that you do this and good soul that he was didn't say it was me, but said he had done it after consultation with various people involved in the issue. The Lusher Motion was defeated.

Those were some of the things, because of my background in the Liberal Party while they were in government, that I was able to do. When we were going to Copenhagen to the Mid-Decade Conference and we had all these meetings to look at the plan of action, I said to Malcolm, 'I would like to give a reception to these people, I think it would be a good idea if we started with social drinks the night before, but we can't possibly do it out of our budget'. He said 'How much would it cost?,' and I said 'I think there are 200 women and only for an hour'. He said 'Why don't we do it at the Lakeside and I'll accept the bill.' So we did that and he went around and spoke to every group.

Copenhagen was very interesting because Bob Ellicott was only there for two days and then I had to be the leader of the delegation. But while he was there we signed the convention and when we were going into the room to sign it the Right-to-Life people were physically trying to bar us getting into the room to sign it. It was terrible. I

Dame Beryl Beaurepaire

Above: Beryl Beaurepaire with husband Ian
and twins Donald and John, 1965
Below: Copenhagen, Mid-Decade of Women Conference, 1980
(Courtesy: Alfa Fotoarkiv, Copenhagen)

got on particularly well with Sarah Weddington who was the head of the American delegation. We had problems with the Communist bloc and in fact the Australians and the Americans were ostracized a bit by some groups so that meant we saw quite a lot of each other to try and plan tactics.

I see her whenever I go to America and she's been out here to stay with us. She was at that stage Personal Advisor to President Carter. Now she's lecturing in Dallas, Texas. She's a lawyer, a very fine woman – very active in the Democratic Party in America. She's wringing her hands in horror at some of the things Reagan's doing, which I am too. This is again this terrible birth of the new right which is so worrying to me. It's worrying to the economy but I think it's more worrying to women than any other group in the community. All we can do is encourage some of the younger women to get more active: they're so complacent. They've got themselves into good jobs with a lot of money and that seems to be all they care about.

I believe in independence and I think the best marriages are those where the two people are independent but dependent, if you can understand what I mean. One of the things I am still arguing with some of my colleagues in the Liberal Party about is income splitting and taxation. And family allowances. I think it is quite wrong to believe that in every family there's only one breadwinner, and then that breadwinner divides the money up evenly. It doesn't matter what kind of economic situation you're in.

We had Meredith Edwards do a survey for us and we found the division of income in families was quite peculiar and you can't be sure that a fellow is going to give the wife enough money. I believe that the family allowances should be paid to the person who takes care of the children and if you're going to means test them you means test them on that person's financial position, herself or himself.

You may say the Beaurepaires have got plenty of money, why should they get child allowance. You're not to know that my sons are giving their wives sufficient money. They happen to be doing so but in some families, like this woman I know, who when she goes overseas with her husband on business keeps telling him she needs more clothes. Of course he likes her to be looking like a fashion plate and he buys her all these clothes. She comes home and sells them and he doesn't know. That's the only way she can get some money. And there are young women who are equally dependent.

I think we're slipping backwards. We follow America and it's the Reagan influence. But why? Why are the women letting themselves be put upon like this?

I'm a feminist in the true sense of the word. If you're a feminist you believe in equal opportunities and rights for women, but you also believe that women accept equal responsibilities. And I would like to believe that Ian's a feminist. And in fact Ian MacPhee has stated publicly that he's a feminist in a reply to a letter to Shirley Walters.

But some women are funny. The late Dame Margaret Blackwood would always say she was not a feminist but in fact she was a strong feminist. I think it's because when the Women's Movement went through burn the bra and all that sort of thing, feminist became a dirty word.

I think that if women were in positions of power we would be much more likely to have a world of peace. But we must be in those positions as women and not pseudo or honorary men. I'm a great admirer of Mrs Thatcher because of the enormous opposition she defeated in order to become Prime Minister, but I think she only got there because she trained herself to think like a man. Unfortunately a lot of women who are getting to the top in organizational and political areas are doing so because they are honorary men, and that's a very dangerous thing.

I hope that the girls we are turning out at Fintona have a bit of 'oomph'. We don't have prefects, we make the whole class 'senators'. The other day I went to speak to them and the headmistress introduced me and said I'd done a lot of community service. I told them that they had received a very privileged schooling and I hoped they would remember that it is also important to give something back to the community and get involved in community life.We make them go off and cut lawns for old people and visit the ill and the mentally retarded. I'm hoping that some of that will stay with them.

I'm slowing down a bit now but I'm still Chairman of the Council of the Australian War Memorial, a soon-to-retire Chairman of the

Board of Management of Fintona, Chairman of the Australian Allergy Foundation, Vice-President of the Australian Children's Television Foundation, Vice-President of the Order of the British Empire Society, a normal branch member of the Liberal Party and a Member of the Board of Management of the Citizen's Welfare Service of Victoria from which I retire every year and they never accept my resignation.

Being Chairman of the Council of the Australian War Memorial has certainly had its ups and downs. I was appointed during the Fraser Government and then reappointed by the present Labor Government. I think the R.S.L. thought it was quite wrong to have a woman as Chairman of the Council, and I did have a bit of difficulty with them at the start.

I was only an officer at the end of the war and not a leading officer. They're used to having Generals and Admirals and so forth. And women didn't really 'count' in the war.

Then of course we had this further difficulty when the Minister alleged the Director was not giving him the correct information and that he was giving the wrong answers to questions in the House. There were more accusations flying around that the Director had done this and had done that and hadn't done the other thing. A lot of the accusations couldn't be proved, but there were three enquiries before the Director was dismissed. The Council supported the Director as long as they possibly could, until the very end.

There is no secret about this, I made two or three trips to Canberra because I got the information that the Director was going to be dismissed, to try and get him to take early retirement on his sixtieth birthday. He could have retired with honour and been given a golden handshake but he still maintained he had done nothing wrong. So it was extremely sad, and dreadful really when he was dismissed. I had to do something I found terrible. I haven't seen him since he was dismissed, but I went up the next day and spoke to all the staff.

I could hardly get the words out. I felt that I had to show the staff that we cared and that the Council cared and explained a certain amount of what had happened so that they knew the true story. Now we have an Acting Director and I hope that soon we will have a new Director well in place and things will be going well.

I still think our main task is to work hard at changing community attitudes. Australia is still a 'lucky' country compared with people in under-developed countries. I get very cross with people who object to some of our money going to overseas countries. We should be much more generous to people in the world who are not as advantaged as we are.

It might sound corny or old-fashioned, but if I've been able to help those people who are less advantaged than me in some way, then I'll be happy. Isn't that what it's all about?

Shaping Business

Edna Edgley

Entertainer and Theatre Entrepreneur

I heard that Edna Edgley was in Adelaide with the Royal Shakespeare Company performance of *Richard III* starring Antony Sher. It had been so hard to track her down as she is always travelling with one of the company's shows that I was determined this was the moment to act.

The voice on the phone was crisp and businesslike and I knew it was important that I arrive exactly on time. I had planned to meet her in the foyer but when she had not arrived within ten minutes of our arranged time I began to get worried. I walked out of the foyer of the Box Office of the Festival Theatre into the inside foyer of the Theatre and saw an elegant straight-backed woman standing by one of the seats. She walked towards me with that surety of step that only dancers and athletes seem to perfect and I knew this was the woman I had been so looking forward to meeting.

'I intended to wait for a half an hour past the set time and then I would have left' she said. Her tone was professional not critical and I explained the misunderstanding. We sat down in the emptiness of the Saturday afternoon foyer and began at the beginning. Even though she must have told her life history hundreds of times, never at any stage did it appear to be rehearsed or mechanical. I hastened to assure her that I had chosen her for the book because without her there would have been no Edgley Enterprises, not because she was the mother of Michael Edgley. She looked at me as if the thought had never crossed her mind. The entertainment business has been her life-blood and certainly her lifeline after the death of her husband. Over 70 unbroken years in the theatre and entertainment business must give her a unique place in Australian history. As head of the firm she kept it all going until her son was ready to take it on. However, the handing over of the reins in no way meant any lessening of involvement. She clearly thrives on the peripatetic life and the variety of people, places and theatrical events. She is confident in the knowledge that she has lived in the best of all worlds and the best of all eras. When the time came for us to part we shook hands and I watched her walk away. For me it had been a glimpse into a world I would never know, for her another day, another show.

I have been dancing with the Australian Ballet on and off for the last 13 years. I was a dancer, of course, all my life. I have done every branch of theatre but opera, strangely enough. Never the singing bit; that wasn't me. But in our days of theatre you had to do a little bit of everything, particularly in Australia. I did my first show when I was six years of age, in pantomime, with a company then called J.M. Tait before they called it J.C. Williamson. That was at the Kings Theatre in Melbourne, which doesn't exist any more, of course.

It was mother who encouraged me to dance, and then eventually my young sister came into the business. I also had a brother, eighteen months older. He's now seventy-seven. My father wasn't all that keen on the theatre, although, strangely enough, he was a very lovely tap dancer. I never did know where he learned to tap. I was a really excellent tap dancer too, even though I say it myself. My mother was the driving force. When I look back and think of what they must have paid for my lessons, I am very grateful. They must have made an awful lot of sacrifices. I was born in Carlton, Melbourne, which in those days was a poor area, my father was just a council worker. Now, strangely enough, Carlton has become one of the 'in' places. Very trendy.

In 1920, I was a dancer in my first pantomime and two men called Edgley and Daw were brought out to star in it. Eric Edgley was then twenty-one and Clem Daw eighteen. They were already established stars in England. Little did I ever dream that in later years, I would eventually marry Eric Edgley. Of course we had to pay for dancing tuition in those days. When I left school I was too big for the small ballet and not quite big enough for the big ballet. The Jenny Burnham women, there were four of them, ran refreshment rooms in all the big theatres in Melbourne, apart from their dancing schools. I used to serve drinks at interval, for which I earned two pounds twelve a week, which enabled me to pay for my dancing lessons.

When I was fourteen, the Italian Grand Opera was produced in Melbourne by J.C. Williamson and they advertised for children in small parts. By then my sister, who was four and a half years younger than me, had become interested in dancing and we were both chosen. It was considered to be very prestigious. They even advertised the children's names who had been chosen.

The more I did, the more I loved it. Twice a week I went to the Jenny Wren School of Dancing and then on Saturday morning I went to class. In the interim I did other odd shows here and there wherever they wanted girls. If you had to audition, I auditioned. And although I say so myself, I was recognized as one of the goodies. There are always certain girls that go from one show into the next and that's exactly what I did all the time. When I was eighteen I did a show called *This Year of Grace* and strangely enough there was a young man in it called Bobby Helpman. Since then, of course, we have worked in various shows together. By 1928 the Italian Grand Opera came out again and the same ballet mistress chose me. By then I was a big girl in the big ballet and for the first time I went to Perth and played in Her Majesty's Theatre. Little did I ever dream that one day we would own it.

In 1931 I caught up again with Edgley and Daw, who had decided to stay in Australia, they loved it so much. I was twenty. I was chosen to be one of the girls in a big musical comedy called *Love Lies* which opened in Adelaide at the Theatre Royal, which no longer exists. I have been coming around with various shows all over Australia and New Zealand for the last fifty-five years. That's an awfully long time, isn't it?

All I wanted to do was work. I never had any boyfriends. I never had time for that because I was going to class and I was working. School had fitted in because it was a must. I was learning piano for two years. I never did any good at that but it was a great advantage being a dancer when they'd say go back to the last thirty-two bars or this or that, at least you knew what they were talking about. I never begrudge that. I even started taking singing lessons but I was no good at that, although I could do a soubrette number. In those days a 'soubrette' was a girl who sang and danced. Had to do a little bit of everything. I never had any men in my life, only my husband.

I think I was always full of ambition. Even when I was quite small, if there were any speaking parts, I was always given them because I had a very loud speaking voice. I still have. Over the years I have done every branch of theatre that you could possibly do and loved every minute of it. Edgley and Daw was just a small family show and we had to do a bit of everything. In those days we changed the programme every week and performed twice a day. That's why I laugh at some of these young people today when they say they are exhausted. Even at the Australian Ballet we are only allowed to work a certain number of hours a day. There was no such thing as Actors' Equity when I first started. In those days you just worked until you finished what you had to do regardless of whether it was Sunday. Time didn't mean a thing. You never watched the clock in those days. You had to be good because there were plenty of other girls as good as you. If you weren't in, you were out. There were lots of similar family shows, like Stiffy and Mo, Roy Rene and his partner, Connors and Hall. They travelled around too but we never played in the same city, naturally.

That's where I got all my experience. In 1932 we even worked our way from Brisbane to Townsville and then up to Cairns. Eric Edgley thought that if we played in Cairns for four weeks we would be doing pretty well. We played eighteen weeks and did two programmes a week. I always remember that the day we left Cairns the little Town Hall clock stopped. The whole city seemed to be sad that we were leaving. They were wonderful days. There's nowhere now that young girls can get that type of experience. It's a different world in theatre these days. Some of these television people go in and do a series. Never done a thing before and overnight they consider themselves stars.

I first went to New Zealand when I was twenty and even now,

there is always someone there who wants to interview me to talk about Edgley and Daw. It's amazing the number of people who still remember them. Mark you, in those days there was no television. We used to have the same people come to the theatre week in and week out. If they came every week, they'd have the same seats on a Monday night or a Tuesday night or whatever. We hold the record in New Zealand for the longest running theatrical company because we opened in Auckland and did twenty weeks there then we played the smalls on the way down to Wellington. Then we used to take the boat to Christchurch in those days. There weren't planes of course. We'd play in Christchurch for twenty weeks doing exactly the same thing, work our way down to Dunedin, play there for another twenty weeks, then by public demand of course (the ads always said that), we had to work our way back up to Auckland. We did what they called request programmes because all those weekly people would write and want to see Clem Daw do a certain number and then they would want to see Edgley and Daw do a certain sketch, and even we girls in the ballet they'd ask for. It took an awful lot of time.

When we were in New Zealand in the beginning of '35, Edgley and Daw decided they would take a show to England but we had to pay our own fares. They took me because I was the ballet mistress and they took about fourteen Australians. We went over on the old *Jervis Bay* and it took us six weeks. They billed the show, as *Seeing the World* and the ad. said '30,000 miles to make you laugh'. I can see it all. It's funny, you don't recall these things until you start talking about them and then it all comes back to you. One of my greatest moments in show business was to go to the Tiller School of Dancing. They were famous, the Tiller Girls, for their line work and here's me, a little girl from Carlton, having worked my way up to this position where I had to go there and choose a line of girls which I did and teach them all my numbers. We played all around England, Ireland and Scotland with that particular show, *Seeing the World*. You could play all the old variety houses in those days for three years without playing one city twice. Well, of course, now they have all become bingo halls or dance halls. Every time I go back to England we go to these different cities and I recall how it was when we worked all those theatres. It's really very sad. So we played in England with this particular review company for over a year then the

Australians we had with us began to get a bit tired. They wanted to come home and Edgley and Daw went back into doing a variety act. They hadn't worked in variety since they left England in 1920. Of course we were there at the outbreak of war and as soon as war was declared, they closed all the theatres and we all became air-raid wardens. Well, as you know, nothing happened in England for the first year of the war, so the people who ran all the theatres in those days, realized that they must open them again, which they did. When we all went back to work in the theatres, they put all the artists on percentage. They didn't anticipate the business was going to be so big, such that after a few weeks they realized that all the artists were getting more than they were entitled to so then they put everybody back on their salaries.

I loved being in England. We were there until the middle of February, and then on the 16th of February, my husband Mick and I were married. We were working at the Hackney Empire in those days, 1940, and by then, because of the war, they were doing twice-nightly performances, which means the first house was 6.30 and the second house was 8.30. As we couldn't go away because we were working, my husband said 'Let's be real devils and take a suite at the Park Lane Hotel', which we did. We used to go to the Hackney Empire and then back to the Park Lane Hotel after the show which was really quite something. I never go to England even now without making a point of passing the Park Lane Hotel where I had such wonderful memories.

When I first joined Edgley and Daw's, Mr. Edgley was the boss to me for many, many years. His first wife died in childbirth during the rehearsals for *Love Lies,* and nobody knew whether he would go ahead with the show or not, but he was sensible enough to realize that it was the only thing to do. I have a step-son Phillip and we're very close, always have been, and still are. Phillip was a very good performer. I stayed with Edgley and Daw all those years and I never left them. After a couple of years I realized that Mr. Edgley and I were beginning to get a bit close and although we were in it together for ten years, we never lived together. It wasn't done in those days. We never lived together until we were married in London at the Registry Office. But we had a wonderful life. My greatest regret is

Above: Mrs Eric Edgley and Mrs Clem Dawe, 1941
Below: On tour with *The Midnight Frolics*
show, with Michael about 5 years old

that he was taken so soon because he was the only one who was responsible for all this Russian scene that came into our lives much later. He was only sixty-seven when he died. These days that's not considered old, as you know. He was eleven years older than I.

While we were working in England, there were six of us altogether. That was with Mick, myself, Clem and his wife, his mother and the boy Phillip, and we were offered a contract to go to Africa of all places. They thought Mick was mad. They said, 'Do you realize what you are doing putting your wife and your family on a ship at this time', because there were more lives being lost at sea than there were by the air-raids.

We played Africa for three months touring everywhere, and then whilst we were there, we had an offer from J.C. Williamson to go back to Australia in 1940 and do pantomime, which we did. The first big show we did was *Funny Side Up* by Eric Edgley, then we did *Thumbs Up*. I was the ballet mistress and still the comedy 'feed' with Edgley and Daw. The comedy feed is the woman who works in all the sketches.

My husband was always the boss. Everybody recognized that. Apart from being a very good performer, he was very brilliant at business. That is where Mike my son gets that from, I should think. It's strange that Mike has come into the business as he is the only one who has never been a performer. My step-son, Phillip, has always been a performer, my daughter, Christine, was always a performer. Mike never showed any ability for it. Just as well, because he's so good on the other side of it.

My husband had both talents. And when we did come back from England, we were also at 3DB in Melbourne for five years doing radio serials. We'd do *Rookery Nook* and those kinds of plays with thirteen episodes. If we knew we were going to do a Tivoli Show we would record in advance. We coped with that and I had Mike in the meantime. Although we were busy, we missed travelling. It was a real family show. Mick had his sister, Dorothy White, his elder brother, Dick White, and his other brother, Les White. It was really Eric Edgley White and Clem Daw White and the mother did the wardrobe. So we formed Edgley and Daw which is what they called it in the *Midnight Frolics* days and we took off touring again, very successfully. I picked up my old role as a ballet mistress and we started the show in Perth.

After touring all the Australian cities, we did New Zealand, a couple of times, and finally ended up in Perth. By that time, I had two children. The Wheat Board, who owned Her Majesty's Theatre, asked my husband if we wanted to take over the theatre. He said yes. We used to do one show a year ourselves. As good as we were, we knew they didn't want to see us for fifty-two weeks of the year. So we brought over shows from the Tivoli and all the Williamson shows. One of the first ones being *My Fair Lady*, which ran for nineteen weeks. It was one of those exceptional shows. It was during this period that Clem, my husband's brother, died. My husband said he would never work again on stage as a performer without his brother, which he never did. We still continued to bring in various shows from the Tivoli and Williamson's and realized that we were getting fewer and fewer shows. The reason was that it cost them a lot less to send their shows to New Zealand than to Perth because whilst Perth is the biggest state, it is still the smallest population. Four weeks in Perth was considered a long season. My husband decided to go overseas and have a look around. He left just before the Christmas of '59, spent it in Japan and went on to most of the countries he had been to before. Suddenly we got a cable from Moscow. We thought 'My God, that's the end of him. We'll never hear from him again'. We were all so ignorant and had a terrible fear of Russia. Anyhow, when he came back, he said, 'It looks as though we will be doing business with Russia'. I thought, 'Isn't this marvellous?'

The very first show we brought from Russia was the *Moscow Variety*. Twenty-five people. We had bought a house in Jutland Parade, Dalkeith by then and the night before they arrived, we were standing on the back deck. It was right on the Swan River, quite a beautiful spot, and Mick looked out and he said, 'They arrive tomorrow. My God darling, what have I done?' and I said 'Whatever you've done, it's too late now, old boy. We're in and we've got to go ahead with it'. But it was one of those things that altered our lives again completely. From the moment the very first Russian company came, it was a fantastic success and by this time, Mike had left school at eighteen and he was beginning to take just a little bit of an interest in the theatre. His father was ill for fourteen years before he actually died.

Up to then, of course, Phillip was working in the theatre with his father and he went to Russia years and years before Mike ever did, because Mike was still at school.

The Russians opened in Melbourne and because they didn't speak English they had no-one to introduce their various acts. My husband decided to use Phillip as a compere. I used to sit through every performance of everything we did. I still do. Even with the Russians, if I noticed there was anything wrong, I'd tell them and they'd accept it because they knew I'd been a performer all my life and I knew what I was talking about. One night I was sitting in the stalls at the Palais Theatre, St. Kilda, and Phillip had been on a couple of times to announce the various acts. When he came on again, I heard the lady in front of me say to the gentleman she was with, 'This boy speaks beautiful English' and the man said, 'They're bloody clever, these Russians'.

Then I went to Russia with my husband and got to know the people. We saw the Moscow Circus and decided it was something we had to bring to Australia. The only problem was where to present them. We had no permanent buildings like they have in Moscow. My husband said, 'We'll build a tent, that's the answer'. So then he said, 'Right, we don't know anything about tents. Who do we deal with?' He chose the Bullen Brothers, which has been a most successful partnership. We brought the first circus out in 1965, which was an enormous success. We made a deal to bring out a circus every three years, which we still do.

Unfortunately, although Mick chose the programme for the 1968 season, he died before they got here. When that happened, the children and I sat down and decided the best thing we could do was to carry on. It was what he would have wanted.

We had booked a company called the Paekschke Ensemble from Budapest, beautiful gypsy violinists. They were really wonderful. Phillip and I toured them all through Australia and New Zealand and we could never understand why the business wasn't up to scratch, because we had never had a failure in our dealings with Russia. We couldn't understand why we ended up losing money on it. The 'crits' were good, they got a wonderful reception every night. Anyhow we dismissed it. Just one of those things. It was the Consul from Budapest who finally solved the mystery. He invited us to lunch in Sydney and said, 'I didn't like to speak to you during the tour because I wasn't sure what was happening'. He went on to tell us that after we had taken them back to the hotel for the night, they would go out to all the gypsy clubs and play. No wonder people weren't paying to come and see them. When they did go back to Budapest, they were all put in prison for smuggling gold in their instruments. They were real gypsies, in the true sense of the word, but lovely charming people.

Another company we brought out was the Stuttgart Ballet Company and that's how I became involved with the Australian Ballet. Ann Woolliams was the Director of the Stuttgart Company and the Australian Ballet asked her to direct *Romeo and Juliet*. She spread her time between the two. She was in Sydney preparing for their last three weeks at the Opera House, and we were there with the Ballet. After the show, as always, we took about ten or twelve of the company out to supper. We still do that after the opening in each city. Anyway, I was sitting next to Ann and I said 'How are your rehearsals coming on with the ballet?' And she said, 'Well, I'm very pleased with them. But I've had one great problem. I haven't been able to find anybody for the nurse'. And I said, 'Oh, really'. I didn't really know much about *Romeo and Juliet* 'Is it an important role?' She said, 'Yes, very'. And while she was talking to me, she was looking me over. She said she had auditioned four people today. They had a lovely appearance, but none of them could move. They were evidently radio actresses. And then she said, 'Of course, how stupid. You're the obvious one'. And I said, 'Oh Ann, don't be so damned silly. I haven't been on stage for sixteen years'. Mark you, I had been involved with our shows all the time, so that I hadn't lost my nerve. If I had completely retired from the theatre, I wouldn't have had the nerve to come back, but I didn't really think she meant it. I brushed it off. I didn't even mention it to anybody.

The next day Peter Bahen, who was in charge of the Ballet, phoned me up. 'Oh', he said, 'Mrs. E., I believe you're going to be in *Romeo and Juliet* with us'. I said, 'Peter, don't be silly. Ann wouldn't have meant that'. 'Oh', he said, 'I think she's very serious'. Anyhow, Bobby Helpmann was with the Ballet in those days, and he phoned me up. He said, 'Now Edna, I don't want any damned nonsense from you. You're going to do the nurse and that's all there is about it'. So then I thought, well maybe they are serious. Mike had gone back to Perth, so I phoned him and he said, 'Well look, Mum, it's purely your decision, but I would insist that they audition you. Don't just let them take you because you are who you are. Make sure'. So I phoned and said, 'All right Ann, I have thought about what you asked. If you think that I can do it. But you should audition me first'. And she said, 'What so-and-so nonsense. You get in there and start rehearsing. The woman who is in your company at the moment is doing a small role and she's over seventy. If she can do it, you can'.

I was sixty-three, mark you. So she said, 'You get with her and start rehearsing'. But she couldn't speak English and I couldn't speak German. It was all done by Marcel Marceau actions. So every day for the last week, I went downstairs to the basement and she and I rehearsed. I had a little bit of an idea of the role when the Australian Ballet arrived a week before we finished in the Opera House with our Stuttgart Ballet season. I had to go in the very first day with all these young kids and I thought they'd be saying, 'Who is this old girl?' A few of them knew me, but a lot of them didn't. Anyhow, to cut a long story short, I did the role. It was one of those things that I created because the role had never been done here in Australia before and it all turned out very, very successful. I've done *Romeo and Juliet* several times and played it all over Australia, and I'm the only one of our family, of which I'm very proud, who has ever performed at the Entertainment Centre in Perth, which we built. Last year the Australian Ballet was going to do *The Sentimental Bloke* for the first time and they asked me if I would do the role of Dolly. There wasn't much dancing in it, only a bit of ballroom dancing in the end. I didn't enter until the last scene but one, but it was just one of those cameo roles and I could create it, because nobody had done that before either. That was lovely. And then we brought out the Bolshoi Ballet last year and during the Sydney season of that they were going to do *Sentimental Bloke* here and they asked me if I could leave the Bolshoi for a week and come over to Adelaide and do it, which I did. So I've been privileged to have worked with them, which is something fairly exciting.

Above: Edna Edgley with
Paul de Masson (left) and
Greg Horsman (right) with
artists of the Australian
Ballet in *Romeo and Juliet*
(Photo: Branco Gaica)
Left: Edna Edgley AM

I've been fortunate to have good health. I always say to Mike, who is into all this health thing, that he is the only one that has ever got anything wrong with him. Every time I talk to him on the phone, he'll say, 'Mum, I've got the most awful cold today'. And I'll say, 'What, not again?' I've always loved crumpets and 'junk' as Michael calls it. Michael says, 'Mum, how you keep as well as you do, eating all that junk, I'll never know'. So I often say, 'If you keep as well as I do and live as long as I've done, old boy, you haven't got any complaints'. But he's the one who has always got something wrong with him. I'm not a big eater. I'm a picky eater. Snacks. I don't smoke. Only on stage when we had to, in sketches, and I nearly used to choke of course, because I have never been a smoker and very seldom do I drink. If we go to dinner, I'll have a glass of wine. But I do walk wherever I can which helps to keep me fit. I'm a naturally healthy person.

I'll tell you what I do take though. A fellow, who is our agent in Denmark, an amazing old man, put us on to Pharmaton. Many people have never heard of it. Just take one a day, they are absolutely marvellous. You can't get them from all chemists. There's only one little Chinese chemist in Sydney who sells them. They're made in Switzerland. They're wonderful. They are teeny little black tablets and I just take one a day. We all do. I attribute quite a bit of my good health to those.

When I turned seventy-five, I realized that I was celebrating sixty-nine unbroken years in the theatre. I'm probably the only person alive now in Australia who could say that. I toured with Torville and Dean this year and when I arrived in Montreal one of our agents showed me an article in the *Montreal Times* that said that Edna Edgley, the matriarch of the Australian Theatre, would be in the audience. The article said a bit about my history and then concluded by saying, 'She's been on skates since the age of four'. I thought that was very, very funny. I've never been on skates in my life. I kept the cutting to show the children.

I was the head of the firm when my husband died, but I can't say I am anymore. When Michael came into the theatre it was great because I'm hopeless with the business side. He is very talented in that area. Part of Mike's success is, not taking anything away from him, his being so young. His father was so well known in this country. I don't think I could have carried on and worked with a stranger. Part of our success has always been due to our being a small family concern. Now, of course, it's got beyond that. Only the other day, Mike mentioned somebody's name and I said, 'Who's that?'. He said 'He's in the Melbourne office', and I said 'Well, really Mike, I don't know who works for us anymore'. But I suppose that's to be expected, especially in the last five years since we expanded into films. That was Mike's decision and it's been very successful, what with *The Man from Snowy River* and *Pharlap*. Mike asks my advice sometimes. I don't know that he always takes it. People often ask me how much influence I have on him and I say, 'I don't know'.

If I had left the business after my husband died, I think I would have died. It's been my life blood. I've often said to Mike 'Don't you ever send me with a show where they're going to say 'She's only here because she's Michael Edgley's mother'. Once it gets to that stage, I'm out. In all fairness, I think I've earned whatever reputation I've got, apart from Mike. I don't want to be in anything because they think I'm his mother and he has to keep me working. I'd loathe that.

I normally sit in on every show we are involved in. I'm here to help the company in any way I can – doctors, dentists, shopping. Because I've been a performer, I talk their language. Mike only comes for opening nights and then off he goes. I'm here to mother them in every respect. When we have the Russians, that's a full day. A few weeks ago, when we arrived in Melbourne on the Sunday and they didn't play on the Monday, I took 120 of them to the zoo in the morning from 11.00 until 3.00. Then they went to their hotel and had a snack and then I took them to a film. There's always one of us along to keep an eye on things. The Russians are the easiest people in the world to handle. They are so disciplined. One of the questions everybody asks is, has anybody ever defected over the years? Never. We've handled several thousands over the years and have never had that problem. They can arrive in a city on the Friday and they perform on the Saturday. There's nobody in the world who could do that. Firstly, Equity wouldn't allow you to do it, and we really haven't got the stamina of those people.

The easiest in the world to handle are the big names, and we've had most of them over the years. They have worked their way up and when they get to the top they appreciate being there and they know how to behave. And as I said, with the Russians, they are the easiest. Even if they go out after the show, it makes no difference. They are still there for their call next morning whatever time it is. They say nowhere else in the world do they get the attention and the organization that we give them when they're out here. From the time they set foot in the country, they haven't got a thing to worry about, only do what they are supposed to do on stage. Everything is organized for them.

We don't ever talk about politics. They don't mention it nor do we. Because we are not interested in that. I don't know anything about it.

Christine, my daughter, is just like me. She lived and loved the theatre since she was born. She made her first appearance in the Borovansky Ballet Company in Perth when she was five and after that all she ever wanted to do was be in the theatre. I don't know if you recall it but she was an aerialist in the *Disney on Parade* we had eleven years ago and was involved in a terrible accident. It was the first *Disney on Parade* we had ever presented. One of the highlights of the show was the big circus scene with six girls on the big trapeze. As Chris was in it, Mike and I used to pop into the theatre every night to watch it. It was a Friday night in Adelaide and we were watching the show. There was a voice-under that used to talk about the aerialists and the voice said, 'And now our lovely aerialists will hang by their teeth', but before he got the word 'teeth' out, the whole thing collapsed. Luckily it was revolving, so it threw the girls out. Had they been still, it would have fallen on top of them and killed them. But they were terribly badly injured. We had to leave them all behind in Adelaide for twelve weeks. It was terrible. It hit the front pages all over the world. Strangely enough, I had just been in Perth not so very long ago and whilst I was there, Chris completely collapsed. They put her in the intensive care ward and said a lot of it had to do with this terrible accident she had, because she had three fractured bones in the pelvis, a fractured base of the spine and a broken ankle, stitches in the forehead. They said at the time they never thought she would ever have a child, but she did – by caesarian, of course.

She was in hospital for the two weeks I was there. So I was very glad because we knew that the orchestra was arriving two weeks after Torvill and Dean finished. As Chris lives now in Perth, Mike and I agreed it was no good coming back to Sydney just for two weeks, I would wait there until the orchestra arrived, which I did.

After Mike sold his home in Perth, I sold mine and also went to Sydney. I bought a lovely home in Vaucluse and I had Chris, her husband and her little daughter living with me. Her husband was a beautiful aerialist. In 1978 we brought out an international circus with an act from every part of the world. He worked as the Great Arturo. He's American. They went together for about a year and then they were married. He handles the circuses for us whenever we bring them out. He does various other kinds of work in Perth and he's doing very well. I keep going back to Perth a couple of times a year at least, and Chris comes on tour with us. Last year, we brought out the Bolshoi Ballet and as Chris speaks fluent Russian, she came as an interpreter. Sometimes she stage-manages the big Russian shows if they don't bring their own stage manager. Next year, we've got the Georgian Dancers coming out again and Chris will be on tour with that one. She's like me. She couldn't bear to give it all up. Of course, our latest excitement has been with Torvill and Dean. They opened in Wembley where they played for six weeks and then they went down into their own home town in Nottingham where we built a special tent for them because Nottingham only had one small rink. They had three weeks off for the Christmas period holiday, and then we went to Canada for the whole of January and played right through there with tremendous success. After that, we presented them in Hobart in the tent, because every tent we've built has had to be bigger and bigger and this one seats 7000 so we played down there for two weeks. From there to Brisbane, where they've opened a completely new entertainment centre, a 14 000 seater and we were the first ones in there. From there to Perth at the Entertainment Centre, they played two weeks there and that's an 8000 seater and that's when I said I stayed over and waited for the arrival of the Symphony Orchestra. After they finished in Adelaide, they went to America for two months. Now they are having time off to go to Germany. They are televizing the show there completely and then we're bringing them back into Melbourne and Sydney where they didn't play this last tour. But they are still under our management. They've been a tremendous success.

It's no wonder that when I wake up, my first thoughts are where am I, and what show is it? I don't have any holidays unless there's a period when we haven't got a show coming in. I often say to the children that if I had a bob for every case I've packed over the years, I would be a millionaire by now. But it's a wonderful life. If I woke up in the morning and didn't have something to do, I would go mad. I've never been a social woman. I am a soroptimist and have been for years. I go to the meetings wherever and whenever I can in any city. They understand if I'm not there. It's only busy people who are in it. They're the only ones who find time to do things.

I very seldom put the light out before 1.30 in the morning. After the show, you go home, have a little snack and do your smalls, which I've always done. I find it helps to unwind to have a little read. I like all kinds of books. Murders and romances. I'm rarely asleep before 2.00. I wake up about 9. By the time you get up and have your breakfast, have a bath, read the paper, it's about 10, unless you have an early call. Sometimes you have to be up at 6.00, depending on the plane.

I say my prayers every night. I'm Church of England. If I'm close by a church wherever we are, I'll pop in for a while. I'm not really a religious person, but I wouldn't go to bed without saying my prayers. I don't know if Michael still says his prayers. I know that Christine teaches her little girl the same prayers I taught her.

My friends know as soon as I hit town I'll contact them. I don't write. There's a lot of publicity about the family. It goes on all the time. And they think, well, Edna's with the show, we'll see her when she comes around. And this applies to every city wherever I go.

I've had two proposals. A very nice doctor, who was my husband's doctor too when I first went to Perth. His wife died many years ago, a very nice old bloke. But no. And then a nice man I met on a boat. Another Michael strangely enough, and I said when you get back to Australia look me up, like all people do. You never expect them to, but he did strangely enough and he proposed to me. He's a very nice man, in charge of a big golf course in Napier. But I couldn't see myself there. Whilst I'm still working, I'm happy. I get lonely sometimes for a man's company, but they're the sort of things you have to cope with. You can't get everything. I've got good friends in the business wherever I go and I manage.

I know if I retired you would never hear another thing about me. One of my grand-daughters is in her first show soon. I said, 'Let me give you a bit of advice, darling. The name Edgley isn't going to be a tremendous help because everybody expects so much of you and there's a lot of jealousy. Just do your best, darling. Do as you're told and you can't do any more'. She said, 'Thanks Nan. I'll remember that'.

We are all very close because even though we're all in the same business, we haven't lived in each other's pockets. We have all got our separate areas. Most importantly, we have a wonderful crew of people working with us. One of the chaps, Andrew, whom I look on as a son, said to me the other day, 'Do you realize, Mrs. E., that I have been with you for more than twenty years?'

I suppose we are unique as a family. There used to be the Bullens and they've split up. It's the Ashton sons that carry the circus business on. Queenie Ashton died years ago.

I feel very privileged to have been associated with the theatre business, to have worked with such wonderful people, and if I had my time over again, I'd do exactly the same thing. I have no regrets in any way, only that my husband wasn't spared to reap the benefit of the hard work he put into this. You look at your children and you think, oh my God, what lies ahead of them? And there's nothing we can do about it, is there? Nothing we can do. You can't help but think about those things. We have been fortunate we have lived in a wonderful era.

Somebody said to me the other night, 'When are we going to see you in another ballet?' And I said, 'It's manners to wait until you're asked.' You just can't push yourself into them.

We've still got lots of wonderful things teed up for the future. Please God I'll be spared and if I am, I'll still continue exactly what I'm doing.

Stella Cornelius

Peace Worker and Businesswoman

Stella Cornelius has declared PEACE on the world. From her home nestled in the native bushland of Chatswood she directs Australia's Peace Programme. The Minister for Foreign Affairs appointed the former manager of Cornelius Furs director of the secretariat for the United Nations International Year of Peace. It's a far cry from selling minks, I thought to myself as I looked at the small electronic village she had created in the downstairs room of her house. As her story unfolded I realized that her commitment to peace has been a lifetime passion. For the last eleven years she has convened peace programmes for the United Nations Association of Australia (UNAA) as well as being involved in the UNAA Media Peace Prize, the Media for Peace Campaign, the Ministry for Peace Campaign, the Australian World Peace Programme campaign, the Women's International League for Peace and Freedom (WILF), the Inter-Religious Council for Peace, she's also a member of the People for Nuclear Disarmament.

There are no scars on this long-time campaigner. Every problem is treated as yet another invitation to a creative solution. She is not battle torn or worn. Her enthusiasm is matched by the never-ending supply of energy she gives to the task at hand. When I eventually left clutching all the literature on Peace she had thrust into my hands I knew that if Australia and indeed the world were in the hands of Stella Cornelius we would all sleep more easily at night.

Her life and work is in fact a recipe for Peace.

A couple of years ago I was at a dinner where I met a business acquaintance whom I hadn't seen for ages. And he said 'Stella, how are you, how very nice to see you. What are you doing these days?' And I said, 'I'm a peace builder'. He looked at me in absolute astonishment. He wouldn't, of course, read the section of the press where he would have learnt about my work. He hadn't seen a report of the Media Peace Prize or heard about our campaign for a Ministry of Peace or checked out what a conflict resolution network was all about. He was absolutely astonished. He had me in a pigeon hole. Stella Cornelius, successful businesswoman. He was about my age and a courteous man and you could see his mind flicking around.

Then he said 'Mmm, yes I suppose if a war broke out it would be very difficult to get people to enlist like I did'. And I said 'That won't be the problem. The next one they are going to deliver to you by room service'.

And I could see the realization dawn on him. Suddenly he knew I was talking about an entirely different ball-game.

And that's what this International Year of Peace is all about. We have to find ways of raising people's consciousness and helping them realize that pre-nuclear techniques of conflict resolution are going to be useless in the nuclear age. Peace has always been a passion with me. Before I started this I was the Convenor of the Peace Programme for the United Nations for eleven years.

Where did this commitment come from? A sense of responsibility which was always with me.

My father left Russia as a little boy of eleven. A few of the family at a time would swim the rivers before they were completely frozen over because they wouldn't be patrolled much at that time.

Father, who was the second youngest, was one of the last to get out. I believe he was, what they now call, an unaccompanied migrant. They gathered together in England and then their parents came last of all. My grandmother died in London and my grandfather went back. To my father, it was an absolutely incredible thing. He couldn't believe it. When one looks back and asks 'Why did he go back?', not for the reasons that my father attributed to him at all but for responsibility in the tiny township, he was the teacher, he was the leader. He had responsibilities to those people that had been left behind.

So responsibility is something which I don't know if there is a little knob up there in your head or there's something in your genes but knowing that *you* have to do something about it *yourself* is something which I've always known.

My mother gave me confidence. I was an only child and her companion and she made me confident about doing what I believed was right and not just accepting things. When I was a little girl growing up in Croydon in the western suburbs of Sydney, I remember the mothers talking amongst themselves saying things like 'Don't let your child mix with "them" – they're a bad influence'. My mother never said things like that to me. She was absolutely sure that if anyone was going to be influenced, it would be them, not her Stella. This belief from my mother did not come out of naivety. She'd had a very hard and difficult life but despite it all, she knew there was something inside you that could still go out there and influence things for the better. That language that 'every individual can be a positive agent of change' didn't become popular until half a century later. My mother knew that in the bones of her elbow.

She grew up in the very, very hard atmosphere in Yorkshire in difficult poverty-stricken conditions. Her father kept on deserting the family. I have to say kept on because that's worse than doing it once. The family kept on growing in between his changes of mind. Her mother died having struggled to keep the family together. When she was thirteen, her father came back, took three members of the family to Ireland where he abandoned my mother with two little brothers in an empty house. She got her young brothers to safety, pulled herself together and out of this life of deprivation. I was born when she was twenty-four, so I knew her as a young woman and she was confident and cheerful.

A lot of my youth was spent on the Murrumbidgee. I remember my mother as the pillar of strength in that pioneer community. She was the person people came to when there were no nursing services. How did she get to be a district nurse? She read about it in the booklets sent out by the Department of Health who were just then beginning to send people booklets about things. She always said that she brought me up that way because she didn't have people around her who could tell you how to bring up little children.

We were small shopkeepers on the Murrumbidgee. We lived above the shop and that was very significant, particularly to a young girl. I was not cut off from the decision-making process. Both parents are working and discussing and you are part of it. There ought to be more of it. This is very much how I'm working now. Alvin Toffler describes it as the electronic cottage. Until recently I was the sort of person who went into the city to work, sometimes seven days a week. No, I'm not a workaholic, I'm a workaphile. I'm a person who likes work. Work is good stuff in my life.

I left school at fourteen. It was 1934 and we were living in Newcastle, in the firm grip of the Depression. My family were not of the generation who made sacrifices for girls' education and there was an opportunity for me to learn my father's trade. So I went to technical college and worked with him in clothing manufacturing. By the time I had finished my technical school education I had discovered the WEA (Workers Educational Association) and university tutorial classes. I got a first class liberal education by going to night classes.

The first course that I ever did was an absolute accident. At the end of my technical school training I went to enquire about something which I'd read about in the paper, not knowing if I'd like it or if I wanted to do any more studying. A very kindly man, seeing a rather lost young person, said 'Look, there's a class about to start, why don't you just sit in', and this class was about logic and I didn't really know what the word meant. I sat there with a marvellous tutor, the late Bert Pellam, and I learnt logic. It was heaven. Here were people who related to you out of their mind and who fully expected you to be a completely thinking person. They were patient when you fell asleep. I've never really been any good at night, even though much of my education took place at night. There are meetings that I've gone to all my life, and all my community service – always done at night after I've been doing something else through the day. But when I want to meet people is at breakfast time. Now I try and organize breakfast workshops whenever I can.

I had a lot of friends who are still my close friends and yet there was an inner loneliness there. Perhaps the result of being an only

Stella Cornelius

Above: Last day at school,
December, 1933
Right: 6 years old, 1926

child, I don't really know. But adolescence was an absolutely dreadful time. I was not the belle of the ball I can assure you. And I so yearned to be. I was serious, probably a bit stolid. I was not one of 'the beautiful people', although I admired them from afar. I didn't know how to play the flirtation games. My mother wasn't good at teaching me that because she wasn't much of a player herself. I went on a trip to Melbourne to stay with my very glamorous cousin who was later to be Senator Sam Cohen, and met his friend, Zelman Cowan. My main reaction was one of jealousy because I could suddenly see that life was giving them things that I was just as entitled to, but wasn't getting. Sam's mother was making sacrifices for his education and talking about his career. I could see for the first time that the game was crook. It didn't create a great revolution in me, but I knew that women were treated differently. I had to realize that life wasn't giving me this sort of excitement.

By the middle of the war I was in Sydney doing war work. I helped in the establishment of a very effective factory, manufacturing hospital marquees and life-belts for the Defence Department. One night we girls went to a dance for the soldiers and I met a charming soldier with beautiful big black eyes and a charming foreign accent. That very first night he told me he was a furrier. It seemed so irrelevant in the middle of the war. Max was ten years my senior and had come to Australia in 1937 to escape Hitler. By the end of the war I was married with a baby and a husband who had been very ill. He was discharged from the Army and his one wish was to get back to his beloved trade.

I was the sort of person who continued to work between breast-feeds. It had been a tradition in our family. As refugees you may not have had the doors opened to you, so you worked harder. I would have loved years at home with small children but it wasn't possible because of Max's health. We just got on with the business with no real idea of where we were going. What we were establishing was to become Cornelius Furs. Max was an enormously skilled tradesman and we had other things in common as well. Like our Judaism. Neither of us was in the least orthodox but we were defined by how others defined us, especially at the time of Hitler. I didn't feel oppressed in my circumstances but I knew from my husband and all his friends about the most terrible oppression and the greatest injustice that they had experienced. I also knew that it wasn't enough just to take the 'aint it awful' line. I felt that it was my responsibility to do something about it.

I remember those times as the most glorious mix in the world. I was already an expert pattern-maker and designer and Max loved teaching me his trade. But parts of it were hell. The work was very hard and the responsibilities were always too heavy. We never planned to build a big business. We just went on doing, day after day, what was the sensible thing to do. We took our responsibilities to our clients and our suppliers seriously and built a good reputation as employers. I also discovered that I was an outstanding employer of women, especially on a part-time basis. By the time people were using the term 'flexi-time' I realized it was something I'd been doing all my life with women staff. I just saw them as sensible devices for using that untapped mine of women's resources. The wonderful things that women could offer you in sensitivity and innovative approaches. I've always felt that people just did not know what they were missing out on by not employing women. My husband absolutely went along with my policy. He did believe that women were people – perhaps not that they were quite equal. Every now and then I'd kick him in the shins and remind him who he was and then he would agree. He had been brought up in the patriarchal tradition. So that even though his head told him one thing, his conditioning often undermined it. In terms of the business, however, he always talked of me as his partner, his co-director.

These years were such a rich mix. I have a great appetite for life. I have a kind of inner strength that helps me smooth out my energy level so I can keep going for a long while. I was always able to be involved in community service work even when I was working long hours in the business. I also did management studies by correspondence and that gave me confidence that I could still study after all those years. I really needed to know about the theory of management because I was probably going to apply it the next day. Sometimes I needed to read ahead in the textbooks for the staff. Max took over the responsibility for the children at the weekends when I needed time to write my assignments. Very soon I learnt the benefits of good accountancy. I loved maths at school.

One of the things I never really did learn to live with, was affluence. It wasn't me somehow. I was much happier with my community work and I was accepted for training as a marriage guidance counsellor. Although I always worked as a volunteer, it was still a professional commitment. I loved the work and I learned a lot that was useful in peace programming. You have to be satisfied with very small gains. I have a very strong belief that because you can do very little, it doesn't mean that you've got any excuse for doing nothing. That's where you need the matriarchs. I don't know whether it's our culture or our genes. I suspect it's a mixture of both, but so many of the attributes of nurturing and caring seem to be more richly given to women. I know some very angry peace-makers, and I'm grateful to their anger and their raucousness and their lack of decorum because they will achieve things, but it's not my way. I will defend their right to do it anyway, except with violence. That is where I draw the line. I feel violence is always counter-productive.

There's always been a mythological figure of the wise old woman and I like the idea of being one of the women elders of the tribe. I'm the Australian Vice-President of the Women's International League for Peace and Freedom. We're not an enormously big group but we do tend to be matriarchs. It was established seventy years ago and we work very happily with other women's groups that attract younger women. We are like a motherly organization in the women's activities for peace. And I love that role. It is very near and dear to me.

Max was never involved in my peace work but he was on the whole supportive of my involvement. About seven years ago, our company was being purchased in stages by another company and Max was about to go overseas. It was a terribly busy time and I wasn't going with him. I remember that he was packing and I was telling him about my new plans for what afterwards became the Media Peace Prize. Max went into his usual argument of 'Why do you want to take on more work? Nobody will appreciate it, etc.' After thirty-three years of marriage we had settled into a way of arguing our viewpoints very comfortably. Usually at this stage I would have given him chapter and verse as to why it was a good practical plan and how my management skills would be useful, but I just let it be. When he came back to me an hour later he said, 'You know that idea for the Media Peace Prize? It's a good one. I think you should do it'. He died overseas three weeks later. But he left me with that inheritance. Although Max's health had been dreadful when we married, it had been generally good. He always operated like a man twenty five years younger than his age. He had so much drive and vitality. The shock of it was awful. I simply immersed myself in work. It was like being in overdrive. The weekend after Max was buried there was a meeting of the Federal Executive of the United Nations Association of Australia. I went along and presented the Media Peace Prize and they said 'Yes, we'll adopt it as a national program'. Basically it is a plan which acknowledges the vital role the media can play for peace and it rewards, esteems and applauds the best of the media in serving the peace process. Anne Deveson is a gold citation winner for her films on overseas aid. I could see that those of us who were working in the peace process did not have the power to go to the media and say 'Thou shalt not do this', by which I mean dishing up all this violence, showing very little of the history of peace. We decided to put the spotlight on positive models. One of my greatest accolades came when a very down-to-earth journalist said 'you know Stella, since you've been doing this it's much easier to get a peace story into the papers these days'. We haven't changed the world but at least we've let people know that the media can serve the cause of peace.

Politically, you know, I cop it from both sides. The Left think I'm giving credence to a wishy-washy attempt at peace by the Labor Government, the Right think I'm a naive apologist for Soviet adventurism. I answer those claims in different ways, depending on what I have time for. My flippant response is to say 'You might think it's a communist plot but the Communists think it is a CIA conspiracy'. What I prefer to do is to lay down evidence to people that polarization is exactly what will prevent you from achieving your stated aim, which is the peaceful resolution of conflict, even if you can't bear the word 'peace'. You do not need an agreement of ideologies to work on a problem together. It is true that it isn't as easy to be a peaceworker in communist countries. They don't have our tradition of allowing and inviting dissent. Once again, the fact that you can't do everything doesn't mean you should do nothing. We do have a positive model in the doctors. They talked to people in communist coun-

Stella Cornelius in the office of the
Peace Program, United Nations of Australia, 1986

tries at the professional level. Communication is one of the attributes of peace building. One of our plans for the International Year of Peace, which everybody liked, is focussed on children in countries right across the political spectrum. Children writing to each other, sending each other photographs, if possible, visiting each other. There is an affinity linking them. Western and communist women are progressing well in this way.

Inga Thorssen, a woman in her seventies, is like myself, a member of Women's International League of Peace and Freedom. She has been a member of the Swedish parliament and she did an indepth research for the United Nations' study on the conversion of military expenditure, military economy, military technology to a peacetime, non-armed society. Ilise Boulding is a Canadian academic writing brilliantly on peace subjects and teaching and organizing in this area.

Leisure? Well, music is good for me. Now that I'm commuting to Canberra I always have good tapes for the long drives to and from the airport. Mostly classical music. Every now and again I expose my ear to new music, but it's a very conscious learning experience for me. Left to myself I could go undisturbed on a diet of Beethoven. I'm a great pursuer of documentaries on television. Occasionally I will turn on something which is absolutely mindless which prevents me from getting on with the next job. Sometimes I need that. I like domesticity. I prepare myself fine food and I like it. I'm a good walker. As I've got a national park at my door, walking is my sport.

A couple of years ago if anyone had told me that I would be working for the government I would have held my stomach and rolled up in a ball of laughter. But it's terrific to have this experience at my age of working with the government. We're in the Department of Foreign Affairs and they have established a new Peace and Disarmament Branch. It's not the Ministry of Peace that we've been campaigning for but it's a step in the right direction. I have established the happiest relationship with the Department of Defence. I'm proud of that. I went in saying, 'Look, I'm not the enemy. I recognize that you see yourselves to be the people who, when all else has failed, will defend the country. What I represent is a societal responsibility to you, in that everyone should do everything possible beforehand to see that conflicts are solved non-violently. You, after all, will be the first people to put your lives on the line'.

Every area where there is injustice is of concern to me. People in the third world countries say to us quite frankly, 'Your western obsession with nuclear disarmament is a bit of a luxury. We're being killed with conventional weapons and guerilla warfare or with petty injustices'.

My daughter is not as deeply involved as I am but she is a teaching psychologist and is going to give a lot of time this year to teaching conflict resolution skills. My son is a lawyer and I often go to him for a serious discussion on how the law can help the cause of peace. He has understood a lot more about what I am doing after he had a period as sole parent. It's extraordinary what a little nurturing can teach you.

I've got a vision of every man, woman and child mastering conflict resolution skills. The global village that Marshall McLuhan promised is here already. Once you have learnt them, these skills can be transferred from solving conflicts in your inner life, in your personal life, in your family life, in your community life, your state life, national life and international life. It's one continual process. To divide it all into tight compartments will serve us all very badly.

I don't know whether I believe in an after life. It's an interesting concept. I don't have any concrete evidence of course, but I am pretty sure that I am committed to this work for more than just one lifetime. I don't feel it a heavy burden. It is one that I would welcome.

Alice Doyle

Businesswoman and Restaurateur

Alice Doyle's grandmother and grandfather opened their first fish cafe on Watson's Bay Promenade in Sydney before the turn of the century. It was closed during the Depression and would have remained so if not for Alice Doyle and her determination to continue the family business. Through hard work, courage and a wonderful sense of humour Alice developed the famous Doyle's Seafood Restaurants which she has now handed over to her family.

Alice is a fun-loving, gregarious woman whose enthusiasm and joy for the sea and all its products spills over into every area of her life. I first saw her one night when I was dining at Doyle's. She was going from table to table, chatting, cracking jokes and signing copies of her cookery book. In the copy of the book I bought she had drawn a little picture of a person fishing and had written beneath it *Just to let you know that if you want to get results in this competitive world, always use the right bait.*

When I eventually interviewed her she showed me proudly around the restaurant and when we came to what is now the dining room she said, with a characteristic twinkle in her eye, 'two of my children were conceived in this room, but I don't tell people that while they are eating'.

After a long and garrulous lunch we looked over at the only other people left. Alice waved her usual having-a-good-time-dears wave, and a woman got up from the table and walked over, bringing a shy young girl with her. 'Alice', she said, 'you don't know my daughter, but twenty-one years ago when I was about to have her and my husband was away, I was desperately trying to get a cab to take me to hospital. I was standing just on the road up there and you pulled up in your car. When I told you the problem, you said 'hop in luv'. We got to the hospital just in time, and here she is. We thought it only right that she should have lunch here on her birthday, Alice was delighted and immediately ordered champagne. After drinking a toast to the girl's birthday I left Alice at their table laughing and talking over old times. Alice Doyle has a genuine passion for people and for living.

My earliest memories are of collecting coke and driftwood here on the beachfront. My mother cooked on an Oldfield stove, and when a westerly was blowing all the wood and coke would be washed up here. The overseas ships were all coal-burners then. They supplied all of Watson's Bay with coke for their fires.

I was born at Watson's Bay, so was my mother and my grandfather. He bought this property in 1883 for one hundred pounds. He had a little shack on it, and fished from here. When he bought a block of land on the beach, he couldn't sign his name – he had to put a cross. Education wasn't so good then, but it didn't matter. He had an eye for beauty, and he just adored this glorious position. You can imagine what it was like in those early days. No footpaths, all the boats at your front door, the nets hanging along the wharf to dry. Grandfather was a fisherman, and he had this little shop. My Grandma would do a bit of cooking out the back – always making scones!

This is where I grew up, in the business, with my parents. President Reagan is six months older than me, and so is Sir Joh Bjelke-Petersen. They never say they're old, but they'd probably say I was. I'm the baby of six. My brother, Harry, was the oldest. He had his seventeenth birthday in Gallipoli.

In 1929 this was a little fish restaurant, but you could also get a grill and afternoon tea. People never came and had their dinners at night-time. We used to call it 'tea' at night, but now I know it's not really proper to call it that. People came here for midday lunch. The bus and trams were running. It was a lovely trip out here, and you'd catch the ferry back.

I met my husband, Jack, in 1929. We were having a twenty-first birthday party for Dolly Woods. Every party in Watson's Bay was always upstairs here, in this dining room. There was nowhere else. Jack came in here with one of his friends on a blind date. I was mad on dancing – the Charleston, the Black Bottom, the Doll Dance. He wasn't a bit like me, he was quiet and didn't dance. I sort of got to like him, but a chap who worked for my parents said to Jack, 'You don't want to get too friendly with that Alice. She tells her mother and father everything!' However, the romance blossomed, and we were married in 1931, at St. Peter's, our little church here at Watson's Bay, where I grew up and went to Sunday School. We had our honeymoon at Katoomba in the Blue Mountains, and when we came back to start our life together, I reckon we had two shillings between us. He was a linotype operator in the newspaper industry. It was Depression time, but I didn't worry about whether he had any money or not. I just thought I would be a glamorous bride, have a nice honeymoon, and a good wedding reception, which we did. That's all that mattered. I thought that things would be just the same as when I was young. Life would be easy, just like young people think it will be when they marry now. I was happy with my lot. I suppose if I had wanted to marry a millionaire or something I would have been disappointed. I wasn't moving in the right circles, and money married money. But I thought Jack was a good man. We were in love, and had no idea of what was ahead of us.

When I left Fort Street Girls Domestic School, I went to Metropolitan Business College, to learn how to type and do shorthand. Then I worked for a little while in an estate agent's office, and then I was a waitress here in my parents' business. I used to go to the Palais and dance my feet off. It was the Charleston era, and I just loved it. Jack and I were direct opposites. He's a Libra and I'm a Leo. I believe in the stars. I can usually pick what people are, especially if they're a bit nutty, like me.

My mother and father had to close the business in 1933. The boats went off the run, the trams were cut down, there was only a private bus service. No money. It was a battle for people. We made this place into three flats. Mum and Dad upstairs, us in the back part, and my cousin and his wife downstairs. We had no money, but we battled on together. We had four sons very quickly. But it was a great place to bring them up because they had the beachfront to play on. They were good lads. I never had an ounce of worry over them.

Then the war years came, and Jack went away. He was in radar, and then he was involved in printing a newspaper for the troops to tell them what was going on, and to keep up their morale. I stayed here with the boys, and I sort of woke up then. I knew we had to get started. I had been in a daydream, but I realized after the first baby was born that we had no money. Although Jack was never on the dole because he had a trade, I was sick to death of paying everything off. Not that I wanted much, but I remember the first rug I bought – I paid it off at one shilling a week. I was so proud of it, I went all along the beachfront showing it to the women I grew up with. It cost fifteen shillings and sixpence. When Jack came home from the war in 1946, I said, 'Can I open the restaurant downstairs again?' He said, 'No. It's too much work. You can't.' I said, 'Well, how are we going to get on?' He said, 'You'll just have to battle on and try and save'. I said, 'Save? How can we – with what?' My father was a wonderful man to us, but he died in 1947. So I just went over to the Council and said, 'I would like to open the cafe on the beachfront'. They said, 'You can't – it's been made residential'. I said, 'Oh no, have another look'. He took out another file and said, 'Well, you're just in time. In three months it will be a residential area'.

I thought, 'Whatever am I going to do – three months, and someone living in the place. It was my dearest friend, Maggie, who married my cousin, and I couldn't ask them to go. You'll never believe how it happened. I used to love to take the kids with me and play tennis and swim. One warm afternoon I came home and thought, Maggie's had her washing on the line long enough. I'm going to take it off.

Maggie used to starch the tea towels, she was fussy – not like me. The tea towels were great big linen ones then, like sheets, nearly. Maggie came out and said, 'What did you take my clothes in for?' I said, 'I want to put mine out – I've been out today, and I'm going out tomorrow to have a game of tennis.' She got so annoyed she said to her husband 'We're going'. So that night she went to my cousin's

Above: Jack and Alice Doyle re-
open the Ozone Cafe at Watsons
Bay, March, 1948
Left: Alice Doyle, 34 years old

sister over at Willoughby and said, 'We're not going to live down there any more'. But then I had another hurdle. My sister's daughter was waiting to get a place, and my mother said, 'You'll have to be fair – you'll have to give her half of that place'. So we gave her half of downstairs, in the front, and we opened the little entrance. I had about four tables working. I managed there for about twelve months, and then, all of a sudden, they got their place, and they moved. So, if I hadn't taken Maggie's clothes off the line, it would never have been opened!

Jack wasn't keen. He said, 'You do it if you want to'. He thought that I would not be able to handle it with four sons. They were never neglected, though. They will tell you themselves that every day I had that business, when they came home from school there was always hot coffee or hot cocoa, and a chocolate cake. Every afternoon of their lives I was here. I always had a big saucepan of toffee so that all the kids got an apple on a stick. I was an expert apple-on-a-stick maker! I used to make them for all the kids in the district because I loved cooking. I couldn't afford to give them the apples, so I said, 'You bring your apple from Mum with a stick, after school'. I had the toffee on the boiler, simmering, and I'd dip it in. The apples used to come with great big holes, where they'd banged somebody on the head with it.

Jack and I had plenty of blues over all this, as you could imagine, but everybody has to work at marriage, anyway. If you want to get on for your kids' sake you can't move out and leave your children. You've got to put yourself second. They don't believe in that today. If people would only work at it, it would work.

The major sources of our blues were that my husband would work and I'd do the talking. Anyway, we got it started, but we didn't have any money. So I wrote to the War Veterans Affairs – it was called the Soldiers Rehabilitation – they were giving £60 to any carpenter or builder to get started again, if they'd been away. I thought we had a good chance of getting some money. They wrote back and said they were sending out an inspector. He was an old ex-colonel from the first war I think. He and his wife had the Sunday stroll. I was looking through the curtains down there and the old place was so dilapidated downstairs, still in its original state. He knocked and said, 'We're just looking around'. I got the report back to say that they thought it was a bad risk and they could not loan us the money. That was another dampener. Jack said, 'There you are, we haven't got the money to start'. He was always frightened, because Depression is a frightening thing. You saw what your parents did, how many people went bankrupt.

Jack was working, still at the linotype at The Merchant and Traders' Association. So I said, 'Well, we've got one shilling a week insurance'. It was about seven pounds, and my mother loaned us about ten pounds. I went to the auction sales. I've got the first books at home somewhere where I'd paid fourteen shillings and sixpence for cutlery and a few seersucker table cloths. We cleaned the fish out the back, but the kitchen was nice and clean. I'd work in the day, and Jack would go to his work in the day, and to get a bit of extra money he worked at the *Mirror* at night and at the *Sun Herald* on a Saturday night. But he would have to go and buy the fish and bring it from the market.

Jack was down at the bank one day and somebody said to him, 'Can you smell fish?' And he said, 'Yes, I can'. It was all over his clothes. He was cranky about that. All the while I didn't take any notice, I was just crying on the inside and laughing on the outside.

I'd get him off to work in the morning, get the kids off to school, then I'd fillet the fish.

I had a girl from around the Bay to help me serve while I was cooking on a couple of pans on a gas stove. My mother was in her glory, because she'd been in business all her life. She was my biggest inspiration, and every Mothers Day I write a tribute to her. She was a most wonderful mother. She never went anywhere; she lived for her family. She used to come to see me at school when anything was on, and she would be the most old-fashioned mother there. She would wear a black hat, grey gloves, and grey lisle stockings. All the other kids had young mothers, but mine was forty when I was born. She would always be up there, though, sitting watching me, whatever I was doing.

When she knew we had opened the business, she was so excited. She'd have batches of scones ready for people. They got a big meal here for two and six, with scones and home-made jam. We were losing at the start, but she didn't mind about that. That was encour-

agement. I always write in my books, 'You've got to throw out a sprat
to catch a mackerel'. When I think of my mother I think of her with
flour over her slippers, flour all over the kitchen. They were her
happiest times.

We started with each day's takings. We had days when we
couldn't get fish. Jack would go everywhere, and I'd ring up my
sister Flo and say, 'You've got to go down to Rose Bay to get some
fillets of fish, but don't let them see you bringing it in'. We were
starting to make a profit, and to get a few more nice things, a bit
more cutlery and crockery. But it was always the best of food. Jack
used to say, 'You don't know whether you're making a profit or not'.
I said, 'We're getting by'. He said, 'You wouldn't know. As long as
you're talking to people, you wouldn't know how much is made'. I
said, 'We'll give it a few more weeks'. It started to get busy, and we
were getting some notable people. We had about eight tables, and I
put some out the front.

Then I taught Jack about cooking fish, and he got right into it. My
mother made beautiful soup upstairs, and we had one of those dumb
waiters. She'd sing out 'Scones!' and they'd come down in the dumb
waiter.

My mother taught me how to cook fish, though. She just loved
cooking, and it always had to be the best. The fish was wiped over
first, and cleaned properly.

My sisters and brothers didn't want to take over the business, but I
just loved it. When I got married, life was going to be bright and
rosy, but I found it was going to be a lot of hard work. We had no
money, and we had to do something. I didn't want to go and live in
the western suburbs after living on this beachfront all my life. The
only way I could do it was to try and get this property, one day. For
ten years we worked here and lived here. We got really famous in
that short time. The manager of Kellogg's at that time, a Mr. Roach,
an American, rang me up and said, 'I want a table'. And I said, 'We
don't book any tables, we haven't got the room. You'll just have to
come and wait in the queue with the rest of the people'. Jack was
cooking in the kitchen when Mr. Roach came in, and said 'Where's
my table?' He'd had a few, I think. I said, 'I told you, we haven't got
one'. He said, 'You know what you can do with your fish?' And I

said, 'You can do the same with your cornflakes, and don't forget the banana!' Everybody was treated the same.

Gough Whitlam, anybody who came, all had to wait in that queue. Nelson Eddy said, 'I'll sing a song if I can get a seat at your place'. And I said, 'I'll help you in a duet'. I used to sing while Jack cooked in the kitchen.

The business started to really go ahead. But then, sadly, my gorgeous mother passed away. I had her for ten years in the business, and without her we wouldn't have made it. We'd all be working until about two in the morning, scrubbing down the front. We didn't worry about sleep. It was terrible at times. Sometimes I thought we could never go on because we were working too hard. But I think stress is good for you, and that's what made our kids. Hard work. The children knew our problems, and they knew that we had our moments which weren't the happiest, but we managed, because a terrific big love was there, I suppose. I don't know what I'd do without Jack, now, and I don't know what he'd do without me. You've just got to try and overcome your obstacles. You've just got to cry and let it out. And then get on with it.

After my mother died, the property had to be sold because, naturally, my brothers and sisters had to get their share. The place was evaluated at £7 000. This was in 1958. So I said to Jack 'We can't let the old property go, and we can't buy it ourselves. We'll have to sell our business to buy the freehold on the property'. You can imagine how sad that was. But there was no other way, and I couldn't let the property go into the hands of strangers. We sold our business to a Frenchman for £7 000. You can imagine the dreadful shock! But we bought this from the family. We lived upstairs, and I made a flat for the Frenchman, and we showed him how to cook. It was a terrible ten years.

Anyhow, I searched the *Herald* every morning for businesses that were for sale. I saw the Pier at Rose Bay, and raced down there to get the lease. We decided to have an all-seafood restaurant. I knew in my innermost thoughts there was nothing as wonderful as seafood. We had eaten so much of it all our lives, and I still wasn't sick of it. I thought, 'Seafood is the answer'. And we were really the first in Sydney to serve nothing else. The kids were older, then, and they were able to give us a hand. We worked very hard, day and night, at the Pier. It is difficult being with your husband twenty-four hours a day. You've got to be very strong to stand it. You've got to learn how to cry. Because underneath it all you know the person is honest and true, and loves you very dearly. But you live under enormous pressure. I can honestly say I haven't got a bad temper, but I've got a most wonderful husband. We've stuck it out together. But the times were different then. We weren't raising kids when all these drugs were around. I sent them to Sunday School, sometimes they didn't go. They used to go to the pub when I didn't know. They all married young, they didn't stay at school long enough to be academic. They all got jobs. But they always knew that whatever we did, it was for the family.

Any money we've made, we've put back into it. We're selling the most expensive food of all, it's the most expensive food in the world, seafood. Everyone thinks we're millionaires. We have six great-grandchildren now, and twenty grandchildren. I suppose our great-grandchildren will have to pay off the rest of the mortgages. This particular part of the restaurant we are sitting in now has never been free of a mortgage. When I think of the dear old place my grandfather bought in 1883, for one hundred pounds, and he erected it! In 1908 they put a front on it, which made it two storeys, and Grandma and my father and mother ran the Signal Tearooms. And I look at it now!

Anyhow, it took us ten years of hard work at Rose Bay before we walked back into it. I'll never forget the excitement. By that time the family were older, and able to take it on. It was the beginning of a new life, but it was also a little sad for me – I was getting older.

In 1969 we bought the Watson Bay Hotel. We had four places operating at that time. In 1970 we had bought the Watson's Bay Wharf and remodelled it, and we had the Pier at Rose Bay, and Manly. Our son, Tim, managed that, and if we ran out of fish we'd have to send for it by boat. By the time you got across that crossing at South Head, though, it wasn't worth it. Tim came back to Rose Bay. So the four boys were working all of the businesses. We sold the hotel in 1976. We are definitely not hotel people. We worried too much about the people who hang around pubs. The rooms in the hotel were never let. Our son used to give them to all the people who were hard up. We never knew who slept there. I wasn't any better. I'd see a woman lying in the gutter and bring her to the hotel. We'd delouse them and feed them. How could you leave them? So that's all we used the hotel for – all the deadbeats. But that's what life's about. It's people who make life. My mother was my beacon – you have to love speaking to people and being with them if you're in business. So much love has gone into this business from my mother and my grandfather.

We have won three major awards for the best fish restaurant in Australia, but as long as we win customers, I don't give a continental about those. As long as the garbage man keeps coming, Mr. Everybody. The worker keeps us going. He comes with his wife and kids, and they love it. You can't get complacent. The customer is always right – we need every customer we can get. That gets drummed into our grandchildren while Dad and I are alive, and while our sons are alive. Customers talk – you don't just lose a customer, you lose all their friends as well.

I don't feel inferior to anyone. Do you know, I met Prince Charles and Princess Diana, when they were last here, and I had a conversation of five or six minutes alone with them. I met them at the luncheon at Parliament House – we were invited! I was so excited! I never thought that Jack and I – fish and chip people! – would ever speak to Royalty. But it was just as if Fate meant it that way. We were just standing near the table, and the Princess left Mr and Mrs Wran and came across in our direction. I said 'Hello', and the Prince came over, too. And I wasn't even spellbound. It was just like the girl next door, with a frock on she had got from Katies – although it was probably pure silk! I said, 'Gosh, it's great meeting you – I'm so excited. I'm very happy for you both, and it's lovely for you to come to Australia, and it's a lovely day, and the whole of Australia and the whole world is excited about you and your baby, and we wish you lots of happiness, and I hope you're not the queen and king for years and years!' So the Prince said to Jack, 'Are you a Member of Parliament?' Jack was all dressed up in his good clothes, and looked nice. He said, 'No, I'm just a plain working man'. She asked about my children. I showed them my coronation medal from 1911. It was the highlight of my life!

Alice Doyle outside Doyle's Seafood Restaurant
(Photo courtesy of John Fairfax and Sons)

My grandchildren, of course, are more impressed with photographs of me with John Travolta, or sitting on Elton John's knee. Always with the man! I suppose I always was a bit of a flirt. But I was never really naughty. I just loved to dance. I love music. It makes me cry – especially the music of my era.

I think Australia would be better if a few more women could run it. I think Hazel Hawke is tremendous. She works for the welfare of young people. I think she's a woman like me somehow. Women are the strongest. I know they have been dealt some terrible blows and everybody can't stay with a man but I think sometimes that you've got to think of your children. But she's stuck by Hawke hasn't she? She has.

I was only looking at the Governor, marching on Anzac Day and he's a great man, but I thought why isn't a woman there? Women have got feeling for people. They're mothers and they know what people want in this world. People are frightened to speak to governors, if it's a man, but they are not frightened to speak to a woman. It's always the mother image and they feel they can tell their mother anything. Women should be running the place.

There are so many wonderful women. I know women who work for the mission and St. Vincent de Paul who get no recognition from the government. They do it all for nothing. They've got to ring up and ask for furniture, chairs, blankets and sheets to supply these young kids who haven't got a home. They know they are going to get rebuffed. They know someone's going to say 'another miserable phone call about wanting something' and they've got to take that all the time. Those women are never spoken about but they are the great women of Australia. They are forgotten.

I would love to have had a daughter. Of course I had four sons, but I do miss having a daughter. I couldn't have any more. I did have a miscarriage once, it was a natural one and they didn't tell me what it was. I often think perhaps it was that daughter. And another disappointment is that I've never had a granddaughter called after me. I'd love them to call one Alice. Now it's a fashionable name.

I hope that they'll try and keep this property because it was such a terrific slug and hard work and tears to keep it going.

We have been overseas a couple of times. I made Jack go. One night, in 1962, I came home from the Pier. It was Anzac Day and it was on a Thursday, and I was reading the Sunday papers and we were there sitting on a chair, having a cup of tea about 1.00 in the morning. The boys were in the business then, and I said to Jack, 'We're going away', and he said, 'Where to?' and I said, 'England'. He said, 'You must be crazy. We can't afford it', and I said, 'Yes, we can. We'll borrow the money and we'll go. Let them manage the place. I would love to go to England, I've never been'. Father came from England and I could always visualize the cobbled streets. Everything's got to be done immediately. Next day I rang up the booking office and we could only get a berth on the maiden voyage of the *Canberra*. We could only afford tourist.

If there's a puddle of water in the night-time and lights are shining on it, I think I'm at sea. Driving along, I just get carried away. Flowers, trees, hibiscus, just carried away. I love the sea. Anyway we had a gorgeous trip and the *Canberra* broke down about twice. It was its first trip through the Canal. It was just wonderful and we just stayed at rooms at Victoria and climbed up all the stairs. The year after I said we were going to Japan on the *Canberra*, and we had a wonderful time. When we got to Yokohama, the Entertainments Officer said, 'Mrs. Doyle. We have selected you to give the flowers to the hostesses in Japan'. When we went away just a few years ago, on the *Fairstar* to Japan, the Entertainments Officer asked me again if I would like to give the flowers.

My average day? I get up about seven, usually. Sometimes I get up about half past four and go down and make a cup of tea. You must get up if you're awake, because if you're lying in bed you think too much! It's a sad thing, getting old. You wonder how you can stand it. You get pains and aches, and you drag yourself up. Then I go up to the shop, and I know everybody there. I take my sister for a drive and shopping, which is great. Then we come down here in the night time, and I meet the people. Every Friday night I'm at one of the restaurants, and through the week I come down and eat. I do most of my entertaining here. I have a terrific zest for living, but I do believe in the hereafter. I suppose the good Lord will have a waterfront for me. He knows I love the view. I never forget to thank Him for the beautiful flowers I see every day. I love God, although I don't go to church enough. I ask the minister to dinner, to square off! St. Peter's is such a tiny church that I said to him, 'You know what you should do at Easter? You should put a sign out the front about three weeks beforehand saying "Come early and avoid the Easter rush", and I might come'.

I don't watch much telly, except the news and current affairs. And I still love to cook. I make scones every day for something in the office. Want to know an easy way?

Dissolve a good tablespoon of butter into a saucepan, add a cup and a half of milk – melt the butter a bit first, so as to make the milk warm – about a pound of flour into a basin, a couple of tablespoons of sugar. Sugar and flour in the basin, chopped up dates or raisins, or whatever you've got. You've melted your butter and the milk is lukewarm. Add a beaten egg into the saucepan – don't worry about another dish, put it into your flour mix-ture, then the fruit. Have the oven very hot, with the top rung in your oven. Put the mix onto the table, where you work it with a bit of flour . . . roll it if you want, but you needn't. Just cut bits off it and onto a tray, then into the very hot oven. That's the secret. A hot oven, and in ten minutes you've got some lovely scones. No art.

If you love doing something, it's never a trouble. My cookbook is in its sixth reprint now. All the money goes to charity. I write in every book – poems and jokes and drawings. I write a lot of letters to people. I sit at my window and watch the moon – I'm moon mad, but I don't often meet many people who love the moon as I do. I keep a diary, and at the top, with the date, I draw the moon in its different stages. I know every one of its faces. I'm on the cusp of Leo and Virgo. Leos are real leaders, they always want to take over, but Virgos worry because they are perfectionists. Everything has to be right. Jack's a Libra, which means he's not a risk-taker like me. But we've lasted the distance. When we had our golden wedding, I sent out three hundred invitations, which said: 'As it's a golden wedding, I expect something in return! I'll settle for a tin of golden syrup, because we were married in the Depression'. No other gifts were accepted, and there was a prize for the best decorated tin. It was a fantastic turnout. I sent the tins of golden syrup to the mission, and

Above: Golden Wedding Anniversary, 1981
Below: 'There was a prize for the best decorated
tin of Golden Syrup.'

Colonial Sugar came out and took photographs.

It's a lovely life to be amongst people. The other night a family came in, and one of them said 'David's very sorry he couldn't come'. And I said, 'What a shame. He must be getting a big boy by now. How old is he?' They said, 'Seventy-four'.

I once said to Bill Peach, 'You do all these beautiful walks, but you've never done TBA Avenue from the Gap to the Glen'. In the olden days, TBA stood for 'Tickle Belly Avenue'. Sounds so tame, now. I think the young kids of today are brainwashed with sex – I feel sorry for them. There are more things in the world than sex. I get my kicks from looking at the view and the flowers. It's funny. Now that we can afford all those things we never could, we don't need them. It's been a long struggle, and now the boys have taken it over. I realize I wasn't born to be selfish – I gave away what I could. The moon will do me.

Shine on, Harvest Moon!

Shaping Thought

Joan Campbell

Potter and Sculptor

Whenever I think of Joan Campbell I hear the lap-lap-lapping of the sea that washes up against the old stone walls of her workshop. I had never seen the Indian Ocean before and as I stood in the wind with Joan, gasping at the vast sky and the intensity of the clear light, I knew why she had chosen to work in this part of Australia. Everything she creates seems to hum with the joy and the awe with which Joan sees the world around her, a world she recreates in flowing elemental shapes.

This world-renowned artist has never done anything by halves. Like a child in a magic cave, I stepped through a hole knocked in the wall and saw Joan Campbell's enchanted world of Bungle Bungle. She saw the original for this vast reconstruction while she was hanging out of a helicopter as it swooped past the huge sandstone formations in the north-west of Western Australia.

Each day presents a new challenge to this woman. She has fought and overcome many obstacles: the death of her third child, years of psychiatric illness, and most recently cancer. Over the past ten years she has also been a campaigner in the arts and a member of the Craft Council. A leader in her field – raku pottery – she showed me around her warehouse workshop and talked in a quiet but animated way about the various forms I was seeing before me. It would be a gross understatement to say I had never seen anything like it before. Everything she creates is coupled with a philosophical understanding of what she is trying to do and why. Her words flowed as confidently as the sea that repeated its hypnotic rhythms.

As the light disappeared, we went back to her cottage which she and her friends had renovated. It too was a work of art, making the best use of every available source of space and light. We talked and talked, long into the night.

If the death of her child was the catalyst for her creativity, the birth of each new work is testimony to the joy that she feels in living. I hope some of that joy and vision is conveyed in this brief glimpse into the life of this unique artist.

I feel the landscape and the sun in this part of the country is part of me – like my own tribal area. It's that affinity with one's own land, one's own place, one's light and colours. There are qualities peculiar to this part of the world that are very intense and very real and I hope they find reflection in my work.

I didn't grow up in Western Australia. In fact my early years were spent walking a lot along Geelong Common. I had two older brothers and one younger. We were fairly crowded in our house and our parents realized we needed space. We were all allowed to have our own tree in the park opposite. Mine was a small elm tree which I could get up without my brothers' help. I could sit up there for three or four hours if I wanted – just dreaming. I made up stories and fantasies about fairies and gnomes and wove dandelion chains for my grandmother. My brothers were imaginary cowboys or Indians. No one came out and said, 'What are you doing up there? Get down'. My parents just believed that we must have had a good reason to be up there and would come down when we were ready. There was a big gliding club on Geelong Common and I loved watching them. I later learnt to fly. I think we were very lucky that we had that chance to give our imaginations free rein. I believe that there's a basic creativity in everyone. In some people it's nourished and in some it's not.

Father was an engineer, a sort of inventor. Not a conformist at all. Mother was a wonderful mother not only to us but to her six brothers whom she'd also brought up. During the war years she had all her brothers and sons away and she wrote letters to them all the time.

We always said that mother didn't have a hobby, but then I realized after she died that it was writing to everyone in the family and keeping up the lines of communication between us. When we moved from Victoria to Perth she wrote to one of them every day and if they were sick, she would make a journey to the city to buy a card and send it every day. We'd say, 'Why don't you just buy a half a dozen cards?' and she'd say 'But if I was there I'd visit them each day'. We realized she was doing something very special.

My parents were a very loving couple and we were all brought up in a warm atmosphere and encouraged to make or do everything. If my brothers wanted to sew my doll's clothes or I wanted to help Dad with the car, no one would criticize that. I don't think my parents had any particular philosophy about it, that's just the way they were. I'm sure my first attempts with clay stemmed from my early memories of building endlessly in mud. In Victoria, compared to Western Australia where it's sandy, you could actually build things in mud and they'd hold their shape. It was an endless source of fascination to me.

Father was very scientifically inclined. He invented things which were patented. We always had radium in a lead box in our house. His grandfather had gone to France and met Madame Curie who told him what kind of ore you would find radium in. When he came back these prospectors went out and found Radium Hill in South Australia, and the family had the leases until the government took them over in World War I. So father had some of this magical radium in a lead box which he'd trot out on Sunday nights and do experiments with it and tell us amazing things. When I was about five or six I remember trotting around the corner to my girlfriend and saying, 'You know, Joany, if man splits the atom, the whole world will change'. I didn't have a clue what I was talking about of course. He passed that sense of fascination with men trying to explore such things on to us. Later on when he died of cancer and my brothers had cancer and so have I, one could reasonably suspect that it was due to the exposure we all had. In those days everybody thought it was a great healing source of energy. It was going to cure all our complaints. We didn't know how thick the lead in the box should be.

So it wasn't a conventional Australian upbringing in that sense but we lived in a pretty typical Protestant Australian neighbourhood. I remember when an Irish Catholic family moved in at the end of our street. The girl, Mary, came to a girls club camp that I was at and when we all went to have a shower in the morning – we were just thirteen – Mary had pubic hair and it was black. I thought that's because she's Catholic and Irish. I quite liked school, particularly maths and physics. Dad used to take me to the woollen mills in Geelong and I'd be totally fascinated with how men could actually make all those parts mesh and work together.

We moved to Perth when the war broke out. I was fourteen. My father only expected to be here about a year but he was poisoned twice with chlorine gas in experiments. He wasn't allowed to continue with his work so he did an incredible thing. He and one of his friends built a set of dodgem cars, which were probably the first in Australia. I looked after my mother in those war years because all my brothers enlisted once they were seventeen and my father was always in his workshop. I worked at the airport, helping to dismantle aeroplanes and re-build them. I was the only girl in the plant but that didn't seem odd to me because of my upbringing. They just treated me like one of them, and taught me a lot of things about mechanics and carpentry.

Towards the end of the war I was desperately anxious to learn to fly. One of my uncles had a plane and employed a pilot. So I thought if I get qualified commercially I can be his pilot. I worked as a secretary to earn the money for the flying lessons. I was about seventeen. I can remember going solo and thinking how clean it was up there. It felt so free and beautiful. But I hadn't even completed my training when I had an accident and wrote off an aeroplane. I just flew straight into the ground. The plane was smashed to bits and I was left hanging upside down in the harness. The man over the other side of the field said he thought, 'If she's alive I hope she doesn't pull the pin, she'll fall on her head and kill herself'. But I didn't. I didn't even have a scratch or a bruise. All I could think was, 'What the hell did I do wrong?'

It was a little hard to tell my parents what had happened. My Dad, the truly creative person, was immediately interested in solving the problem. Problems are either a source of frustration or a source of using what you know to discover something you didn't know before.

Joan Campbell in 1958 with husband Jim and children
Gregory, Suzanne and Debra   Inset: 16 years old

That was always Dad's approach. It was probably the reason we had dared to tackle a lot of things because we knew he'd respect our reasons for doing it. I flew again, of course, in the next couple of days and then I had another medical. That doctor diagnosed that I had long sight in both eyes. Once I had the correct glasses I was fine. I loved flying over the house and giving them a wing so they could see me. But I realized that my mother was absolutely freaking out. I was her only daughter and it worried her sick. I thought 'It's not worth it. If it's doing that to my mother it's not important'. So I didn't continue with it. What's the point of making someone else's life miserable for your own enjoyment.

So then I got married – it seemed like an interesting thing to do. During the war our house was always full of friends of my brothers' or mother's and Jim was brought along to my twenty-first. I thought he looked like Spencer Tracy, a nice rugged type. He was a nice man and everyone said 'Why don't you get married?' So we did. People today analyse everything but in those days you didn't. We seemed to be the same type of person. In actual fact we were totally different. Everyone told him to get a safe job in the government. In actual fact he quite liked it and ended up being deputy head of the Department of Labour until he retired a few years ago. In those early days we were just like any other young suburban Australian couple where the man had been away at the war. They'd been in a man's world for years, so Saturday nights were always bring your own Gladstone bag with half a dozen beer in it. We didn't have enough money to do anything else but sit around having a drink and a laugh and a sing song. But I found that being a housewife wasn't all that absorbing. I'd get the housework done early and then I did everything you could think of. I sewed and crocheted and went to the parents meetings. I played golf and went to fashion parades – all the things that the *Women's Weekly* was telling me I should do. And yet inside I kept thinking I'm just filling in time, why am I doing all this? Don't forget, this is nearly forty years ago and there weren't a lot of work opportunities available to women, and I wasn't educated for the ones that were.

I had three children, my third child was stillborn, but I had four babies. I loved their childhood. I used to make up fantastic games to play with them. I'd bung them all in prams and go into the bush. We'd be cowboys and Indians and I'd be crawling around in the dirt with them. It was great fun living at the beach because we would make sand castles all day and it didn't cost any money. I had six pounds a week to keep house. I sewed all their clothes. But we were no different from anyone else. We were all just struggling to educate our kids and look after our homes.

When I lost my third baby it was really a major shock. I was two weeks over-term and I knew there was something wrong. Jim was away and I got my brother-in-law to take me to the hospital. The baby was stillborn. It had strangled at birth because it had moved in the excess fluid. Jim was isolated on a station and couldn't get back for five days until the Flying Doctor plane brought him. So I had to handle our parents and family who came to see me. I had to fix up the funeral. I kept saying, 'It's all right. I'm all right'. What I didn't realize was that because I thought I had to be brave and noble and not cause anybody distress I carried around a whole lot of unresolved grief. My arms would quite physically ache to hold the baby that the body had been conditioned to have. I can really understand how young women snatch babies out of prams. I thought that given time nature would heal these things. All I had to do was just keep going. But it really made me question the meaning of life for the first time ever. There was this perfectly formed big black-haired baby boy who looked just like he was asleep. I kept asking myself, 'What is life?' I started to read every philosophy book I could lay my hands on. Then I thought I would be confirmed in the Church of England. I listened to all the teachings and followed all the disciplines. Jim didn't come to my confirmation and didn't really know what was going on. After about four or five years I thought 'This isn't really for me'. It's fine and wonderful for most people but I keep feeling that the ministers and the Church got in the way of God. I believed in God, but felt that God wasn't a form. I began to read really seriously. Then when I was really questioning I began to spin off, really spin off. I would have visions and things. Quite crazy visions. I actually drew up all the plans of a church. The minister who'd been like a family minister believed everything that I told him because, I realized later, he himself hadn't had those experiences. Later when I went to India, some of their spiritual people made me realize why the Hindus have gurus in that sense. The true guru is the one who has been through all those experiences. Their role is basically to level off all the time and just bring you right back to earth and not go off on some head trip like that. This young man wasn't able to do that. One night I got up from bed and went out into the middle of the road and just passed out completely. They picked me up off the road when they found me and didn't know what had happened, including me. So they called the doctor and said you'd better hospitalize her. They gave me electric shock treatment for five days and I was unconscious for five days. The doctor didn't think I'd pull through. He didn't know what was going on. Nobody did. I'd had a dinner party the night before. What was going on inside me, no one knew. I was carrying on this normal life out there doing everything right and having this trip inside.

I've had a friend since I was eighteen who is a theosophist, and a very remarkable lady. She heard that I was in hospital and even though I was allowed no visitors, she got in. I remember hearing this voice saying, 'You'll be all right now. You've been over the edge. You won't do it again. You will be all right now'. She saved my life because she was the one person who got through to me. I became conscious next day and then I discovered I'd had a breakdown. I freaked out, because I thought only insane people had breakdowns. I immediately became terrified of me. They'd blown my mind. I didn't know half my clothes, I didn't know half my friends, I didn't know half my house. There were gaps where you'd remember an apple but couldn't remember a banana. It was just awful. They sent me home with all this dope and said, 'You have to stay on that'. I hated that. I couldn't remember what had happened. It was about three months before my memory came back. I rang the doctor because I thought my head was going to fall off, it was shaking so much with shock. I talked to him about it and he said, 'Now look, there's nothing bloody well wrong with you. You're just a bloody creative woman and you're not using it. I can't do anything for you. You can do it for yourself. Just keep taking those tablets because if you don't you'll freak out again'. I said 'Well, I can't live taking tablets'. And he said, 'Well, you've got to take them now'. I said, 'I'm going to break them down', and he said, 'Well, not too fast. And ring me every week'. So I started taking myself off these things and it went on for about nine months. I was on a four-hourly thing and by about three hours I would start to feel shaky and I'd think, 'Oh, I don't know whether I'll see it out. I want to go to five this time. After four hours I'd be thinking, 'Oh jeepers, I really want to go to a four and a half'. I'd be terrified that I might do something and hurt somebody. I was so destroyed as a human being that I couldn't walk from my kitchen to my bathroom without being frightened that I might do something that was bad. And nobody talked to me about it. My family just looked at me terrified and they didn't know. They were loving and caring, but they didn't understand.

I went to see the doctor again and he said, 'Well now you had better do something'. Everything we went through I seemed to have done. Finally we got around to pottery and I said, 'That's the stuff you do with clay, it's cheap I could dig that'. I went to a ladies pottery class in the mornings. What I learned from that experience was that the worst reason to do anything is because it's going to do you good. The next thing I tackled was an oratorical competition in Western Australia. A friend convinced me that if I could stand up alone on a platform in front of people and just speak naturally from the heart it would do me good. And give courage to a lot of other people who were still struggling. I still felt only half a person but I took a gamble on myself. My main fear was that it would send my head spinning off again. Anyway, I won the female section. It was then that I decided to start work seriously with clay. Even if it took the rest of my lifetime I just knew that if I could acquire enough knowledge and skills then life would begin to flow through it.

But also at that time, I began to get really shaky again. I was off the tablets and one morning I woke up about 4 am and thought 'No I'm not going to get out of bed again'. And I turned over and made myself go to sleep. When I woke up in the morning I was all right. It was a real lesson in having faith in yourself and your own capacities. I knew that if I started taking those tablets again I would always be dependent on them. Throughout your life I think everyone has the chance to make a choice – it's a gamble – about the kind of person you eventually become.

I had one more stint in hospital and I remember waking up in that room, sitting up with my back against the wall saying to myself, 'Please don't let them do that to me again. Please don't let them come in here'. It was the first time I had really remembered how terrible the shock therapy had been. I do feel there is something basically inhuman about that treatment. When I saw *One Flew Over the Cuckoo's Nest,* I knew it all. I remember Jim and I driving east to see the family and looking out the window at a farmer sitting on a tractor and thinking, 'How can he just sit there all day? What does he do with his mind?' Mine was just spinning around all the time. My family certainly thought I was very strange during that time but although they couldn't help me they believed I would get there. Jim is a totally calm, conventional, rational person who didn't understand but just continued trying to lead a normal life. It was all buried emotions. The hardest part were the hours alone each day. In fact, it took me about two years to really get over it all.

When I began really working with clay I started to feel a lot better and I had great fun with a huge wood-burning kiln. It was three times the size it should have been because I got the wrong plans. My Dad helped me build it in the back garden. We took six weeks working eight or nine hours a day. It was the most complex and inefficient kiln ever built but I thought it was beautiful. I even rang up the local minister and asked him to bless it. He was a bit taken aback but Dad and I stood in the back garden whilst the minister blessed it in praise of the work that will come forth to the glory of God. And then I spent the next four months blowing everything up. I just couldn't work out what I was doing wrong. I asked the men in the brickworks and all they'd say was 'Oh Joan, they all fire differently, love'. But I was determined and I believe that when you are really seeking a solution to a problem your antennas are out everywhere. One day I was listening to two men talking about the fuel ratio of a diesel on their boat and suddenly it came to me. The problem was the air–fuel ratio. It's an English kiln where the atmosphere is heavier than that on the western coast here, where the breeze comes in at ten o'clock and shoots the fire up. So I raced to the junk yard, got an old Kookaburra gas stove and took the door off. I raced home, rang Dad and he came over and with his help I had the means whereby I could control the air coming in under the fire. I had a couple of years of wonderful firings after that. I'd sit up all night with the fire and I learned that the force of the firing was part of the creative process. I learned about the rhythm of working with natural forces and not resisting them. But listening to the fire I knew about its character and what it was doing. I fired with coke and wood, then later with oil and now eventually with gas. I have been years watching these flames dance around. It's like a woman in labour, you have to work with it and help it. I was getting incredible red and blue pots when I was trying to get an ordinary brown glaze. I remember being introduced to Shiga Shigeo, the Japanese potter and he said everyone was trying to get reds and blues and couldn't. And later on Nicolas Vergette, a wonderful American potter came to Australia for a conference and asked if he could come and plod around in my back yard. He just kept saying, 'I don't believe it. You don't even know what you've done, but you've done it'. I once gave a talk on 'I don't know what I did or what I do but I'm doing it and I don't know where I'm at but I'm there'. Basically that still applies, but it certainly did then because I was working in total isolation from what was going on in the rest of the world. There weren't many books or magazines and people didn't come by very often. Mean-while, of course, I'm still cooking cakes for school fetes and scream-ing at the athletics. Whilst I was preoccupied I made sure I was there when they came home from school. Mind you they might have had to get the tea because Mum was firing the kiln.

When we came to summer I couldn't fire the kiln because of the fire restrictions so I decided to build some little wood kilns. Then I read in one of the few books available, about using a lacquer to fire it quickly, and that's how I started doing raku, which is my own form. But I never did it in the sense that the Japanese practise it with a whole philosophy that goes back 800 years. The stuff I produced first was very strange looking but I persisted. Then I dug a hole in the ground, lined it with bricks and got one of the home-made oil burners that Dad had given me and fired it with kerosene. I had only one pot in the middle of the kiln and the fire circled around it. The roof was a plough disc with a hole in the middle. That was my kiln. I worked and worked and gradually things started to happen. By the end of the year I had about two hundred pieces and I'd buried about five hundred. They were the weirdest looking things. I said to my Dad 'How will I know whether it's yuk or not?' He said 'There's only one way'. So I rang the Richeymans who had the Old Fire Station

Gallery and they set up a show. I don't like to go to my exhibitions at all. Once you've done your work, it's history. You have to move onto the next thing. I've never kept a piece of my own work. Anyway Ric rang me and said 'The exhibition is amazing. Everyone's very excited about it'. I thought 'Oh, it's just because it's different'. In the next couple of days I got a letter from a woman I didn't know who had written a poem about the exhibition. I was so moved that I sat on the front step blubbering my eyes out. I knew the work had communicated at the level I had aimed at. It's those things that keep you working.

I had another show the next year which I floated on glass. Then my father was told he had cancer. It was totally inoperable and he said to the doctor, 'I don't mind dying, but I hate not trying to live'. So he asked to be given the latest treatment so they could find out something that might help young people with cancer. He was given five weeks and he lasted nearly twelve months. When he was finally in hospital he seemed to be quite excited about discovering what actually happened when you die. He wasn't sad at all.

Just before he died he told me he wanted me to go abroad to see what was happening there. I wasn't all that keen but one night when we went down to the beach and put on the lights so the men in the Sputnik could see them, I stood there looking up into the sky and thought 'There's a professor in America that I really want to ask about some problems I've been having with the kiln'. Then I thought, 'Oh no, he's so famous and I'm just a suburban housewife playing about in the backyard'. Then when I saw the Sputnik I thought, 'Isn't it stupid that these men can talk to the whole world and we are too frightened to even write to each other'. So I wrote to him and that correspondence gave me the courage to go away and experience the most wonderful things. My work kept growing and expanding – literally. I discovered that large scale is my natural scale. I kept having to re-design kilns so I could fire the pieces.

All I was doing was making my life interesting. I wasn't trying to be anything. I was invited to an International Symposium whose Academy I had been elected to after winning an award in London which I knew nothing about. I just got this letter which said 'You can now use these letters after your name'. I thought it was hilarious – me with-

Above: Working with students from Goroko Teachers College,
Papua New Guinea   Below: In the workshop, 1986

out two bob to my name. I was determined to get there so I made two hundred black and red ashtrays for Hammersley Mines. I don't ever want to see them again but I got there and it was the most amazing and exhilarating experience of my life. I realized that you shouldn't ever feel inferior with whatever your lack of skill is as long as you try every day to expand. For me it's a steady process of learning.

When I returned I realized that I had to find another building in which to work. More houses had been built alongside us and the neighbours were worried about the noise and the smoke. When I found this workshop on the edge of the ocean, my work changed with the influence of the magnificent sunsets – all those wonderful pinks and blues and lemons. For the last ten years I've had trainees here and they've been terrific times. My biggest show was a large portal which has been very symbolic of my life. After two failed attempts I decided to build it in one and then build the kiln around it. I started building inch by inch until I had two columns about seven feet high spanned by four foot six inches unsupported. It took me three weeks up a ladder and there were about six people in the workshop saying, 'We don't believe this'. I never believed it would fall down.

It was while I was building that I picked up the phone at ten one morning and was told that I had cancer. I had, of course, been through the tests, and they were positive. I went to see the doctor and he explained that it meant massive surgery followed much later by a radium implant. I said, 'I'll do everything you ask of me for the next twelve weeks as long as you don't tell any lies. But I've got an exhibition to finish'. Before I went to hospital I was determined to finish the portal. As there was no time to build a kiln around it we sawed it up into five pieces and gave it its first firing. At least when I went to the hospital I knew it wouldn't crumble away. To me it was the symbol of life.

As I had been meditating for twenty years I was quite calm about going to the hospital. I knew I had to save my energy and become almost an observer. So I put myself into the hands of these two scientists whom I knew would do their best. They removed the cancer from the uterus and then I had to go back a month later for a radium implant. I went back to work after twelve weeks and my friends helped me set up this mammoth exhibition – the portal was the piece-de-resistance. We were all there doing the final touches when someone came through with a ladder, swung around slightly and knocked the portal. The whole thing crashed to the ground. I couldn't believe it but all I thought was 'Well, that wasn't to be'. We dragged it away to a back room and got on with the Press Conference. One of the things I learnt in India was not to be attached to anything. That doesn't mean that you aren't loving. Some people find it very hard to grasp intellectually. I think I have probably been at this stage of non-attachment longer than I realized. It's about loving and giving without possessing. When I realized I really wanted to have my own house Jim understood. So he has a unit in Perth and I have my cottage in Fremantle. He's retired now and needs to be with his friends and clubs and he comes and stays with me a couple of nights a week. He lets me be myself and that's a mark of real love. I respect his space and he respects mine. We have never had to stay locked in each other's bosoms all these years. Love can take many forms, ours is just a different one.

I was born in 1925 so I have begun to think about what I'll do with the rest of my life. I always said I wasn't going to have a retrospective of my work until I was eighty, but a sculptor friend of mine had a major exhibition to celebrate her eightieth birthday. It was a stunning exhibition. So now I think I'll have my retrospective when I'm ninety because I've still got a lot of things to do.

Dame Mary Durack

Author and Historian

'For many years now I have lived in three generations, following many a vague and winding track in search of missing clues and facts long buried in the mists of time.'

So begins the Foreword to Mary Durack's family saga, *Kings in Grass Castles*. There is something about her directness of gaze, her willingness to listen, and an underlying strength of will that brings to mind phrases like 'pioneering spirit'. When I went to her family home in Perth it was clear to me that she had squeezed me into an already busy day. She says she finds it hard to turn people away, and so is always over-committing herself to a wide variety of projects.

We sat in a glassed-in room from where we could see the birds that flew in to gobble the food that she had put out. Together we tried to trace the map of her life, and she kept getting up from the table to pull out one book after another, showing me photographs or reading me small excerpts. One recollection led swiftly to another and I trailed around after her with my little tape recorder, trying to get it all down. She read her words with the same care and respect with which she writes them. There is a different look which comes into her eyes. Writing is the special place to which she goes, which is hers alone.

While I was there the phone rang several times, mostly people with requests. She always took time to listen and try to help. I felt drawn into a life as vast and diverse as the country which she and her family have traversed.

Eventually she took me to another study in the back garden and showed cabinet after cabinet overflowing with her father's diaries and all the research she still had to carefully piece together for yet another volume of the family saga. Seeing it all reminded her of how much work she had ahead. I waited on the front verandah for the taxi to come. There can be no time for small talk when every moment counts.

I think this sort of oral history is a very good thing and I'm trying to encourage it for various reasons. So much of our history has been lost.

There are a lot of women who have done extraordinary things absolutely unrecorded – one of them has recently died. You wouldn't have ever known Patty Clancy would you? She was ahead of her time. She was a journalist to start with and then she ended up being Secretary to the United Nations and she went round and round the world. She was living in New York most of the time. But I said to my niece who was her niece, my sister married her brother, 'You should write her life. It's quite incredible'. It was only when she died and I went to see her sister in Sydney who had all these papers and newspaper cuttings. I always knew she was remarkable but I had no idea she'd done all that.

My very earliest memories are not exactly brilliant or bright. When I was a few weeks old – I was born in Adelaide in 1913 – my mother came back to Kimberley – they had no city home at that time – with my elder brother and myself. I can very clearly remember, before my mother's face, the Aboriginal woman who used to carry me around absolutely patiently and lovingly. She would sit down on the edge of the billabong in front of the homestead with a little bent pin or something and catch these tiny little fish. I can remember seeing them wriggling and that was a great entertainment. And I also remember being on a ship. I didn't know what it was at the time and it was swaying around, I took my first steps and I remember feeling very proud. The ship was going from Wyndham to Manila where the family were sending cattle. Mother spent her early summers in Manila. People say, 'Well you and your family were brought up in the bush' but that was not so, because just before my sister Elizabeth was born, my father decided that it was time that he got a place in

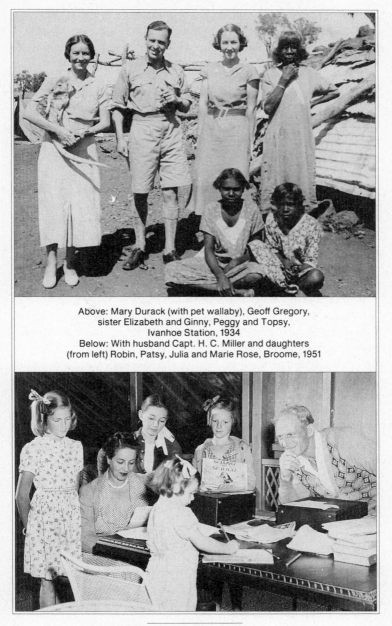

Above: Mary Durack (with pet wallaby), Geoff Gregory,
sister Elizabeth and Ginny, Peggy and Topsy,
Ivanhoe Station, 1934
Below: With husband Capt. H. C. Miller and daughters
(from left) Robin, Patsy, Julia and Marie Rose, Broome, 1951

the city. There was no education in the north, there was nothing. No flying doctor service or anything like that. It was very sad, how many of the families that did try to rear children, how many of those children died. Fever was rife and it killed children off as well as adults. So we were not brought up in the bush and we didn't even go back for our holidays because there was only the ship service between Fremantle and Wyndham and that would take two to three weeks there and back and in any case, we couldn't travel around. So we just were city-bred children. It just happens that my first little memories were of the place that I've always felt was my spirit home. When I got back to it I felt as if I'd come home.

Actually it was Ivanhoe Station, the Kimberleys, one of the four or five stations our people had. They all adjoined each other and we went from one to the other, but Ivanhoe was my spirit home and I think that that was where I began. And it still has an extraordinary effect on me.

I would love to be there. I go up once a year or sometimes twice. As a matter of fact, as years have gone on I feel I belong anywhere in Australia. I don't mind whether it's the heart of Sydney or heart of the desert. I'm perfectly at home. But I think I'd prefer the desert. I've stayed in most parts of Australia and lived for quite a considerable time in Broome when my husband was running the air service between Perth and Darwin and this was his half-way home so we lived between here and Broome. The children went to school quite a lot in Broome and I loved it there and we could fly around and get on the planes or the bus.

I have an elder brother – he's there now, up in the north. And he's worse than I am. He just can't keep away. He was the only one who remained with the station after my father sold out.

But the north was always very close to us because my father was to and fro. He was general manager of our pastoral company and he was more than half a year in the north and then we would always see him off and come down excitedly to meet him at the boat and he always brought us something interesting. A bird or a pony or something or another. We were living in Perth then. As a matter of fact, only last night my sister and myself were at the announcement of what was being built on our old home in Perth on the site. It was very sad when I passed it a couple of months ago and suddenly found it was razed to the ground. It was one of the few really old homes left in Perth. It had been business premises for a number of years, but it was still the same shape and the same place. We were asked to put some of our books down in a time capsule.

It's going to be a big business premises. They're calling it Durack Place. My father didn't build it. He bought it from Henry Parker who was a member of parliament and very prominent. He had built it in 1896 for his family and first of all we lived in Claremont around the corner here in Goldsmith Road. My father was then put into parliament and moving by train – before the days when everybody had a car – and coming home at all hours of the morning. He got a bit sick of that so he decided to get a house near enough to Parliament House in the city and that was 1919. When we moved in there, it was always a very happy sort of a home. My brothers went to the college over the road and we went to the Loretto Convent just a few doors down. We knew everybody in the whole of Adelaide Terrace, all the old people.

My father was the Member for Kimberley. He was extremely interested in doing all he could to help to develop the country and the roads and better means of transport. As a matter of fact from the back of that old home of ours in Adelaide Terrace the first air service began. Major Norman Brearley came back from the war and my father was in parliament with his father-in-law. I've got a book of his (Brearley's) written by Ted Norman, the Australian aviator. Well Dad got to know Norman Brearley and told him that aircraft was not only for warfare and for stunts, it was something that was going to become of civil significance. My father believed in it entirely and he said he could have the backyard of our house which ran from near Adelaide Terrace down to the Esplanade. It was very big and he was told he could have the place for his hangar and use the Esplanade as the runway. And the only rent he would want for it was that he would like to go on the first flight when he founded the air service. So that was duly accepted and my father did go on the first flight but it was rather tragic. The two planes set off and one of them crashed. And the two young men on it were killed. So that was a rather bad beginning but it didn't stop it. It became a very important air service bringing the north close to the south. In 1934 my husband's company got that from Brearley so we were very much connected with it.

I don't remember one particular person being a major influence in my life. It was just that we did know a lot of people and everyone was in and out of our house, Dad being not only a Member of Parliament but very much a citizen and interested in people.

The family was gregarious. My father perhaps less so than my Uncle Jack who was down here managing the office and between the two of them they knew everyone practically in Perth in those days. Mother had many, many friends whom we loved. Mother was certainly gregarious, very capable and a much loved woman. She was very beautiful. She was always the person everybody stopped to look at. When she came to a school concert all the kids would say 'There's Mrs. Durack. Isn't she gorgeous?' And she was. I'll just show you a little picture of her. They called her the Grand Duchess till the last. Mother lived to ninety seven.

She died only in 1980 and she was beautiful to the end, very stately and always beautifully dressed. She had a companion help but she would water the garden and all those little things and it was only a week before her death that she went into hospital with gangrene of the leg and they were talking of amputating it and that was dreadfully distressing for us but she evidently decided her time had come and so she just quietly died. She had had a marvellous life and she lived quite a lot in the Kimberleys. She'd go sometimes with Dad, leaving us with a nurse and staff – those were the days when people had staff. Perhaps she was a great influence in our lives. Nurse Stevens was a great influence. She came out as a girl from London and went to Laverton as a nurse in 1900 and came back from there and went into the maternity hospital with a friend of hers and that was how mother first came in touch with her because two were born in that hospital. Then somehow or other Nurse decided she would come and live with us as mother's companion-help and she delivered the last two sons. Six altogether, four boys and two girls. I was number two. The last one was born in 1920.

This Nurse Stevens was a modest sort of a woman, but she was a great reader and in the days before radio or television she read to us and we just sat there doing our sewing, our little doilies or painting our little pictures. She would read for hours and what she got through was amazing. She introduced us to Dickens. That was one of our great favourites. Even Walter Scott, all those writers. She would imitate the accents. Sometimes she'd go to sleep and we'd wake her up to get on.

I was always writing. It never occurred to me that I was a writer, not for a minute, but it was a sort of game. I can remember thinking at the age of five or six it was clever to be able to make words rhyme and make sense. And I'd go around sort of making words rhyme, but I couldn't make up lines and one day, and this was my first literary effort, I came out into the garden and said, 'The bees are humming, so summer must be coming'. I thought that makes sense, it rhymes. So I went and wrote that down and put a few more lines to it and it was like children would do a crossword puzzle or something like that. It was a form of amusement. Anyhow I was writing verse from the time I was six and mother would read it out to people coming in. She was very proud of me but I wasn't suppose to know. I'd just listen outside the door. Once or twice when she was talking to someone up in her bedroom I'd be under the bed. It was just interesting to hear what the grown-ups were talking about. Eventually I'd come out and say I've been listening. Naughty child, oh dear, oh dear. Then they got down to the stage of looking under the beds for me after that.

Professor Murdoch, Sir Walter as he was, was a very great friend of my father's and he was interested in a child writing verse so he said to Dad when I was about fourteen or fifteen, I was writing plays then, he said, 'Let her go and get on with this'. I had my junior exam and was in sub-leaving when he let me go back to the north rather than stay down and do another year of school. Whether he was wise or not I don't know. That was how I came to leave school at sixteen rather than seventeen.

And the other great influence in my life as a writer – you've heard of Dame Edith Cowan – if ever there was a matriarch, she was. She was the first woman member of parliament in Australia. Dame Edith lived near Kings Park up in Melbourne Street, a nice Sunday walk, but she had a daughter called Dirksey Cowan. She was Edith Dirksey I think, the mother. I would take a trip around either Saturday or Sunday every few weeks. Dirksey and I would go for walks in the park and come back and have cups of tea with mother. Dirksey was one of the founders of the Historical Society and I can remember her telling me about the story of Western Australia, which was fascinating to me. It was just like listening to a novel. She mentioned on one occasion an extraordinary Aboriginal called Yagan and told me the story in brief. They called him the Bronze Apollo. She said, 'I feel we should have a statue to that man in this park'. There is one of him now. I said I'd like to write. 'Has anyone written about him?' She said it was all in the papers at the time, back in the 1830s. I said 'Where would you see those?' And she was the one who introduced me to the Archives, the public library it was then.

I was absolutely fascinated. It was much more interesting to me to go and look through those old newspapers than going to the films. At sixteen or seventeen I wrote a thing about the early Swan River. It was the story, including Yagan, to do with the early history of Western Australia. It was never published as a book but parts of it were, to my surprise – we did also know the editor of the *Western Australian* and the *Western Mail* – and they published episodes of it. That was my first publicly published work, except for the book which I wrote as a child of ten and my parents were persuaded to publish by Walter Murdoch and Mrs. Muriel Chase, who was a remarkable woman. She was one of the founders of the Silver Chain. Do you know about the Silver Chain? Looking after care of the aged. Wonderful concept, it's still going. She also did the Children's Page on *Western Mail*. She was Aunt Mary and strangely enough I became Aunt Mary in later years after she had died.

The book was called *Little Poems of Sunshine* by an Australian Child. As a matter of fact I was a bit upset about it because I was teased at school and the teachers really thought they were probably done by some other member of the family. I can remember being sent outside to sit on the verandah at school and write a poem. They wanted to prove that I could do it. And I sat there and sulked and didn't do a damn thing.

Then I began to write plays. I wish I had some of the things. My sister and myself began a weekly magazine, weekly or monthly, that we called 'Kookaburra and Kangaroo'. I was Kangaroo and Bet was Kookaburra and this was for our father. To be sent to him when he wasn't with us. Someone's got them. They were just about what the family was doing, making up stories about this one and that. 'Kookaburra and Kangaroo' was a great delight to my father.

My sister did the illustrations. She didn't take it very seriously. Most were secret caricatures of the girls and the teachers, which were priceless. She was always talented in that way obviously. But we never thought of it in that regard.

So in 1929 when I was sixteen we went back to the country. I was my father's chauffeur. He was never terribly keen on driving but he loved to have someone and I got my licence in Broome when I was just turned seventeen. Then I was officially allowed to drive the old man around. That was wonderful, driving around the stations and in and out of Wyndham. He just liked company. At that stage I didn't lift a finger on the domestic side of the stations. We did later but not then. There was always a Chinese cook, Aboriginal staff and the manager and his wife were responsible for keeping the house in order. But my great amusement, apart from driving around with Dad, was getting out on the mustering camp. The horses are trained. You push them on – cutting the cows out of the mob and you'll get the one you're trying to get out. A real game.

I was still writing. Before that whilst I was still at school, I was doing plays for the younger children just to entertain the family to start with and then, for good causes, they were put on at the Assembly Hall and grown-ups were acting in them too. Great fun. I did one on Charlotte Corday, that was a fascinating subject, the one that was guillotined. I think I played Charlotte Corday in that. I don't know what I called it. Then we did another one based on Egyptology. One of the nuns at school, old Mother Gertrude, was a great historian and she had a great love of Egyptian history and she did hand that on. Up north I started to write station sketches and they were accepted by the *West Australian* and the *Western Mail*. When my sister joined me she began illustrating the sketches and we got to having them published in the *Bulletin*. This was the heart of the Depression years and we had stayed at Ivanhoe helping the manager, old Bill Jones, who had been thirty years manager of the place, but he was getting feeble. He went away and we thought he was going to hospital but he didn't come back. While he was away we took over the management of Ivanhoe which had only Aboriginal

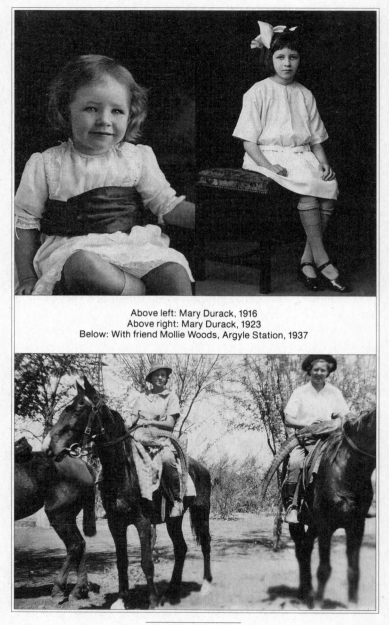

Above left: Mary Durack, 1916
Above right: Mary Durack, 1923
Below: With friend Mollie Woods, Argyle Station, 1937

staff. At that time there had been a Japanese cook but he'd gone home to his family and we didn't employ another one. We took over the cooking and the general supervising of the thing, but it wasn't an impossible job – they were a wonderful lot of Aborigines. The stockmen were wonderful. Johnny Walker, who was the head stockman and the tribal leader, was a bloke who's still with us at Bungladoon. He must have been like Yagan, the Bronze Apollo, when he was a boy he was beautiful. Tall, handsome, not outgoing, very polite but he was the tribal leader and he wasn't coming on in intimate terms, back-slapping or anything like that with the whites. He was a marvellous bloke, and totally trustworthy.

Bet was about eighteen and I was twenty when we took over. It was 1934, or 1933. I still think of these Aborigines as my brothers and sisters and aunties. They stay here when they come. One of my tribal sons was here for Christmas. Jacky Saval. He's an extraordinary character. We did have a fond relationship and it has been maintained through the years and they work on my sister and myself like real relatives. Drink is a big problem, but I've never gone on to that reserve and seen any of our people drunk. It's not that they knew I was coming, I would just come.

Sometimes I have to be careful about the ones that have recently died. We have to be careful not to mention their names. It brings his spirit back.

We never attempted to learn the language because they spoke all right and we'd speak to them in pidgin with a few words of Aboriginal thrown in and out. I'm sorry in a way we didn't. It was difficult to find out what was *their* language because there were so many.

They made it known to us that we were welcome at any of their ceremonies or corroborees but there were secret ones – right out into the hills and we didn't even know. But the ordinary wet season gathering of tribes from all over would be held half a mile from the house on the river bank. You could even hear them from the house and they always made it quite clear to us that they hoped we'd come. An hour or two would be enough but we did and then the women had their sacred life. I think they thought, 'The poor girls they've got no company'. Professor Elkin, the anthropologist whom my father had known, asked my father whether he could send an anthropologist up to investigate the women's life and whether there was any sacred or secret life of the women. Well my Dad said, 'Yes', and when he heard it was a woman anthropologist because they were the only ones that Aboriginal women were likely to talk to he said 'Oh there's an anthropologist coming. You'll have to look after her'. We thought, 'What a bore'. And the anthropologist was a girl not much older than we were, a couple of years at that, Phyllis Kaverry – she became a famous anthropologist. We said we'd speak to them and say she's a friend and trustworthy and see if they'd let her come. They agreed. So this was a big breakthrough. The book that emerged was called *Aboriginal Woman*.

They really loved Phil. She moved off from us to other properties and then came back from time to time. When she went abroad we said, jokingly on one occasion, 'When we've saved up enough we're going too'. We had a postcard someone sent us of Trafalgar Square, 'We'll meet at the north lion there'. And we did and saw a lot of each other in London.

The Aboriginals on the station were part of the family in their own way. They didn't live in the house or anything, but they were looked after and mostly there was an affectionate relationship. There would be a few examples where it wasn't but for the most part they were happy associations.

We couldn't have carried on like that because they couldn't have gone on not getting any education and not getting wages. There were usually forty to fifty on each place. The bush camps with their relations were all fed by the stations and looked after if they were sick and taken to hospital if necessary. It was paternalistic, but it hasn't really in the long run done any good. When they introduced wages the station would only need three or four stockmen and perhaps two women. They could only afford to pay what they presumed they needed, not feed a camp of about thirty or forty others.

It couldn't have gone on the way in which it did but it meant that the people that weren't employed drifted to the outskirts of the settlements. On social service they got into the drink and gambling, with nothing to do. The kids would be going to school there. Paternalistic as it was, from the outside it looked like a form of slavery.

The employment thing is very difficult for Aborigines because they're increasing. For a while they were declining and my father said by the time my life's over there'll practically be no full-bloods left. The elders had said the Dreaming's over. There's nothing to have children for. They suddenly found a reason. More money. Suddenly they all began to have children again. '54 I think it was. There was a lot of abortion, a certain amount of infanticide but whether they had another form of contraception I never got around to asking.

It was a very big property. At that stage it was Avern, a huge property. There was Ivanhoe, Argylle, Nury, Avern and Woollata, huge properties. It was seven million acres, whatever that is in modern terms and half the size of Ireland, nearly the size of Belgium. I have just been asked to do a talk on how our properties nearly became the New Jerusalem. It was quite extraordinary. In 1937 Dr. Adolph Steinberg came out wanting to buy our properties because he said that this man Hitler was going to kill them off by the million and the big Jewish, wealthy people in America would subsidize this if it could be a place of refuge. Dad was inclined to say yes. The family was very much against it because Dad had said he didn't want to leave the boys with the responsibility. It went on being discussed until 1945 or 1946. Menzies was in agreement, the next Prime Minister Curtin in 1945 said we cannot have the introduction of one mass of people and they were talking about 75 000 families. 75 000 was peanuts to what they have brought out but you do wonder how 75 000 enterprising Jews would change the whole country.

The family was continuing to run all the properties including my brothers' and cousins' and friends'. We were on the road but we were fifty miles from Wyndham. Our nearest neighbour would have been sixty miles or so, but we never thought it at all lonely. The house was a charming old place, too, with a tower on top. We'd get up and see people coming. We'd get up at night and play guitar.

My sister and I did everything together. We'd go for swims every day down in the river and long walks over to the pools and the hills.

First of all they published our work as a series of articles but later brought them out in book form. By that time, I was always writing.

There were plenty of things to do, when I wasn't heating up bread and cooking beef. We were getting three pounds ten a week between us and we got extra for the books. Dad had insured us when we were kids for two hundred. Bet was twenty-one and I was twenty-two or three, so we had enough to go abroad. I didn't particularly want to leave, but Dad didn't want us to get bedded down in the bush. He was keen for us to go so we went on a meat boat from Wyndham and we had a year away or thereabouts. We had a flat in London and went over to Ireland and saw our uncle and lived with him for a bit and then around Europe and Sicily and then down to North Africa. When we were in Tripoli, a man who was a very nice bloke married to an American said, 'You'd better get home. War is going to break out and you can be trapped here and you don't know what it'd be.' His wife joined in and said 'He's not going to let me stay either.' We wanted to do all sorts of other things but he got us on board the *Escalina*, an Italian ship and we did get back. That was one of the false alarms of the war. It didn't happen until nearly two years later.

We got back in 1937 and went back to the stations for a short time. Then my sister decided she wanted to go to Darwin and get a job. She went into the hospital as a nursing aide and I came down and got on to the *Western Mail* as Julia and Aunt Mary were doing the children's things. We did picture stories published as sort of serial stories in the *Sun*. But it's a real muddle here, the story of our lives. My book *Keeping My Country* was published about May.

I met my husband for the first time when he took over the air service from Norman Brearley and it became Roberts and Miller. That was 1934. He had already started an air service not long after he got back from the First World War in South Australia. I think he started first in Victoria and then South Australia. His partner was Sir Macpherson Robertson the great chocolate man, and my husband was Horace Clive Miller. There was certainly no idea of romance on our first encounters. He was over twenty years older than myself, but when I took a job with the *Western Australian* he would often be waiting outside at lunch time and we'd go to lunch. But he was to and fro and I'd see him then. When I went away on my holidays, the end of 1938, I went up north and had a few weeks of bliss. He wrote while I was there and said will you meet me in Melbourne and get married? And he enclosed an engagement ring. And I thought that's mad. I didn't even tell the family.

As Dad and mother were in Canberra at the time, I was coming down that way and then coming back. He was there to meet me and so I said, 'Yes', I had thought that it was time that I made a home of my own and this man was someone whom I felt suitable for my way of life. He appeared to be very keen. I can't say there's anything I've regretted and in a way our lives did fit in. He was in a sense, a sort of loner. He had the best of both worlds, as I told him. He was a married man and a family man and he was also a bachelor. He could move around anywhere he wanted to and did, because he had planes. We had very happy times particularly in Broome, where we had the house when the kids were growing up and Horrie and myself could fly around to the stations. He loved going and it was a way of keeping in touch and even after my father sold I could go any time I wanted.

We moved in here in 1939 when our first born, Pat, was a baby and it has been our headquarters ever since. It's too big and nobody will want it for the whole house. They'll want it for the two blocks of land which are very valuable, but personally I don't want to bulldoze it down. I need the space at the moment. That's my file room and study down there and there's a flat up top where I used to work. My husband died in 1980, a few months after mother. He was active but he was terribly upset when he had to give up his driving licence, because he had a stroke.

I wrote all the time. In the early days I wrote a lot at night. I had a girl living in, helping me with the children and sometimes coming in the day to take them for a walk to get them out of the road. I did a lot of work for the ABC reviewing books, writing plays and little sketches and things for radio. My sister was then married and living in Melbourne and we went on doing things between us. She was in Melbourne when she illustrated *The Way of the Whirlwind*. I'd done the story some years before and we went on collaborating. I wasn't absolutely devoted to my writing as far as I remember. I wanted a life of my own, apart from the family, to which I was very devoted also.

I seem to have done it fairly effortlessly, never had a miscarriage or any great troubles. Four girls and two boys. Three girls to start with and one of them was so like my old man she just took to flying from the time she could practically toddle. My old man wrote his own story, *The Earlybirds*, which was the history of aviation from his perspective. He wrote under my persuasion. He didn't want to write about his childhood at all and I said, 'But you have to say what your background was and where you started,' which he eventually did. It was only until the time he took up with Robertson Miller. The next part of his story has just been published in the book called *Speck in the Sky* by Frank Dunne.

My daughter Robyn has written a book called *Flying Nurse*. The dear girl died in 1975 and after that her husband and myself put together her letters and things in a book called *Sugarbird Lady* which sells for the Flying Doctor Service. It was cancer. No-one realized. She married the Federal President of the Flying Doctor Service, Harold Dix. They brought back together about seven planes across the Atlantic and Robyn flew solo from Europe on one occasion. She would have flown solo anywhere.

A plaque to Robyn's memory has been erected in the Administration Wing of the Royal Perth Hospital. An educational foundation has also been established to help train nurses to fly and encourage their study in special techniques at the Royal Flying Doctor Service. She was absolutely devoted to the service and was answering the phone for the flying doctor a few days before she died.

Darling Julie was a hostess for ANA and also got herself around the world. She married and by one of those unpredictable sort of things, when she was pregnant, some sort of thrombosis suddenly hit her and she died. It was terrible grief to lose the two girls like that, but they are both buried up in Broome with their father. I think they've left a space there for me.

Patsy, the eldest girl, was one of the air hostesses in the company and got herself around the world in that capacity, then went to London and got a job with the BBC. Can't imagine what it was. She always got jobs. She then met the Australian flier, whom she married, Bob Millett. She married him in Canada and their first child was born in Canada and then they came out here and had another son and her husband said, 'I want a truly Western Australian name for my son.' We had all sorts of funny ideas about that and I said, 'Why don't we call him Yagan and be done with it'. He'd never heard of Yagan. So we gave him the book and he came back next day and said it was the only name for his son. So my eldest grandson is Yagan.

Andrew started off as a draftsman in the company, his brother's company, and then he went into surveying – he's a real bushman, can't keep away. He's up in the old Dream country, on the diamond mines, a survey job and he just loves it up there. He had quite a bit of his childhood there.

John, the last boy, is a jeweller. He says, 'I'm not a jeweller, I'm an artist'. So that's all right. He's doing beautiful work. He had a business in Broome, where he spent much of his life, and then he did well enough to get himself away for seven or eight months on the Continent and recently back, and is setting himself up in Fremantle. He felt that this was the time to come there but he does beautiful things – things around chains, earrings and all sorts of things and many things on Australian themes.

Marie-Rose, the youngest, is married with children. She is an artist and teaches part-time at the technical school.

The sale of the stations had gone on and off, on and off for years. Ever since the New Jerusalem idea. And before that too. Dad sold them finally in 1950. It just wasn't our family, it was also the partners. My father could have bought them out and kept it for his own, which two of the boys were suggesting. We survived the Depression years when the stuff was hardly worth sending to market and then walked into the arms of the Second World War and that was a difficult time. Of course the price did go up during the war and that meant the offer was more than it would have been before and my father felt that he would prefer not to leave the responsibility to the boys. He had been keen to encourage his youngest boy David to finish his engineering at the university, which he did. He then survived the war in the paratroops and the next boy, Bill, had done his architecture and was well into that and Kim was an agricultural scientist. Reg had been going to be a doctor and did some training towards that, but was brought back until after the Depression and then by that time he was married and kept on one property when Dad sold.

The one most upset about it was Kim because he had begun to experiment in ways in which the country could be improved. He's a biography in himself. Extraordinary boy. It was through Kim that the dam came to be there although he said it was too early to put in the dam, but he had begun to show that you could grow all sorts of things. He had also warned that you had to give it time to know how you were going to cope with the natural things, diseases, insects and the bird life. All these problems. Sugar grew, but we were up against the Queensland market. All sorts of difficulties, but he went on. He formed the first research station on the Ord River and then went over and started a rice growing place in West Kimberley, Aliveringa, Camdown, and he didn't want to sell. He did try to talk Dad out of it, and Dad said, 'but why?' And he said, 'because it will kill you.' And Dad said, 'Kill me, it might give me a chance to relax for the first time in many years. Take your mother for a trip'. Kim stood at the foot of his bed when he breathed his last and he said, 'I didn't mean it literally Dad'. And he had signed it away a few weeks before. On the day Dad died the old homestead burnt down.

I was with Dad when we heard it come over the wireless. The manager and his wife were away and a kerosene heater blew up. It was extraordinary. The end of an era. I continued to go there to see my brother and his family on the place they'd kept and my cousin who was still managing Argylle Station. And of course to see all my Aboriginal family. Dear old friends and old stockmen. It was only in 1972 when I saw the waters of the Ord covering the place where the old homestead was that I suddenly felt I've got to go on with the book. I said I wasn't going to do any more about it. I had all the material in the family library. I brought it back and started on the other book, *Sons in the Saddle*, 1983.

From the 1950s I became very much associated with Dame Ida Mann, who died only a couple of years ago. She was head of Morphields Hospital, the first woman ever to be head of a major hospital. She got interested in the eye problems of the Aborigines and that brought her in touch with me. We saw each other up north and I went around with her quite often. She had a place down at Busselton which she would go down to for two or three days a month or more and whenever possible I would go down with her. I'd do more work in three days in that beautiful place looking out over the Bay, than I could do sometimes in three weeks at home. Then I could bring the children down in the holidays – the younger ones – and it was a wonderful working place. We had no 'phone. People always coming to stay and so forth, but it was wonderful.

Ida left her autobiography, *The Chase*, which is shortly to be published. Professor Ian Constable and myself have been collaborating. It's being done here by Fremantle Arts Centre Press. It is a most remarkable woman's life story and she was certainly a dear friend and much missed.

My life has been very mixed up with the artistic world. I was a foundation member and president of our branch of the Fellowship of Women Writers. Many other things too, like PEN, the Australian Society of Authors and for several years I was on the Aboriginal Cultural Foundation. One of my great present preoccupations is the Australian Stockmen's Hall of Fame. I like to encourage in any way I can, that's why I've got mixed up in the Hall of Fame to begin with, when the family think I should be better employed. I think they feel too much time and effort goes into it. I should be finishing the next bit of the family saga. I'm not getting on with enough. There's just as much as there is in any of the other books. It's just amazing. I had no idea there is so much material. I've researched the whole thing. Got it all indexed, all the names and all the dates and my father's diaries are all abstracted and tried to join the letters with the other material. I never intended to write another part of it when I did *Sons in the Saddle*.

I think I have always tried to do too many things at once. Not always my own fault, only because I get involved and it's not always easy. People say you've got to learn to say no. It sometimes can take me half of the day to say no, or more. You've got to write letters and all sorts of things.

A lot required one to be out and about giving talks at this, that and the other thing, but not of my own choice. I've never belonged to a Bridge Club or a Card Club or a Sports Club – might have done me good if I had. I do plenty of swimming and looking for shells and things and go wading out over reefs in Broome with the children. I go to the theatre, not a terrific lot, but I do go.

I make a lot of plans, but they aren't always able to work as I anticipate because I never know what's going to crop up next or who. Or what's going to happen in the family. I have more or less become philosophical about the fact that I live as I have to. I have got a goal to finish that book, and a few other immediate goals before I can even get back on it.

I used to write at night, no television in those days. My husband was away quite a lot. I don't think it daunted me, just took it for granted. Always had good friends, that's meant a great deal, and many lifelong friends started from the beginning of the Fellowship.

I make a list every day. I live on my own, when I am on my own. There's usually somebody staying. I do need the space at the moment because I've got so many rooms for books and documents.

I never agitated for women's rights. I've always just taken it for granted I've got them. It never occurred to me I didn't have rights. I don't think I had time to think about it. I did what I more or less felt I had to do and that was it. I wouldn't have wanted a permanent job. Taking on things like running writers' schools just for a week or two at the university vacations in the various states of Australia has done me for jobs.

I knew most of the women writers in Australia. In this state for instance, among our early writers and early members of the Fellowship was Katherine Susannah Pritchard, Henrietta Drake-Brockman, Molly Skinner, and many more. That is a Fellowship of Women Writers, with which I'm associated. I think I'm patron of it.

To tell the truth I don't get as much time for reading as I would like to. I try to keep up with the literary magazines and the *Bulletin* and a few other papers, and a few books which are sent to me to comment on.

I don't really think about politics. I've always had a perhaps unfortunate capacity of seeing both sides of every argument and I think that's possibly the novelist in me. In our family we've had the extreme left wings who've gone right, and the extreme rights who've gone left. I've tended to vote Labor but it doesn't mean I don't believe it's a good idea for someone to stick to a party no matter

Dame Mary Durack, 1986

what the party is saying. I just believe for myself, I have got to try and think who is talking the most sense now.

In 1978 I was made a Dame. I didn't know what to say. I just called together a few trusted friends and said I think this is going to be more of a burden than anything. It's hard enough to get to work now and if the Dame is put on all they'll want you to do is opening things and shutting things. However, my friends said, 'No, you can't refuse. It would be ridiculous. You'll be able to help people,' so I said 'all right'. It might have been nice for the family, but they're not that sort of people.

I'm a nominally practising Catholic. I have also written the story of the Catholic Mission in Kimberley, *Rock on the Sand*, I hope from an objective point of view, because of finding so much in the drawers and cupboards of the missions. I have a great admiration for what the Catholic Church has done in the Kimberleys and much of it was absolutely ignored. Wonderful nursing and teaching sisters who-have given their lives. Even when they took over the leprosy problem thinking they'd never be able to get into the white community again. But it didn't work out that way. As a matter of fact, the leprosarium in Derby is my hostel when I'm in Derby.

I don't know about an after life and I don't think any of us are meant to know. My little grandson came in to me the other day and said, 'Come clean Grandma, when am I going to see Grandpa Horrie again? Under what circumstances?' I tried to explain the spirit to him and then he found a dead bird. I said, 'You go and bury it' and he said, 'Will it go to Grandpa Horrie?' and I said 'Yes, its spirit will probably go to Grandpa Horrie.' So he went and buried it and an hour later he came back dragging it by its tail in the sand. 'You didn't come clean Grandma, it's still there.'

I can't imagine being absolutely sure. We hope. It's just beyond me. You still talk about them. There it is. I miss them, of course, but you just have to be sensible. No good sitting down and moaning. Back in the saddle. I do pray for strength, for the power to concentrate more than I do. Whether it does any good I couldn't tell you. All I can say is, I hope to finish this book that I've undertaken. I'll do the best I can. At least I'll leave enough for other people to be able to go on with. There's nothing the matter with me as far as I know, radically. Apparently good health. I never really was a smoker. The days when everybody automatically smoked I'd find I'd left mine to burn down on the table while I was doing something else. I don't think about my diet. The quickest meal is fine. I sit down to the evening meal about seven o'clock and see the news and then what I do then depends on what has to be done.

I don't work much at night. Maybe letters. There are many things I want to see and do and there's not many evenings I'm left to my own devices. Depending on the time of the year I'm usually up at seven. I can't live without a diary. It's not a philosophical diary, just enough to put down what I did and to know what I have to do as the days go on. I also stick photos in to remind me of where I was.

The family can have the diaries if anyone wants them, it will be up to them. My father never thought of his diaries as being anything. Probably they are one of the most extraordinary records in Australia because he started when he was nineteen and kept on until the week he died. It's really quite incredible.

My grandchildren are writing better poetry than I did at that age. They put it into competitions and they usually win. It's important to the family that I go on writing. They just take it for granted. The only problem is there's so much still to be done . . .

Kath Walker

Poet and Aboriginal Activist

I began to think I would never be able to coordinate a time when Kath Walker and I could get together. She is always flying around Australia or the world on behalf of her various causes. Finally I pinned her down to a day but I had to wait until she had returned from Moscow where she was participating in an international disarmament conference, followed by a trip to New Delhi where there was a conference on the renewal of grass-roots cultures. The one thing Kath Walker is never short of is energy.

Unfortunately time didn't allow for me to visit her at Moongalba – her sitting down place on Stradbroke Island. Instead she caught a ferry and a taxi to the hotel where we had arranged to have lunch.

As she had only a couple of hours before she had to return, we dispensed with the usual small talk, ordered our food and wine and dived headfirst into a life that is as rich and varied as the culture from which it takes its strength. Kath Walker is among other things a writer, a teacher, an actress, an artist and an Aboriginal activist. And above all else a wonderful story teller.

She told me she once worked for Lady Cilento as a domestic cleaner. I told her I thought it was marvellous that here she was side by side with her in a book on Australian matriarchs. She expressed no surprise at this as she had already appeared in a photographic exhibition next to her.

Nothing in Kath Walker's life seems to have really surprised her.

As I followed the tale of her life I felt as if I was on a raft with her, on a river adventure. She took us over rocks and boulders and even cascading down a waterfall or two and I never knew where the next bend would be. But I always felt I was in safe hands. Unfortunately we had to stop because of our time limit but the next time I see her I'm going to sit down with her at Moongalba and continue the journey that I feel I've only just begun.

I wasn't born a radical, the education system made me into one, because it made me write with my right hand when I was a natural left-hander. I was going to get up and destroy the whole world at five. If I'd found a way I'd have done it. In those days you were classed as a freak if you were a left-hander. And it had to be corrected quickly so that you wouldn't keep growing up to be a freak.

I cannot write with my left hand but I do everything else with my left hand including eating my food. You know those old fashioned ebony rulers, the round ones, they used to rap my knuckles until they were sore and bleeding. I can still feel the pain. My brother was left-handed but he just picked up the pen with his right hand and said, 'O.K. I have to write with my right hand.' I felt that they were robbing me of a beautiful gift my ancestor gave to me. My earth mother. I didn't like it.

I loved reading and always came top in English and the Arts. I remember once when there were five in our class taking my report card home and my father going mad because I came fifth. I thought that was pretty good coming fifth but he saw it as me coming last in the class.

Doesn't everyone feel like that about themselves. They should. Being Aboriginal didn't worry me in the least. I knew I wasn't lesser. I left school at the age of thirteen to work as a domestic in a white household for two shillings and sixpence a week. I used to rush through my work and when the mistress was out, read all the books. Although the libraries were filled, I was not supposed to touch any of the books. I used to touch them all right. I remember once reading a book called *Droll stories from France* when I was about sixteen. My mistress came home and caught me in the act, and, oh my God, did she come out at me. 'Reading that filthy book', and I thought, if it was so filthy why have you got it in your library. It didn't seem filthy to me at all, seemed rather boring to me.

So I'm self-educated. The ironic thing is now I'm lecturing at universities all round the world. Strange that isn't it? I always knew I wasn't better than them but I was as good as them. The political awareness came when one day when I was about twenty, I was up at the butcher shop, and in those days they used to wrap the meat in newspaper. I took it home and because I was an avid reader I'd read everything and there was a little article complaining that Aboriginals weren't allowed in a shop in Bundaberg.

I thought the man talks just like I feel. The name of the paper was the *Guardian* and I discovered it was the communist paper. So I joined them because I liked the way they talked. I couldn't join any other party because they had the White Australia platform. The Communists were saying that all people were born equal etc. I'd always known this, but here at long last I was hearing my party saying it. I didn't stay in the Communist Party long because they wanted to write my speeches. They wanted me to say what they wanted me to say. I said 'No, can't do that. I'm no parrot'.

But what I learned in the Communist Party was a hell'va lot about politics which stood me in good stead through life. I joined the Labor Party but there are more racists in the Labor Party than there is anywhere else in the world. I stood for the Greenslopes seat in 1969. My campaign director was a wonderful man, and we'd walk into a Labor Party meeting or Labor Party industrial place and one of the men would say, 'How's the squaw going', in front of me. And Reg, was so upset about it, he'd look at me and we'd walk out. Nothing was said because I didn't want to bring the subject up and see the pain on his face any more.

The fellow who was in the local council at the time, a Labor Party man, refused to stand on the same platform with me because he was afraid that his name would be linked with me and a bed. He said, 'I can't stand to lose my good reputation'. I said, 'What makes you think I'm going to try to go to bed with you'.

I lost a lot of the socialist votes for two reasons. One I was a woman and two I was Aboriginal. I got a university student to do a survey on it and he said that the attitude was, 'Well if we get her into parliament we're going to be the butt of every joke that goes on around our work. To have a woman and Aboriginal at that representing us in the House'. So the Labor Party lost votes although I polled a lot of Liberal Party members because the women said we want a woman in Parliament and they backed me.

But it was the Labor Party Socialists who refused to vote for me. Men, men, men – but still I love 'em. We have to educate them. Year by year. I don't believe in Woman's Lib. I'm going to fight for people. I was liberated the day I was born. Any woman who's not liberated today deserves all she gets. It's her own fault. Even in the Aboriginal movement I will not join women's groups. I don't even fight for Aboriginals either. I fight for all people.

As a young girl growing up I knew nothing about sex. My mother was brought up in that narrow-minded bigoted attitude of the Catholic Church and they were a damned sight worse than what they are now. I will never forget the first day I found my pants red. I was so ashamed. I didn't know what I had done wrong, and I kept it to myself for three days. Going out and washing my pants all the time. One day I couldn't handle it any more. I went to my oldest sister and told her and she said, 'oh that's nothing'. I found out it was perfectly normal.

There were seven of us in the family. I was second youngest. My sister introduced me to the Modess pad and said, 'You are going to get this every month'. I said, 'Forever', she said, 'just about'. I said, 'Oh my God it's the end of the world. Fancy having to put these damn things on every month. How awful'.

In a traditional Aboriginal tribe if a woman was menstruating she wasn't allowed to eat with the tribe. The eldest brother would put the food outside the gunyah and the woman was not allowed to be seen by the tribe for five days. She was considered to be unclean. She has to cut the grass, put down new matting and then burn it. Only one of the grandmothers, the tribal elders, would attend to her.

I knew my husband from way back. His aunty was married to my cousin. I think I was frightened of being left an old maid. Everyone laughs at me when I say that. I thought the first guy who proposes to me I'm going to accept, so it was him. It only lasted about ten years. By these standards that's a long time. Still I got two good kids out of

10 years old, on Stradbroke Island
Inset: Playing cricko in Brisbane, 1938

it. I worked hard and paid off the house. As well as working as a domestic for Lady Cilento from nine to three, I took in washing and swung an iron.

This went on until the kids were in their teens and then I was working in a bacon factory. I came home to my lounge and I found half of it burned with a cigarette. My kids had been in primary school at the time, when I took on the bacon factory. So I went up to my doctor, (it wasn't Lady Cilento), and said 'my kids are running mad' and she said, 'What is your position, what do you want to do? Do you want to make a career for yourself or do you want to rear your children?' I said, 'I want to rear my children.' So she said, 'You know you are entitled to a pension, so why don't you go on it?' So I did.

I had no intentions of becoming a writer. I used to do it to inflict myself on to my friends at socials. I wrote lots of things just for my own amusement. Then a friend of mine who had read my work said, 'Why don't you join the Australian Realist Writers group. They might be able to help you?' I said, 'oh I've nothing to do, I think I will.' This is where I met Brod Hall and Tom Shapcott and they were the babies of the team then. What I liked about the Realist Writers was you'd put your manuscript down with no name on it and then everyone read a manuscript not knowing whose manuscript it was.

This was a great help to me, so I kept going with my writing. Then a few years later Frank Hardy was having a book launching at New Far and they said, 'Kathy come along and say a couple of your poems'. It was 'Son of Mine' that I recited. This grey-haired, old man came up to me and said, 'Have you written many poems?' I said 'a few'. He said, 'How many?' I said 'I don't know'. He said, 'Thirty, fifty?' I said, 'Oh in between'. He said 'I'd like to see them'. I said 'OK' and he gave me his address. Well I went home and threw the address away and forgot about him. But he was a very persistent old man and he found out where I lived, obviously through the Realist Writers, and wrote to me and said 'what about those poems you promised to send me'. So more or less to keep him off my back I sent him the poems. Then he wrote and asked me would I go and see him.

I rang my friend Kathy and said, 'I don't know what this old man wants to see me about, he might be a dirty old man, will you come with me? She said she would and we often laugh about it now. You couldn't have met a nicer, more beautiful man.

He said, 'I sent your poems to Mary Gilmore and she's charged us with the responsibility of teaching you how to put them into manuscript form for publication'. I still didn't think they were that good. He said, 'I'm prepared to write the foreword.' I didn't even know what a foreword was! His name was Jim Devaney, a well known author, poet and critic.

About a fortnight later as I was in FCAATSI (The Federal Council for the Advancement of Aboriginals and Torres Strait Islanders), I was asked to go to Sydney to launch the petition for the referendum to change the Constitution to include Aboriginals. We got a ninety-three per cent yes vote on it, Holt was in power when it happened.

Anyway I had one day off and they said, 'What would you like to do on the day off' and I said, 'I'd like to meet this marvellous poet called Mary Gilmore'. She was ninety-four. They took me out to meet her. When I walked in she said, 'Sit, girl'. She handed me my poem and said, 'Read'.

She gave me some advice then and I've never forgotten it. She said, 'Girl, these are not your poems. These belong to the world. Never forget you're the tool that wrote them down only'. She said 'I want to make sure that they go into book form'. So on I went with the referendum business, getting people's signatures all over Queensland.

When I got to Rockhampton a fortnight later, I opened a paper which said Mary Gilmore had died. I saw her a fortnight before she died, which made me rather sad. But I was glad that I'd met her. So then Jim Devaney showed me how to put this thing into book form and we submitted it to Angus and Robertson. Beatrice Davis was the one we saw. She saw *We're a Weird Mob* at the same time and knocked both of them back, as not being up to standard.

Then we submitted to Jacaranda Press at the time. They were looking for unknown writers and prepared to take a risk on it, because they could get a grant from the Commonwealth Literary Fund.

During Book Week I met up with Judith Wright. I'd just got word through that the Commonwealth Literary Fund had OK'd the grant.

I said, 'Judith, guess what, my book's going to be published'. She said 'I know. I recommended it.' They'd sent it to Judith for her assessment. And then she said something that made me feel very proud of myself, for a little while anyway. She said I envy you your writing of 'Son of Mine', I wish it were mine. High praise.

So that started my career into the writing world. We went into seven editions in seven months. I'm the best-selling poet in Australia. I rank next to C. J. Dennis. He's way ahead of me, but I have a chance of catching him up because he's dead and I'm alive. I don't know if I've got a lot of years to go, but while I'm alive there's hope. I don't worry about dying. I don't look to the future, I live for the present.

I want to be able to get up in the morning, look myself fair in the eye and say, 'I've done my best, win or lose or draw, I've done my best'. I still do that. And that's a nice way to live, a fulfilling way to live, whether I'm planting, or whether I'm mowing the lawn (I've five acres of land I mow, regularly), or whether I'm fishing, which is my favourite pastime, or whether I'm painting. I love painting. Do you know Janet Holmes à Court wrote to me and said she had seen some of my stuff and she said, 'It's exquisite'. Another compliment, which I was proud to have.

I always painted but I didn't want anyone to know about it because it was my little pocket I'd crawl into to save my sanity. I used to just paint and then throw the books into a cupboard. One day I was spring cleaning my cupboard and I had all my books out in my caravan. Dr Ulli Beier, who's a German who came out here to get away from Hitler, had rung me and said 'I'd like you to be one of the editors of this magazine, "Black Writers of the Pacific", that I'm thinking of bringing out. I'm coming up to Brisbane, may I come across and talk to you about it?' I said 'Yes sure'. In the process of talking about it he saw all the books I hadn't put away.

'What are these', he said. I said, 'I do art work to keep my sanity intact in this mad world'. 'These should be in frames', he said. 'You've got to exhibit these'. I said, 'No I don't want to because that's the only thing I have private in my life. You're not taking my last storm hole away from me'. He said, 'Oh Kath, that's not right'. Then what Mary Gilmore said to me hit me fair in the kisser. I said 'Oh, go with it'. This was last year.

Well he forgot all about me being editor of this magazine, I might add. He went home, he put them all into frames. I had an exhibition in his house in Annandale in Sydney, and I sold quite a few of them. The National Art Gallery bought six of them. We had cloth materials with my designs on and that sold like mad. Amazing. I remember once when I had to go to America, on a Fulbright Scholarship and they wanted me to do a tour of America. So I had to send over to America my curriculum vitae and all this jazz. So a friend did the curriculum vitae and she said, 'Here what do you think of this'. And I read it and I said 'I haven't done all those things'. She said, 'Kath you have, I've done research on you'. 'My God, I said 'I can't believe it'. It's true, I am a workaholic. God help my family if I ever get sick because I'd be a terrible patient. I'd drive them mad. They'd have to put me in a home, or have a big ward nurse to stand over me and make me behave myself. I'm impossible to live with.

I've been called an Activist but I think I'm fairly conservative. During the Civil Rights Movement, when so many really wonderful white people, genuine people, wanted to learn more about us, I ended up lecturing all over the place. Universities and schools. I remember a speech I gave in Adelaide. Actually Nugget Coombes wrote about it as 'Kath Walker's Espionage Speech'. I had been up to Canberra to see Charlie Perkins about getting a friend of mine in to see Wentworth who was the Minister of Aboriginal Affairs. Anyhow while I was in Perkins' office I saw a copy of Coombe's speech about Aboriginal health to the Royal College of Physicians in Melbourne. Right across it in big letters was NOT FOR PUBLICATION.

When I arrived in Adelaide later that day I found a copy of this speech in my bag. So when Jim, who had lined me up to talk at Adelaide University said to me, 'What are you going to talk about tonight?' I showed him the speech. He said 'Kath, this is hot, where did you get it?' I said, 'The less you know about it, the better'. He said 'I can't allow you to do this. They'll arrest you. This is espionage.' He was biting his nails down to the bone. I said, 'I'm determined to do it, Jim, are you going to help me or not?'

He said 'I'll help you but my God, I don't want to stand by and let Security arrest you'. 'They wouldn't dare', I said. So that's when the famous words of Nugget Coombes came to the public. 'An Aboriginal child that is born today has a much better chance of dying than a white child,' etc. There was this hushed crowd in the auditorium while I'm reading it out and Jim's sinking lower and lower in his seat and looking over his shoulder. Anyway when I'd finished a chap got up and you could have heard a pin drop. He said, 'Kath if you'd given those statistics about the white race, the Australian government would have called a state of emergency immediately. I bet you a pound, that the media here will not print a bit of it'. They didn't either.

We sat up all that night and we sent a copy to every man in the house of Representatives and Senate. Nothing. They put a blanket over the whole thing. The only one who published it in full was a South Australian woman who was writing a newspaper for Aboriginals at the time. The media just closed ranks. They were told to. Jim said, 'Why didn't they arrest you?' I said, 'All hell would have broken loose if they'd touched me'.

After the FCAATSI movement folded up I got very sick, I hadn't had a holiday in seven years and my son, Vivian, came up to Brisbane from Sydney.

He was the one who had run away from home and I didn't know where the heck he was. He was being very obstreperous, as I thought. So I rang the police and said 'I don't know what's happening to him'. They said, 'You can list him as a missing person. Have you got any photos of him?' I said, 'What will happen if I list him as a missing person?' They said, 'We will advertise it in the papers'. I said 'what if he is doing all right?' He said, 'That's the chance you take'. I said, 'No I won't list him as a missing person'. I had to go to Sydney, to launch *Dawn is at Hand* and the people who had seen the publicity about it said to Vivian 'Your mother's down here'.

Vivian had rung up Jacaranda Press and said 'I'm her son, and I want to know where she is living'. I told Jacandra Press not to give my address out to anyone or my phone number. When the Agent came to see me with the Press man about three days later, he said 'oh there was a young chap rang up and had the cheek to say he was your young son'. I said, 'What name did he give'. 'Vivian'. I said 'he is my son, and I've been looking for him for the last two years. Where is he?' 'Oh he gave me a phone number but I haven't got it on me'. Two more days elapsed and he finally found it in his office and phoned me with it. So when I picked up the phone to my young son, he said, 'Mother, if you hadn't rung to-day I'd have listed you as a missing person'. I thought that was ironic. Oh boy.

Anyway, this time when I was so weak Vivian had been to see my doctor who told him I was absolutely worn out. So he said 'Mum, sell the house and get back to the island'. So I did. I took a year off. But eventually it got boring and I remembered that all the time I was in the Civil Rights Movement I had wished I could just go somewhere to recharge my batteries. I thought, 'Why can't I build such a place here on Stradbroke'. So I applied for the old mission called 'Moongalba', which was all bush then, saying I wanted to approach the Federal Government for enough money to build a museum and art gallery.

Then I spread the word around to the entire spokesmen and women of the Aboriginal world saying, 'If you're tired bring a tent, pitch it and get away from it all. Save your sanity'. After I was there for about three months, two deserted women came in with eleven kids between them. Just to have a rest. I looked at all these kids and tired mothers and the kids all frustrated and fouled up. I phoned the university students who'd helped me clear the land in the first place and said, 'I want eleven university students down here in a hurry', and they came.

I lined up all the university students and I lined up the kids and said, 'Right, pick your brother and sister'. And the littlest one picked the tallest one. Little Mickey picked Peter, who was a med student. And I said 'OK now, mothers don't need to have a holiday away from their kids, they need a holiday from the responsibility of rearing their kids. So while the mothers are here, you people are responsible for the kids, what they want to do and what they don't want to do'. And they said 'yeah, we'll be in that'. They had one child each.

The kids had a ball and so did the mothers because they just sat and gossiped. Cooked when they wanted to, didn't if they didn't want to. They just pleased themselves. When the holiday was up and the families had gone back, the university students said 'can we be exempt from any of the chores around the place, we're buggered'. I said 'I think you'll go back with more respect for Mums when you go home'. They said, 'We didn't know it was so hard rearing kids'.

What came out of that was the thought 'why don't I bring primary school kids in here, and the mothers can come with them. So when I have twenty-five kids I say I want five adults. For the last seventeen years I've had 26,500 children on the land. White kids as well as black. And if there were green ones, I'd like them too. They don't have to be a special colour. I'm colour blind, you see. I teach them Aboriginal culture, I teach them about the balance of nature. How every animal, every bird, every living thing has a place in the society and there's room for us all.

I teach them about Judith Wright's poetry, which I love. I think she is the greatest poet in the world. I teach how to cook food Aboriginal and Torres Strait Island way. When the kids come in they have full responsibility for themselves. The parents sit back and have a holiday. It was from those first two women that I got that idea. One group rang me from Wacol Aboriginal Hostel and said, 'How many can we bring?' I said, 'Twenty five'. Seventy five turned up and I said, 'Can't you count' and they said, 'What happens when they get on the bus at the last minute without any clothes or anything. Do we throw them off the bus?' So I said 'Oh bring them in'. So there was seventy-five and about seven adults.

The adults kept doing everything. 'This is wrong', I said. 'You're not to do this.' But they wouldn't stop. So I ganged up on them. I got the eldest of the kids and said, 'Why don't you take over and do that for yourself'. They said, 'We want to and they won't let us'. I said 'well, get up there and call a meeting, and say you want to run the camp for the last week on your own'. They were there for three weeks. The adults were absolutely worn out, for the first fortnight. I was growling and carrying on something terrible. Anyway the kids went up and told them they wanted to run the camp for the last week. The adults caved in, they were too tired not to. The kids said, 'Will you back us', and I said, 'This is what it's all about. Responsibility'.

I like teaching, especially kids. When they were going back home I said, 'I want your medical doctor at Wacol to check every one of these children when they go back'. They told me that after he'd examined them, he wrote a prescription that said 'recommend three more weeks at Kath Walker's Place'. There wasn't one sick kid amongst them. That's the part that's good. That recharges my batteries. I've got a whole stack of kids coming in this year. I'm booked up six months ahead of time.

The last writing I did was up in China in 1985. I was so inspired by them. Oh what a beautiful country. I wrote seventeen poems on the track. I was invited, together with Professor Manning Clark, Rob Adams of the Australian Council for the Arts, and Eric Tan who is of the Tan Dynasty but now living in Perth as a surgeon, married to an Australian wife. He compares notes and up-dates stuff in surgery here and in exchange they give knowledge of acupuncture and herbal medicines.

The Deputy Director of the Queensland Art Gallery led the deputation. It was wonderful. At my art exhibition I was asked to recite my China poems to music. When I heard the tape I couldn't believe how good the poems sound with the didgeridoo and the flute. As a result the book is being published here and also in China. It's pretty exciting to be translated into Mandarin.

I have always lived by my instincts. Sometimes I can be walking across the land and it's like an invisible glass comes down in front of me and I stop. It's like something is saying 'Back out'. And I do. It could have been a snake close by or anything. I get big instincts and I obey them, especially when I chose my acting parts. I trusted instinctively in Frank Heimen when he made a short film about me called *Shadow Sister*. I'd never heard of him before when I agreed. The result was an international prize for my acting and a place in The Black Hall of Fame in America.

When Bruce Beresford rang up to ask me to play the part of the eccentric old woman in *The Fringe Dwellers* I knew the book was good even though I'd never heard of him. My grandson, Denis, was also in it and he didn't even recognize me when he first saw me in the role. I loved doing that but I've knocked back a lot of scripts because they are just roles for token blacks. I'm not a token anything.

I was once asked by Wentworth to take on Charlie Perkins' job, and I said, 'I'd have to sign a paper telling me to shut my mouth and keep it shut. Give it to somebody else'. Public servant, oh yuck! That's one label they can't tag on to me. I'll work for Government

Above: Launching her book *Dawn is at Hand*, 1968
Below: Kath Walker today

without pay but I'm not going to take pay off them. They buy you body and soul.

I've been emancipated from the day I was born. No one buys or sells Kath Walker. Don't ask me about the things I hate. Hate is not part of my vocabulary. If I ever had it, I threw it out years ago. That's the dirty little, four-letter word I do not want to have anything to do with. I get angry, when either my people or other people do the wrong thing, I blow. But I don't hate them. I love them. I can't even hate people like Bjelke-Petersen. I think they are silly people. I feel sorry for them.

If I had any advice for young women of today it would be don't fight the men. Educate them. I like men, they're nice people. Slightly silly. Oh God, I'd never marry again. I had affairs but since AIDS is now around, I don't even have affairs any more. I masturbate. It's the safest way. I like making love to myself. It's beautiful. This business of sex. When the kids come to me all dewy-eyed I say, 'What you look for in a man is mateship. Forget about this love thing'.

I've told at least thirty-five men in my lifetime that I'll love them forever. All that usually exists between man and woman is passion. The desire to get rid of their dirty dishwater. True love exists between man and child. Of course if you get the right mate, you're lucky. Very few people have. I've had a few mates but it went out of the window as soon as they started getting possessive. I'd say 'Don't call me your woman. Time to part company, goodbye.'

What should exist between man and woman, black and white, is mateship and being able to live together. But all you can do is give the young the benefit of your experience. I'm not going to dictate to them what they should be doing. That's their responsibility, not mine. I just want to be able to look myself fair in the eye and say, 'Win, lose or draw. I've done my best'.

Lady Phyllis Cilento

Author and Medical Practitioner

Lady Phyllis Cilento was unfortunately not very well on the day I flew into Brisbane to interview her. She was however sitting comfortably in her living room which overlooks the Brisbane River. After a lifetime spent in improving the health of other people, she told me that her own health had not been too strong of late and that she needed a lot of rest. She was also still recovering from the recent launching of her autobiography and all the media interviews. The details of her rich and fulfilling life are there for us all in her book and what follows is a brief but still intense conversation that I had with her. I did not attempt to stay long because I could see the answers to my questions were causing her to use enormous amounts of energy and to tire very quickly. Her eyes however were bright and alert and flashed from time to time when I suggested ideas with which she disagreed. She's straight and to the point. As she told me, 'There's never been any frills for Phyllis'.

Matriarchs are a good thing to have in a country. The family all call me the matriarch, but I had to be one because Sir Raphael, my husband, was away a great deal. You see he was an administrator and a tropical disease expert. When we were up in New Guinea and then Malaya he had to go away on surveys.

I was left alone with the children. I had my first baby in the little town of Telok Anson on the Perak River where Raphael was stationed as a medical officer. Events dictated that he had to confine me himself, with my mother holding the chloroform mask while he delivered the baby boy. I had engaged a Chinese amah, or nurse, and despite all my London lectures on child care, I learned a great deal of practical experience from her. Before I was out of bed, other mothers from the European colony were bringing their babies to see me.

At the end of the year the Australian government invited my husband to study tropical diseases in other countries and to take his diplomas in England, with a view to directing the Tropical Institute in Townsville, North Queensland. So I returned to Sydney with our one-year-old son – still breast-feeding.

During that time of waiting I started on the diploma course in public health, but although I attended lectures and did practical work, it was impossible to finish the course. That was when I first became interested in nutrition. After some time as the Director of the Institute of Tropical Medicine, Raphael was sent to the territory of New Guinea to establish a comprehensive medical service.

Our second child was born just before I followed Raphael to Rabaul. Although the management of the house and the care of what became three children took up much of my time, I had, like all Europeans, a staff of native help and a nurse for the children. I found the social life and the bridge-playing quite unsatisfying so I started private practice. Then when we settled in Brisbane, in 1929, a year after the fourth child, I started a limited private practice.

Domestic help was easily available in those days and I always had my consulting rooms in the house. My practice became centred around maternity cases and growing families and in 1932 I was instrumental in starting the Queensland Mothercraft Association. Then Sir Raphael went away to work for the United Nations and we were three or four years apart. I had all the kids at their growing period and I had to have a firm hand on them.

Then I went to the United States to join him. Since 1929 I have conducted a weekly radio session on mothercraft, written articles for a women's magazine and had a weekly press column. From 1930 to 1934 I was an honorary physician at the Brisbane Hospital for Sick Children and the first lecturer in mothercraft.

How I managed it all I don't know. Of course I did always have a

Dr Raphael Cilento, Dr Phyllis Cilento and
baby Raphael, Malaya, 1928

nursery/house-maid and a cook/laundress. But I had boundless energy and good health. I've always followed a good diet and never had sweets or junk food. We just had ordinary good food. Meat, at least once or twice a day. I'd like to ask a question. What is the difference between red meat and white meat? Nobody's been able to answer that question. The saturated fat of meat is very well balanced in most cases especially in pasture-fed animals.

I was always independent. My parents wanted a boy, you see, and so they brought me up as much as possible like a boy. I couldn't bear dressing in girly clothes and I used to strain my hair back. But I wasn't competitive with boys. I simply didn't worry about them. I always believed I could do anything. When I was a little girl I secretly always wanted to be in the circus.

I had been to the circus and seen people riding on the backs of horses and standing up and being trapeze artists. I thought how wonderful it would be. Then, I don't know, life just went on. My parents gave me the opportunity to learn everything. They had me taught singing and voice production, which has stood me in good stead over the years in broadcasting and lecturing.

My father had me taught everything to further my education. Like gymnasium and rowing and swimming, he taught me to swim when I was five.

I was interested in my work at school and I did a public examination for ten solid consecutive years every November from the time I was fifteen to the time I was twenty-five.

You had to work for examinations and I was one of the dux of my school and then I went to the university. I really wanted to be an artist. But I chose medicine because I thought I could do more good in the world.

I was in the Student Christian Movement and I used to go to conferences. A lot of my friends had dedicated their lives to do something good and they went to the mission field, but I read about the Oxford Movement and the work they did in the East End. I thought that was the sort of thing I wanted to do. I was doing Arts at the University because my father believed in a good education. He said, 'You must have a good degree in Arts at the University or Classics or something?'

So when I started I did modern European history and English and then I switched over to medicine and that meant a year of science before you could start. So I did six years more. We were always very independent at the university. There was a men's sports association and women weren't in it, but we were allowed in.

I went to their meetings with another girl who was an independent young lady, Millicent Proud. We were allowed there on sufferance. But there was a very strong feeling in Adelaide at that time that, well, females were only females.

I see no reason why women shouldn't develop their minds. If you were to take my own life and career as an instance, I always believed a woman should be a good wife and mother and look after her children but could follow a career as well. Have it all.

I think it's wonderful that women should exert their own faculties and develop their own potential but not at the expense of their femininity. My sex education consisted of a book my mother bought called *What a Young Girl Should Know* and on Sunday morning she used to take me into her bed and read it to me.

So I learnt how babies came. But not how they got there. That wasn't until I was doing botany and physiology at school. Suddenly it dawned on me that there had to be a daddy as well. Quite late. And then in my medical career what I didn't know about sex would fill a library. I ran V.D. clinics and all that sort of thing but I had no idea about it.

As far as contraception was concerned the only thing we knew when we were married was a little sponge or Wendell's Wife's Friend which was a quinine pessary and that was very irritating. The sponge used to get lost. I've always been a member of the International Family Planning and the Population Council and I get their works every week and the other day they said there was a wonderful new contraceptive and that was a little sponge! I've written a book on practical birth control.

Eventually I got on to the diaphragm and so forth and that was the great thing. I've been in the family planning movement since it really began. But it wasn't 'quite nice' for ladies to be in such things. But I'd been in England with Marie Stopes. I always had radical ideas, especially for a woman.

I remember when I was coming back to be married and I suddenly said 'I won't be married. I want to be myself'. I went and had my hair cut off as a sign. It looked awful. I went to the best place in Regent Street, but still I looked awful when I got home.

We were engaged in my last year in medicine.

I had a few boyfriends beforehand. One of them was killed and the other one didn't believe in women doctors and so on. But I was very glad when I finally married. I knew that this was the right thing, and he was the right one. I never ever met anyone as interesting. So I never worried about other men.

Because I was left alone a lot, I didn't have time for flirtatious ideas. I had to be a matriarch and look after my family and my practice.

There have been so many highlights in my life. I mean each baby was different and a terrible thrill. I do regret that I never had time to do any senior degree. I was MBBS. I didn't get much time to paint but I've been doing some flower paintings with felt pens because they are easy and I enjoy it.

I had a cataract a year ago and I had to give it up. I'll go back to it now that I've had lens replacement.

People often ask me if I had a message to young women what would it be? I would say, fulfill your potential as a woman mentally as well as physically. I think a woman hasn't attained her full stature until she's married and has a child. Then she knows what life is. Otherwise she really doesn't. We were formed and made to have children and to carry on the race and to be the link between the past and the future. We have to do it and no one else can do it.

One of the things I don't like that has developed is the degradation of sex. That is something precious that is given to us not only for the procreation of children but for the companionship and pleasure within a personal relationship. I don't think it should have become so degraded.

I've never been interested in politics. My husband stood for Parliament once and then the Senate. I used to go around with him but I wasn't terribly interested. My main interests were nutrition and mothercraft. I wrote my first book on nutrition in 1934 and have gone on writing about it ever since. I've written a book about drugs. And now there's the Lady Cilento Foundation for research into nutrition.

Lady Cilento at home

The family always say that the first thing I still ask is, 'Have they had their dinner or do they want something to eat?' You know in all my six children, twenty-six grandchildren and ten great grand-children there's not been one who was born unhealthy and there's not one with an illness. Nobody with asthma or anything like that. Mind you I think you should choose your genes pretty carefully. I had good Scottish, Welsh and English ancestry.

My great love is still art. And it's a strange thing but all my children as they have developed have gone back to some kind of artistic expression. My daughter Ruth is a painter and a sculptor as well as a psychiatrist. David is a doctor and also paints, does stained glass and carves. Even Diane in her old age, is starting to paint pictures. It's lovely.

I don't see anything of Ralph. He's a neurosurgeon in New York. David, Carl and Ruth all call in to see me every week. Margaret's in Melbourne and I see her when I stay with her or she stays with me. Now who else is there?

Well, Diane is up at Karnak and she comes down to see me when she can. She came down specially for the launching of my book and to promote it with me on television. That was fun, but very tiring. Instead of growing apart from each of my family, we've all grown closer. I think it's because we've got common interests and like talking about the same things. Sometimes we argue about medicine and research. I usually convince them around to my opinion. I'm a part of my children and what they are doing. I've always had the opportunity to study in my work and that's important.

I think it was Churchill who said it was happiness to work with something you loved.

Now of course since I have had a cataract and various other disabilities, I can't go downstairs to my nutrition clinic like I used to twice a week. I have a good partner and she does most of the work. But I do miss it.

I find that there are a lot of things I can't do. I have to depend on other people and that is very galling. But anyhow I'm very happily situated. I have this house which I've given to the family and they look after it. It has a lovely view of the river. Just a treasure.

I can take a certain amount but I mustn't have too long interviews or too long visits from people. They come and stay and stay and stay and I feel it the next day.

I never really thought of writing about my life. I never kept a diary properly. But I did feel when I got to ninety, I should put it down.

I'm a Patron of the West Australian Heritage and I'm very keen on the older people writing down their reminiscences about what times were like when they were young. If that is not written down now it's lost – for ever. Everything's changing so rapidly that the younger generation coming on, won't remember – it will all be forgotten.

Women haven't always valued their experiences enough to write them down. Only the people like Jane Austen and those 'phenomena' I call them like Elizabeth Barrett Browning and those other authoresses of that date. They were remarkable.

But they were so under the thumb of their parent and their male relatives that they didn't have a chance to call their soul their own. So they burst out into writing it down and expressing themselves. No man has ever told me what to do. I listen to them and say, 'Yes dear'.

That's the secret.

I remember having great arguments with my husband saying I want to do it one way and he'd want it another way. We'd have an argument and I'd put my ideas and he'd disagree and say I was talking a lot of nonsense, and I didn't know what I was talking about. Some weeks later he'd come up with the same ideas as if they were his own. I'd say, 'Isn't that clever that's just exactly what I think'.

You have to be careful of men's egos. They're very sensitive about them.

I don't think there's anything wrong with my ego. The important thing is always to believe in yourself.

Author's Note
On 26 July 1987, Lady Phyllis Cilento died. I consider myself to be very fortunate to have met her and recorded what was probably her last interview. This book is the richer for it.

Biographical Notes

MARGARET WHITLAM (1919)   A.O., Dip. Social Studies
1975   Member National Women's Advisory Council
1977–79   Director Commonwealth Hostels Ltd
1977–82   Director Sydney Davee Co
1978–87   Council Member Sydney Teachers College
1978–80   President A.C.T. Council of Social Services
1982   President Council Sydney College of Advanced Education
1982   Chairman of Board of Governors of Law Foundation.

HON. DAME ROMA MITCHELL (1913)   CBE 1971, DBE 1982
1962   First woman Queens Counsel in Australia
1965–85   First woman judge in Supreme Court in Australia
1979–81   Chairman, South Australian Parole Board
1981   Chancellor University of Adelaide
1981–86   Chairman, Commonwealth Human Rights Commission
               National Chairman Winston Churchill Memorial Trust
               National President of the Australian Association of
               Ryder–Cheshire Foundations
               Member of Australian Committee United World Colleges
               Member of Council for Order of Australia

BETTY MAKIN (1926)   City of Sydney Australia Day Community Medal 1984
1981   Chairperson Management Committee South Sydney Council CYSS

EDNA RYAN (1904)   Ph.D. (University of Sydney)
1958   First Woman Deputy Mayor Fairfield
1965   First Woman President of Local Government Officers' Association
               Set up Meals on Wheels in local area
               Founder Residential School for Mothers and Children
1974   Advocate for Women's Electoral Lobby in National Wage Case
1978   Advocate for Women's Electoral Lobby in Maternity Leave Case

1985   Awarded Honorary Doctorate of Letters, University of Sydney.
PUBLICATIONS
Gentle Invaders (with Anne Conlon)
Two Thirds of a Man

DAME BERYL BEAUREPAIRE (1923)   OBE

1969–77	Member National Executive YWCA Australia
1970	Vice-President Citizens Welfare Service
1973–76	Chairman Victorian Womens Section Liberal Party
1974–76	Federal Women's Committee Liberal Party (Vic.)
1976–87	Vice-President Liberal Party (Vic.)
1973	Chairman Board of Management, Fintona Girls School
1977	Member Federal Women's Advisory Committee Working Party
1978–82	Convenor National Women's Advisory Council
1982	Chairman Council Australian War Memorial
	Member Board Children's Television Foundation
	Member Board Vic. 150th Authority

EDNA EDGLEY (1911)

1920	First public performance
1925	First performance with Italian Grand Opera
1965	First tour of Moscow Circus
1974	Performed as Nurse in *Romeo and Juliet*, with the Australian Ballet Company

Shows brought to Australia include *Moscow Variety*, the Moscow Circus, *Disney on Parade*, the Stuttgart Ballet, Torvill and Dean and recently the Bolshoi Ballet.

STELLA CORNELIUS (1919)

I rang Stella Cornelius recently to ask her for a personal biography. All I received in the mail were the latest handouts on Conflict Resolution. Consider this the summary of her life and her work.

THE CONFLICT RESOLVERS SELF-CHECKLIST

1. WIN-WIN

What's wrong?
What outcome do I want? I need to get clear about how we both could win. I want what's fair for all (both of us).

2. THE CREATIVE RESPONSE

Let me choose a positive approach to this. What will this mean here? What can I use this as a good opportunity for?

3. EMPATHY

When I really listen and understand, what are they actually saying (or implying)?

4. APPROPRIATE ASSERTIVENESS

If I'm soft on the person (respectful and caring), I have the right to be hard on the problem (I don't have to put up with it!). What assertive action should I take?

5. CO-OPERATIVE POWER

How can I make it clear that I want us to solve this problem together?

6. MANAGING EMOTIONS

What's stirring me up? What am I telling myself this situation implies e.g. They don't respect me? They aren't listening to me?

Am I overdramatising or distorting? I won't say or do what I will regret later. I'll choose my response rather than have it choose me.

If necessary, I'll take time out for some physical exercise or relaxation to restore balance. Or perhaps I will write a letter and not send it that day. I'll tear it up or write it more constructively when I've calmed down.

7. WILLINGNESS TO RESOLVE

Me unwilling – What's my pay off in not solving this?

What am I still too angry about? What am I too frightened of?

Them unwilling – I'll make statements like:

'I'm here to solve problems;'

'I'd really like to fix this, how about you?'

and try to gain or have implied in the goals of the conversation their commitment to resolution, too.

8. MAPPING THE CONFLICT

What is motivating me?

What are my needs?

What are my anxieties or fears?

What is motivating them?

What are their needs?

What are their anxieties or fears?

9. DEVELOPMENT OF OPTIONS

Am I thinking too narrowly about the solution to this? Can I come up with a creative idea that will mean everyone gets more of what they need?

10. NEGOTIATION SKILLS

(a) What do I want? What is my hierarchy of wants? (The most important up the top.)

(b) Do I have a bottom line? A place of no compromise? Can I express this bottom line in terms of my needs rather than solutions, so that there can be flexibility in the negotiation?

(c) Look at areas of difficulty within the context of the areas of agreement. What do we already agree about?

(d) How can I include the objections rather than ignore them?

11. BROADENING PERSPECTIVES

Should I be so sure I'm right and they're wrong? Their needs are valid precisely because they are their needs.

Has our solution included or somehow reflected their point of view?

12. THE THIRD PARTY MEDIATOR

Check myself for the right attitudes for this task. 'I'm for you, but I'm not against them. Can I help you understand them better? In the space of my unconditional acceptance is there anything in your attitude or behaviour you'd like to change?' Let's figure out what's fair and how we'll go for it.

Do I, myself, need this sort of help?

ALICE DOYLE AM (Service to Restaurant Business and Community Service), Sydney, N.S.W.
PUBLICATION
Doyles Fish Cookbook, now in its 7th print, the royalties of which are paid to the City Night Refuge of the Sydney City Mission and St Luke's Hospital, Potts Point.

JOAN CAMPBELL (1925)   MBE 1978

1972	Foundation member of Crafts Council of Australia.
1973	Foundation member of Crafts Board, Australia Council.
1974–77	Member of Australia Council.
1974	Awarded prize, International Academy of Ceramics exhibition held at Victoria and Albert Museum, London, England.
	Awarded Caltex Ceramic Award.
1975	Elected to International Academy of Ceramics, Geneva, Switzerland.
1979–81	Member of Western Australian Arts Council.
1980	Participant, World Craft Conference, Vienna, Austria.
	Foundation member of Crafts Council of Western Australia.
1980–83	Member of Community Arts Board, Australia Council.
1980–82	Vice-President, International Council for Apprenticeship in Crafts.
1983	Member Claremont Art School Foundation.
1985	Member Review Panel Visual Arts Tertiary Education.
1986	Member Arts Advisory Panel, Western Australian Institute of Technology.
	Member Arts Education Consultative Committee, Commonwealth Tertiary Education Commission.
	Awarded Roz Bower Memorial Award (National) for services as Community Arts Developer.
1987	Foundation Fellow Curtin University, Western Australia.

COMMISSIONS AND EXHIBITIONS

1974	Exhibited Faenza Ceramic Exhibition, Italy.
1981	Exhibited Carmen Dionyse International Invitational Exhibition, Ghent, Belgium.
1981	Sculptural commission, Presbyterian Ladies' College.
1982	Sculptural commission, Music Department, University of Western Australia.
1984	Sculptural commission, Orchard Hotel, Perth.
1986	Sculptural commission, Ralph Sarich residence.
1986	Commemorative sculptural commission, Swanleigh Homes, Perth.
1987	Sculptural commission, Williams residence, Sydney.

Represented in collections:
Parliament House, Canberra

National Gallery of Australia, Canberra, A.C.T.
Victoria and Albert Museum, London, England
Tennessee Art Collection, U.S.A.
National Gallery of New Zealand, Wellington
Auckland Museum, Auckland, New Zealand
McDougall Gallery, Christchurch, New Zealand
National Gallery of Victoria
State College Art Collection, Victoria
Art Gallery of Queensland
Brisbane City Art Collection
Queen Victoria Museum and Art Gallery, Launceston, Tasmania
Tasmania Museum and Art Gallery, Hobart
The Christensen Fund
Art Gallery of South Australia
Art Gallery of Western Australia
Shepparton Art Gallery, Victoria
Bunbury Art Gallery, Western Australia
Newcastle Art Gallery, New South Wales
Australian Museum, Sydney
Power House Museum, Sydney
Curtin University, Western Australia
Work included in many private collections and galleries.

DAME MARY DURACK (1913)   DBE 1978, Hon. D. Litt. University of
Western Australia 1978, OBE 1966.

1958–63   Hon. Life Member Fellowship of Australian Writers and President
of the Western Australian Branch
Hon. Life Member International P.E.N. Australia, Sydney Centre
Member Australia Society of Authors
Member National Trust
Member Royal Western Australian Historical Society

1982   Member Australian Society of Women Writers (Australia) and
presented with the Alice Award.
Former Executive Member Aboriginal Cultural Foundation.
Director and Patron, Stockmen's Hall of Fame and Outback
Heritage Centre.
Awarded Commonwealth Literary Grant 1973 and 1977 and
Australian Research Grant 1980 and 1984–85.
Awarded Emeritus Fellowship 1983–86 from Literature Board of
the Australia Council.

PUBLICATIONS

1935   *All-about*
1936   *Chunuma*
1938   *Son of Djaro*
1941   *The Way of the Whirlwind*
1943   *Piccaninnies*

1944	*The Majic Trumpet*
1955	*Keep Him My Country*
1959	*Kings in Grass Castles*
1963	*To Ride a Fine Horse*
1964	*The Courteous Savage*
1976	*Yagan of the Bibbulum*
1963	*Kookanoo and Kangaroo*
1964	*An Australian Settler*
1964	*A Pastoral Emigrant*
1969	*The Rock and the Sand*
1976	*To be Heirs Forever*
1977	*Tjakamarra—Boy Between Two Worlds*
1975	*Swan River Saga*
1983	*Sons in the Saddle*

PLAYS

1968	*The Ship of Dreams*
1972	*Swan River Saga*

Numerous scripts for the Australian Broadcasting Commission Drama Department Young World etc.

Libretto for the opera *Dalgerie* (music by James Penberthy) 1966. Replayed at Sydney Opera House 1973.

PUBLICATIONS IN COLLABORATION WITH OTHERS

1952	*Child Artists of the Australian Bush* (with Florence Rutter).
1974	*The End of Dreaming* (with Ingrid Drysdale).
1984	*The Land Beyond Time* (with Olsen, Serventy, Dutton, Bortignon).
1984	*The Stockman* (Mahood, Williams, Willey, Sawrey, Iddon-Ruben).

KATH WALKER (1920)

1920	Member Aboriginal Arts Board
1964	Writer and Educator
1972	Managing Director Noonuceal – Nughie Educational & Cultural Centre, Queensland.
1974	Senior Advisor to Australia Contingent to Wotlf Black Festival Arts Nigeria.

PUBLICATIONS

1964	*We are living*
1966	*Dawn is at Hand*
1970	*My People*

LADY PHYLLIS CILENTO (1894), MB, BS

1921	Lady Medical Officer Malaya and New Guinea
1924–27	Lecturer, Mothercraft and Obstetrical Physiotherapy, University of Queensland.
1930–35	Founder and President Queensland Mothercraft Association.
1935–48	President Queensland Medical Women's Association.

1938–47	Founder President Business and Professional Women's Club, Brisbane.
1975	Member N.Y. Academy of Science.
1974	Queensland Mother of the Year.
1980	Queenslander of the Year.

PUBLICATIONS

Enjoy Your Family
A Guide to Parents
Plan Your Family
Practical Birth Control
Square Meals for the Family
All About the Pill
Care for your Eyes
Vitamin E
The Versatile Vitamin
All About Drugs
You don't have to live with Chronic Ill Health
Ailing Heart and Arteries
Vitamin and Mineral Deficiencies
You Can't Live Without Vitamin C
Nutrition of the Elderly
Nutrition of the Child
Medical Mother
The Cilento Way

Acknowledgements

The South Australian College of Advanced Education provided a research grant for me to cover some of the expenses of the interviews. I thank them for their support and belief in the project.

The women of the Registry of the Magill Campus typed the manuscript and particular thanks must go to Meg Burchall, Ros Leane, Carol Harnett, Lyn Lang and Judy Wrobsel.

My thanks to Julie Watts for her early support and encouragement and to Margit Meinhold for her sensitive editing and never-ending enthusiasm.

My dear friend Lindy Powell was as always a source of strength and honest feed-back.

Without Mary Beasley I would not have the inspiration or the strength in myself to continue my work.

My father Irwin Mitchell has always believed in the excellence of anything I have undertaken.

And finally my thanks to the women in the book who have convinced me that the best years are still to come.